The darkness slowly (...)
demons beat him i(...)
But instead of swee(...)
himself in the cemetery where his
family had been laid to rest.

Aubrey was there, still dressed in her pink hospital gown, her eyes covered with thick gauze. She sat, weeping, upon the grave of his sister. As he went to her, she looked up at him, and in a voice filled with emotion she begged him not to give up.

Please, Angel, she said. *Please don't give up on me.* She touched the headstone, running her fingers along the inscriptions. *On either of us.*

The child turned her face to the grave. The earth began to churn. Angel watched with a mixture of wonder and horror as a tiny hand broke the surface like some pale, exotic flower.

The hand beckoned to him.

And, in his head, in this state that was more than dreaming, he heard her voice, his sister's voice, like the wind whispering through the trees.

It said, *Please.*

Angel™

Available from POCKET PULSE

The Essential Angel Posterbook

Available from POCKET BOOKS

ANGEL™

soul trade

Thomas E. Sniegoski

**An original novel based on the television series
created by Joss Whedon & David Greenwalt**

POCKET PULSE

New York   London   Toronto   Sydney   Singapore

Historian's Note: This story takes place in the first half of *Angel*'s first season.

An *Original* Publication of POCKET BOOKS

POCKET PULSE published by
Pocket Books, a division of Simon & Schuster, Inc.
1230 Avenue of the Americas, New York, 10020

™ and © 2001 Twentieth Century Fox Film Corporation.
All rights reserved.

ISBN: 0-7434-0699-0

First Pocket Books printing May 2001

10 9 8 7 6 5 4 3 2 1

POCKET PULSE and colophon are registered trademarks of Simon & Schuster, Inc

Printed in the U.S.A.

For my evil twin, Christopher Golden. Without his friendship, patience, expertise, and an occasional kick in the pants, this book would never have been done. If you were a girl we'd be going steady.

All hail The Big Thumb!

PROLOGUE

The obscenely fat woman in the flowered house-coat jumped up and down in an insane dance of victory, bells ringing and lights flashing. Her nametag announced her as Donna. She undulated her way up from the row of *Dollars and Sense* contestants and onto the stage, a winner.

"Friggin' cow," David Bentone muttered. In a booth at the back of Hurley's Pub and Grill, he flicked the ash from his cigarette into an ashtray and leaned slightly into the aisle to see the television hanging over the bar.

He thought about the four losers who let Donna get up on stage instead of them. If he ever had the opportunity to be on *Dollars and Sense* it would be him up there with the white-haired host, not a three-hundred-pound housewife from Michigan.

He took a sip of his beer, careful not to drink too

much. It had to last until he figured out what he was going to do about his current predicament.

On the TV, the host was explaining the next game to the enormous *hausfrau*. Donna looked like she was in shock, nodding her head slowly, mouth agape, as she tried to understand the rules.

Moron, Bentone thought.

The host made a half-witty comment and the audience laughed uproariously. He finished the explanation and showed the woman what she might win.

The crowd went berserk as the curtain rose on a brand new Mustang convertible. Donna nearly lost her mind. The host was wise enough to step back out of the way of the three hundred pounds of screaming, bouncing flesh.

Bentone imagined himself on stage with Bill Burton, the MC. He would be as cool as winter in Alaska, talking to the man with the perfect hair and teeth as if he did this kind of thing every day. The people watching at home would think only one thing: *This guy's a winner.*

Bentone crushed out his cigarette and got himself another from the pack resting beside his beer. The cigarettes, the beer, and the game show helped quiet his nerves, but they couldn't erase his problem forever.

What would I do with a new Mustang? he thought as he took a long pull off his smoke. Bentone knew what he would *have* to do: sell the damn car and use the money to pay off some of his debt to Benny the Wrench.

A waitress appeared by his booth with her tray. She wore so much blue eye shadow her eyes look bruised. Then again, a place like this, maybe they were. "Get you another, hon?"

Bentone shook his head. "I'm set." He lifted the mug to his lips and took another delicate sip as he watched her walk away.

In the real world, David Bentone had not won a new Mustang convertible, nor was he able to sustain the illusion that he would ever be given the chance. But he owed some very impatient and volatile men a great deal of money and he had to come up with some way to pay them back.

Up on the small screen, Donna proved to be exactly what he thought she would be. Unable to guess the proper retail prices for Happy Time Popcorn, Big Snapper Car Wax and Chef Pierre's Canned Beef Burgundy, she lost the car and left the stage a loser. Bentone knew she was a loser, but now she'd proved it to the world.

The remaining four contestants were taunted with the news that they would have a chance to win a prize worth more than a hundred thousand dollars, after the commercial break. An ad for adult diapers came on and Bentone turned his attention back to the closed environment of the booth and his troubled thoughts.

He breathed in the stale smell of countless cigarettes and spilled beers. Some of his best thinking
was done in places like this. Running his thumb
along the side of the mug, he felt the coolness of
the condensation, and he forced himself to confront his looming predicament. He'd owed people
money before and always figured out a way to pay it
back.

*Where's the guy as cool as an Alaska winter?
Where's the big-shot winner now?*

Bentone sucked the last from his cigarette and
deposited the filter with the other dead soldiers in
the ashtray. He ran both hands through his thick
black hair and sighed. How could he have gotten
himself into such a fix?

It was a question he had asked himself many
times over the last twenty years. He never seemed
to learn, never seemed able to change.

It was supposed to be a sure thing.

Little John Fabonio worked a window over at the
Hollywood Park Race Track. He had the inside
scoop on a horse named Mother's Milk that supposedly had what it took to blow away the competition.
When Bentone found out that the horse was born
the same day as his five-year-old daughter, Aubrey,
he knew it was an omen. Problem was, he thought it
was a good one.

It should have been the opportunity of a lifetime.
All the other deals he had mistakenly thought were

the real thing were just a warm-up to this, a precursor to the big payoff.

All he had to do was reap the benefits of a sufficient wager. One simple bet.

Bentone didn't have the money. A back injury had kept him out of work for the last six months. This gift from the gods had landed in his lap and he didn't have the cash to take advantage of it. But he knew where he could get it. So sure was he of Mother's Milk's imminent victory, he paid a visit to his favorite loan shark, Benny "the Wrench" Giordano and borrowed double what he currently owed, with an interest rate of thirty percent. Once he won, Bentone figured he'd have more than enough to pay off his debt and still have plenty left to play with.

The large, leathery-skinned loan shark looked more like an animal than a man, with thick tufts of fur sprouting from the backs of his rough, squared hands. That day, he sat hunched over the table as he counted out the money into two stacks. Then he had looked Bentone in the eyes.

"You better be sure about this, my friend. Money like this . . . You don't pay, we sell your organs one at a time to some rich freaks in South America. I don't even ask what they do with 'em."

The ominous words held no threat for Bentone. He had taken the stacks of cash and placed them carefully in the bottom of a shopping bag. As far as he was concerned, Mother's Milk had already won and by that time the next day he would have repaid his debt to the Wrench in full.

So much for that, he thought, and snorted derisively as he recalled his own foolishness. He took a small swig of beer and rolled it around in his mouth before swallowing.

The waitress passed by again, not even bothering to look in his direction. With a nervous hand, Bentone took another cigarette from the pack and lit up. On the TV above the bar, the afternoon news had replaced *Dollars and Sense* and the place had started to fill with a lunchtime crowd.

He took a long drag of the new cigarette, holding the smoke in his lungs. The idea of lung cancer didn't bother him much. As long as it killed him quick, it could be the answer to his prayers.

A sure thing. Mother's Milk had barely finished the race, placing a distant sixth.

So now he owed double what he had borrowed plus an additional thirty percent. It wouldn't be long before that thirty percent doubled. Tripled. Bentone didn't bother to do the math, even at half the amount he would still be unable to pay.

He drained the last of his beer as he imagined himself lying on a makeshift operating table in the back of a meat-packing plant owned by Benny Giordano. In his mind's eye, he saw two wiseguys in surgical scrubs sharpening their butcher knives, preparing to fill a rush order for a kidney.

Bentone broke out in a cold, prickly sweat. *No way*, he thought. There was no way he could get his hands on the kind of money the Wrench was expecting him to pay. He had to run. He had to leave L.A. immediately, get a new identity and start over again, someplace where the Wrench and his goons couldn't find him. He had no choice.

He didn't mind going to South America, as long as he could do it in one piece.

Bentone reached into his back pocket for his wallet. Inside, he found two five-dollar bills and an old scratch ticket, not even enough for bus fare out of the City of Angels. He swore beneath his breath, searching the wallet's various compartments for any money he might have set aside for a rainy day. He knew he wouldn't find anything—he'd used up all his rainy days.

Hiding behind his license, he did find a pocket calendar from 1997 and a picture of himself, his wife, and his daughter. They were all smiling; at that moment in time, the happiest people on the face of the planet.

Bentone stared at the photograph and tried to remember if there was ever a time when he had been as happy as he appeared to be in the picture.

A sudden anger welled up within him. *They* were the reason for all his problems. Even though he and June had split up over two years ago, Bentone was still looking out for the best interests of his family.

Everything he did was for them, to give them the best. But was it appreciated? *Not a chance*. The last time he saw his little girl, the ex had been screaming about child support. She had even threatened to keep him from seeing Aubrey if he didn't start providing them with a regular means of support.

They were the reason he owed the Wrench so much money, why he had to leave L.A. He put a thumb over their faces. Maybe leaving town wasn't such a bad thing after all. He stuck the wallet back into his pocket. Maybe he could take the ten dollars, find a crap game and—

Bentone jumped with a start, his heart beating furiously in his chest as he stared straight ahead. He was no longer alone in the booth.

The man sitting across from him nodded his head slightly. He was fortyish, well-dressed and handsome, with jet-black hair, long and slicked back. His eyes were the lightest blue Bentone had ever seen. Ice blue.

Bentone looked around to see if anyone was watching, wondering if this was some kind of prank. But he knew it wasn't. It felt *bad*. He turned back to the man who continued to watch him with a weird, cold stare.

The waitress walked by and the guy lifted a single finger. "Another beer for my friend."

"Look, I don't know you, pal," Bentone said nervously, as he stubbed out his cigarette. "But you can keep the booth. I'm just leavin' . . ."

Bentone started to slide from the booth. He had a sick feeling this guy was working for the Wrench. Somehow the shark had guessed he would run and sent somebody to make sure he didn't. He had to get out of there fast.

The man touched his arm gently. "David Bentone. You are David Bentone, are you not?"

The man spoke with a slight accent. *Probably from somewhere in Europe,* Bentone thought. He pulled his arm away as he stood.

"Nope. Sorry. You got the wrong guy. Look, I'm late for an appointment. Enjoy your booth."

He was moving up the aisle toward the door when the man spoke again. The words stopped him dead in his tracks.

"I believe I can help with your current financial situation."

Bentone turned. "What's that?"

The handsome man gestured to the empty place across from him. "Please, come and sit down. We will talk and you will see that I am not here to cause you any problems. Please. Sit."

Bentone slid back into the booth, eyeing the stranger cautiously.

"Excellent, David." He extended his hand. "Now we begin again, like gentlemen. My name is Anton Meskal."

Meskal's handshake was warm, firm. Bentone noticed some fine-looking rings on the man's fingers and an expensive watch as Meskal withdrew his hand. The guy had money.

"Mr. Giordano informed me of your current debt."

Bentone lit up a new smoke, shaking out the match and tossing it into the ashtray. He leaned his head back and blew smoke into the air. "Let me guess. You and the Wrench made a deal. You bought my marker and now you own me. Is that how it is?"

The waitress with the bruised eyes came back with a fresh beer and placed it in front of David. Meskal had nothing. The man tossed a twenty onto her tray and gestured her away.

"*Own* you, David? I don't want to own you. I want to help you."

Bentone took a swig of beer as he studied Meskal. "Why would you want to help me? You don't know me from Adam and I owe the biggest shark in Los Angeles an awful lot of money. Tell me how I happened to become one of your best friends, 'cause I'm really friggin' interested."

Meskal leaned forward and fixed Bentone in his cold, blue gaze. "I won't lie to you, David. I went to Mr. Giordano specifically looking for someone in your situation. Someone desperate."

Bentone was insulted. He stabbed the ashtray with his cigarette.

"Desperate? Y'know what, I don't think I like the direction this is going, so I'm gonna just walk on out of here. Thanks for the beer. Place like this, you shouldn't have any trouble finding another desperate type to talk to." He turned to go.

"Sit down, David," Meskal commanded, a new edge to his voice. "What little pride you had remaining was crushed beneath the weight of the debt you owe to a three-hundred-and-fifty-pound Neanderthal. Sit down, finish your drink and let me extend my offer. If you're not interested, I'll go on my way and won't bother you anymore. How does that sound?"

Bentone settled back into his seat and pulled his beer closer.

"Excellent." Meskal placed both well-manicured hands onto the scarred wooden tabletop. "It's quite simple, really. I need something that I believe only you can get for me, and I'm willing to take care of your problems with the Wrench in order to acquire it."

Bentone smiled and shook an admonishing finger at Meskal. "I know there's a catch to this. But you've got my attention." He took a long draught of his beer, then wiped his mouth on his hand. "That's an awful lot of money you're talkin' about pickin' up the tab on."

"Are you interested?" asked Meskal, the intensity returning.

Bentone squirmed. "What . . . what *exactly* would I have to do? Breakin' and enterin'? Robbery? I'm not gonna kill anybody," he said. He laughed nervously. "I'm not a criminal no matter what you heard, okay? And if you want someone dead, you're talkin' to the wrong guy."

"I'm sure I'm talking to the *right* guy. I'll only ask one time more. Are you interested, David Bentone?"

Meskal's intense eyes were starting to freak him out. David looked away, glancing about the room, anywhere except the man's eyes.

"Yeah. Yeah, I'm interested. I'd have to be an idiot not to be."

"Wonderful, David," Meskal responded happily. He folded his hands in front of him. "Now, shall we discuss the specifics of our transaction?"

Bentone couldn't avoid the man's gaze any longer. "What could someone like me possibly have that you would want?"

Anton Meskal's lips spread into an unsettling grin. A predator's smile.

CHAPTER ONE

Angel wrenched the slathering canine's head violently to one side, the junkyard dog's neck breaking with a wet snap. He tossed the still twitching body into the path of the slowly advancing pack of dogs in hopes of deterring the animals from attacking further.

"See what happens to bad dogs?" Angel said, as he eyed the savage pack before him.

His investigation into a recent rash of child abductions from some of the poor neighborhoods surrounding the junkyard had brought him to Dead End Salvage. The dogs were supposed to watch over the place, but the average watchdog would never have been this savage.

The pack leader, a mangy, gray-furred beast that looked to be a cross between a German shepherd and a Saint Bernard, bent down to sniff the corpse of its dead pack mate. The dog's wild, glassy eyes never left Angel as it took a single lap at the blood that trailed from the dead animal's nose. The four other dogs watched their leader, sniffing and mewling at the scent of death that now hung in the junkyard air.

The animals' movements were stiff and jerky; a strange, milky film covered their eyes. Angel felt a small pang of compassion for the beasts. It was obvious their actions were not their own.

Of course, compassion could be costly. Angel glanced briefly at his ravaged forearm and the torn material of his black coat. He felt the throb of the bite wounds that bled freely beneath the cloth. He flexed his hand and wiggled his fingers to make sure they were still in working order. There was pain, but not enough to concern him.

He really had no idea what he was up against. Not this time. All he knew was that children were missing, and he might be able to help.

Angel had been reading newspaper articles about the missing children. Nosing around, he learned that a viscous, foul-smelling fluid had been found at more than one of the crime scenes. The police pathologists were perplexed by their discovery that the fluid had come from some kind of animal, but one unknown in the annals of science. Angel could read between the lines. Demon, werewolf, whatever it was, the thing wasn't likely to be something the LAPD could handle. It was up to him. He had started working the case in his spare time. What little of it there was.

Now he was here, bleeding and without backup.

A sixth child was missing and the police seemed no closer to a solution. There was no obvious sign of the supernatural, but with each abduction, the possibility loomed larger that the perpetrator was not human.

Angel had studied maps of the area and decided to begin his investigation in a junkyard that bordered the neighborhoods from where the children were stolen. Amidst the stacks of twisted metal and the refuse of society, creatures that hunted in shadow could easily create a lair hidden from the curious eyes of humanity. Angel and Doyle had agreed to meet at the junkyard at sundown, but the demon halfling never showed. Impatient, and with the possibility that the children still lived, Angel had gone in alone.

He had scaled the razor wire–topped fence with ease, jumping down into the yard. Walking among the stacks of flattened automobiles and piles of discarded appliances, he had begun the search. Angel looked for a sign, something that would tell him if he indeed faced a supernatural threat, and if so, what sort. Only children had been taken and a foul-smelling fluid had been found at each crime scene, which made him suspect that some kind of earth dweller might be responsible. A troll, perhaps.

Angel had little fondness for any of the supernatural creatures that stalked the world in secret, but he had even less for trolls. Maybe because they preyed primarily on children. Whatever the case, Angel hated trolls.

At the moment, however, he was none too fond of dogs, either.

The pack of junkyard mutts snarled and circled him, trying to trap him between them. The pack leader leaped over the corpse of its fallen comrade with a guttural snarl. Angel caught the beast's muscular bulk in mid jump and stumbled backward into a stack of flattened automobiles. He gripped the matted fur of its neck, feeling the powerful muscles coil beneath.

"And me without a newspaper," he grunted, trying to keep the beast's snapping jaws from closing on his face.

The animal's breath was rank with the odor of death and decay, a smell the vampire was all too familiar with. The dog's paws raked at Angel's body, trying to rip through his clothes and the flesh beneath. Angel brought a knee violently up between the animal's legs. The leader howled in pain and rage as Angel threw its thrashing body away from him.

The dog skidded across the ground with a yelp, scattering the others in its wake. Quickly it regained its footing, shook the dirt from its fur and glared at Angel with hate-filled eyes.

The other dogs padded closer under the watchful eyes of their leader. They spread out, licking their chops, nervously sniffing at the air. Angel glanced down. A small puddle of blood from his bite wound was forming in the dirt near his feet.

The four dogs crouched, hackles raised around their necks, the dark flesh of their jowls peeled back to reveal nasty yellow teeth. Angel felt his own transformation begin. The flesh of his brow grew thicker, more pronounced, his incisors elongated to vicious points. In this form he was more in tune with the dogs' savagery, their madness. It wasn't natural.

"Last chance to be my best friend," he growled.

The dogs attacked. Angel lunged to the right, grabbing hold of a rusted metal bumper from a classic fifties car. He wrenched it away from the body of the flattened vehicle and swung.

The bumper connected with the first of the leaping beasts, its jaw practically torn from its face with the force of Angel's blow. It fell to the ground in a heap. The dog tried to stand, but slumped back to the ground and then grew very still. Another of the pack lunged. It ducked beneath the next swing and dove for Angel's side. The snarling vampire thrust the heavy bumper into the dog's mouth, preventing it from burying its teeth in his flesh. Then he brought the bumper down onto the dog's skull with a sickening crunch. The dog didn't make a sound as it flopped on its side, dead. Angel kicked the corpse away. He bared his fangs to the remaining beasts and advanced, holding the blood-flecked bumper.

"Now who's top dog?"

The dogs backed away to join the pack leader; the beast had taken up a defensive stance in front of the rusted-out remains of a black minivan. The three dogs came toward him, barking and snapping their jaws, and then returned to guard the van. Angel realized there was a reason they didn't want him near that particular hunk of junk.

That answered his question. These weren't just watchdogs. Something held an unnatural influence over them. Another of the dogs leaped at him and he swung the twisted bumper. Its spine shattered in mid leap as metal brutally connected with flesh and bone. Angel moved toward the van, holding the bumper menacingly. The wary dogs backed away.

"Do I have to kill you too?" he asked the two survivors.

The pack leader cocked its head quizzically and stared deep into Angel's yellow demonic gaze. The other dog continued to bark frantically.

"I'm the boss now. The pack is mine," Angel said forcefully. "Go." He could see their survival instinct was still strong despite the supernatural influence. He made a sudden move toward them. "Go on, get out of here."

The dogs hesitated, then began to whine, apparently struggling with the power commanding them and their own instincts.

Instinct won. Tails bent between their legs, the two slunk away from the minivan. When they had trotted off a ways, the German shepherd–Saint Bernard mix turned and let loose with a series of ferocious barks as if to warn him not to assume that because they were retreating, it meant he had beaten them. The pack leader padded confidently off into the shadows of the salvage yard, its surviving brother tagging close behind.

Angel studied the wreck of the van. The windows were covered in thick mud and dust that prevented him from seeing inside. The wheels had been removed, making it sit flush with the ground. A powerful stench wafted out of the van. If the dogs' behavior hadn't tipped him off, the smell would have clinched it: Angel knew he was in the right place. He discarded the bumper with a clatter of metal, then reached out and gripped both rear door handles. With a surge of vampiric strength he ripped the doors off their hinges and tossed them to either side.

"Knock, knock," he called out. He might be the scourge of the forces of darkness, but he wouldn't want them to think he was rude.

The inside of the van was stripped down to the bare metal. The stench was nearly palpable. Though he did not have to breathe, he put his coat sleeve to his mouth and nose to lessen the effects of the offensive odor, just in case he was tempted to inhale.

Where is that smell coming from? Angel wondered as he ducked his head and crawled inside.

The stench grew steadily stronger. He felt the movement of air on his face before he found the hole. The metal floor of the van was missing and a large hole had been dug into the ground. With deep regret, he inhaled. The horrible odor wafted up from the tunnel, carried on the slightest current of air, and now that he had gotten a better whiff, it confirmed his suspicions.

Troll. Angel snarled in disgust.

He glanced around the dirt floor and found further evidence he was in the right place: a pink barrette, a tiny sneaker, a broken action figure. The vampire crouched over the gaping hole and felt his rage growing. He reached down and let his hand run over the smooth earthen interior. His fingers came away covered with a thick, awful-smelling substance.

Probably a Duergar, he thought. Duergar trolls were an extremely rare and ferocious breed of earth dweller. They excreted a viscous, malodorous perspiration that acted as a kind of lubricant as they burrowed tunnels beneath the earth. Angel recalled that the Duergar also had the ability to control some of the lesser animals like rats, carrion birds and dogs. Trolls were always bad news, but the Duergar were the worst of the bunch.

Angel wiped his hand on his pants and stared into the tunnel. If those kids were down there, he shouldn't hesitate. But he also knew the last thing he should do was to go in without backup. None of which would have been a problem if Doyle had bothered to show.

Where are you when I need you, Doyle? he thought. It suddenly occurred to him that Cordelia might know where to find him. She was probably still at the office. Angel reached into his coat pocket for his cell phone, then let out an exasperated sigh. He'd left it on the seat of his car, which was parked on the street a couple of blocks from the salvage yard.

It wasn't the first time Doyle had forgotten an appointment, but they had specifically discussed the importance of this job that morning. The smell of troll drifted up from the hole to remind him that he had a decision to make. He made it. Again, he had no choice but to do this alone. Angel dropped into the wretched tunnel. His final thought before being enveloped in a cocoon of stench and darkness: *Doyle better have a damn good excuse.*

Doyle drifted in a mental fog. He didn't really know where he was. It felt as though he were floating in space . . . then suddenly he was in his apartment. Confused, he looked around. His place was much neater than he ever remembered seeing it. *I must have cleaned it and forgot,* he thought, as he took a deep breath of the room's uncommonly clean smell.

The room stank of garbage.

"Doyle?" a voice asked from somewhere in the room.

He turned and looked into the eyes of beauty.

Cordelia Chase was in his apartment. Odd, he didn't recall her coming in. Maybe that's why he had straightened up. It made sense.

Cordelia smiled at him and his heart began to beat faster.

His neck throbbed; a twinge of pain shot up from his throat to the side of his face.

Doyle walked toward her, returning her smile with one of his own. "Cordelia," he said, looking sheepishly from her face to the floor and then back to her. "Nice of you to drop by."

She was still smiling at him. He could feel the warmth of it. *It's like the sun,* he thought, as he looked deeply into her eyes.

His hands began to tremble. Here was the opportunity he'd been waiting for. Cordelia Chase, the woman of his dreams, in his apartment. His immaculate apartment that he didn't remember cleaning. He'd had a thing for the raven-haired beauty since the first time he saw her. When she started to work with Angel, and Doyle got to see her every day . . . well, to say his attraction to her grew was an understatement.

"Francis . . ."

Doyle was startled. She'd never called him by his first name before.

"Francis, there's something I've been wanting to tell you for a very long time."

Doyle was stunned as she took his hands in hers.

Her thumb rubbed across his knuckles and Doyle noticed they were no longer in his apartment but at the office, downstairs in Angel's living quarters.

"Weird," he muttered. But he dismissed the bizarre transition to listen to what Cordelia had to share with him.

She held his gaze with dark, moist eyes and squeezed his hands in hers. "I've had to build up an awful lot of courage to say this and I hope I don't scare you away."

Wet, he thought. *Something's soaking through the back of my pants.*

Doyle pushed the inane thought from his mind and returned his full attention to Cordelia. "You won't scare me, darlin', what is it?"

"I love you, Doyle. I've loved you from the first time I saw you."

For the briefest of moments he heard the melodious music of a harp, but that sound morphed into a cacophony of car horns.

This was more than he ever hoped for—a fantasy come true.

"I've grown more than a bit fond of you as well," Doyle said, as he brought Cordelia's hands up to his mouth to kiss them.

His lips fell upon nothing. He kissed only air. Cordelia now stood on the other side of a pub he often frequented by the name of Taggert's. She held a hand full of darts. It looked like she was getting ready to start a game.

"Are you ready?" she asked.

Was he ready? Doyle knew that in order for the two of them to be happy he had to share with her his darkest secret. But should he risk it? He had waited so long to tell her how he really felt. Now that he knew she felt the same, did he want to chance driving her away?

Taggert's smelled of garbage, rotting vegetables, like his apartment, and he looked about for the source of the offensive aroma. His gaze was drawn back to Cordelia, who watched him expectantly.

Now or never, he decided. *If she can't take the fact that I'm half Brachen demon, well then, it just wasn't meant to be.*

The pain in his neck grew sharper.

Doyle walked across the pub's wooden floor, his feet sinking into it as though it were made of foam rubber. He thought that was a tad unusual.

"Cordelia," he stammered, "I've got somethin' I guess I ought to be sharin' with ye as well."

The darts were now sticking out from various parts of Cordelia's bare arms and throat. Others jutted from her face and scalp.

"Yes, Francis?"

That's a bit queer, isn't it? Doyle thought briefly. "I also have a little secret I think ye should know."

"Go on." Cordelia's entire body now resembled a strange kind of pincushion. She was covered with protruding darts.

Doyle closed his eyes and said his piece. "Cordelia, I'm half demon. My mother was human and me da—well, Da wasn't. I know how you feel about demons and such, and I can understand if ye are a bit frightened, but let me assure ye that—"

"That's great, Francis," Cordelia said, as she typed away at the computer on her desk.

Doyle looked around the office of Angel Investigations and then at the woman with whom he had just shared his darkest secret. The darts were gone from her beautiful body and he was relieved.

"Do ye understand, Cordy? I just told ye I'm part monster."

Cordelia continued to tap busily away at the keyboard. "Ah-*ha*, that's great, isn't it?" she said, staring into the computer screen.

This isn't right at all, he thought. As he approached her desk he began to let his demonic features show. He leaned forward, making sure she could see that his skin was blue and covered with rows of sharp quills.

"I'm half Brachen demon," he said to her.

Cordelia looked up and smiled broadly. "That's great."

Doyle's nostrils filled with the stench of garbage, his ears heard the phantom blare of city traffic. *This isn't right. Not right at all.*

"I've got no money and I want to marry you," he said.

Cordelia continued to grin at him, not bothered in the least by his demonic countenance or his proclamation of poverty.

"Awesome," she beamed.

" 'N Sync is the grandest band ever . . . even better'n U2, I think."

"Oh, I totally agree," Cordelia responded, never missing a beat. She returned to her typing.

"All right, that's it!" Doyle snapped. He lunged forward, grabbed the doppelgänger by the shoulders and shook her furiously.

"What've you done with the real Cordelia Chase . . . tell me!"

The floor beneath him disappeared and he began to fall into an inky void. He heard her voice all around him. But the voice began to change.

"And you wonder why I'm so upset."

Doyle awoke with a violent cough, trying to hack up the thick, foul film that coated the inside of his throat. The broken pavement of the alley was wet beneath him and had soaked through the bottom of his jeans. His head pounded and he could hear the sound of traffic off in the distance.

"Oh, aye, this is paradise," he muttered.

And what the hell am I doing here? he thought. His memories, except for the bizarre hallucination, were fuzzy.

"Who's Cordelia Chase?" a female voice demanded from nearby.

He stared blearily ahead, blinked his eyes into focus, and saw a large, green Dumpster. Someone— or something—was perched on the cover of the trash receptacle in a predatory crouch, watching him.

"What'd ye do to me?" Doyle rasped as he tried to stand.

"Did I hurt you, hon? Poor baby."

A sharp, red-hot pain shot through his neck. Doyle's hand went to his throat. Something was sticking from his flesh. With careful fingers he touched the protruding, needle-like object and plucked it from his neck.

A quill. It was all coming back to him.

He attempted to stand again but his hands slipped in the bits of rotting vegetables that had not made it into the Dumpster.

"Verna. Why'd ye stick me with one of yer quills, darlin'? Did I do somethin' wrong?"

The female demon, her body covered in a fine sheen of long, quivering protrusions, leaped from the lid of the trash container to land catlike in front of Doyle.

"Don't give me that sweet talking 'Danny Boy' crap," she snarled. "You know exactly what you did."

His vision was clearing and Doyle looked into the demon woman's dark, feral eyes. What he saw there was not a monster wanting to murder and maim for the fun of it, but a woman whose feelings he'd hurt.

Doyle had met Verna a week ago at a tavern where he was still allowed to keep a tab. The place was frequented by some of the more unusual denizens of the city. It wasn't the type of place he normally would have chosen to linger, but he was low on cash that particular evening and a mean thirst had been crying to be quenched.

He'd noticed the red-haired beauty halfway through his fourth beer; by the fifth she had taken note of him. Around the eighth, Doyle had learned everything he cared to know about the woman: her turn-offs and turn-ons, where she worked, everything except the all-important fact that she wasn't human. He didn't get that bit of info until sometime around last call when she asked if he would be interested in escorting her home.

He hadn't seen her since. Until now.

With a snarl, Verna brought a quilled forearm up under Doyle's chin. The lethal needles lengthened to press against the soft skin at his throat.

"Give me one good reason why I shouldn't kill you, you heartless creep!"

Doyle touched her arm, careful to avoid being punctured. "Could ye give me a bit of a clue as to what I've done to offend ye?"

The demon woman began to cry. "I thought we hit it off that night—that we had a real special chemistry. And you let me believe it."

Doyle tried desperately to remember what had happened after last call. Verna had snuggled up to him seductively and now he recalled his shock as he watched the quill-like protrusions extend slowly from her flesh. She was a Kashshaptu demon; the toxin that covered her quills was a hallucinogen in small doses and lethal in larger ones.

"You said you'd call," Verna cried sadly. "Why didn't you?"

Doyle thought fast. "I was gonna call . . . but . . . but I lost yer number. I had it in me shirt pocket and it went in the wash. It happens. I'm sorry, really I am."

Doyle had very little to do with the demonic side of his heritage. Ever since the day he had discovered the truth about himself, he had been deeply ashamed and acknowledged it as little as possible.

The phone-number-in-the-wash excuse seemed to dispel some of Verna's anger. She smiled, and Doyle was surprised at how alluring he found her.

A real shame she's a demon, he thought.

"It's just that we had such a nice time that night and you did say you wanted to get to know me better. I thought I would have heard from you sooner and . . ."

Doyle watched as Verna grew calmer and the quills receded beneath her flesh.

"When you didn't call I got so mad. And when I saw you walking into that pub I got furious. Now I'm feeling like a total jerk." She moved closer and looked him in the eyes. "Can you forgive me?"

Doyle put on his most charming smile. " 'Course I can."

She smiled at him warmly, seductively. "So, are you interested in doing something tonight, angel?" she asked, biting sexily at her lower lip.

Doyle violently slapped his forehead in frustration. "For the love a God! Angel!"

"Who?" Verna demanded, a hurt expression already starting to spread across her face. "Who's Angel? Another one of your bar conquests?"

The quills were beginning to show again, their tips glistening with toxin.

"He's a guy, Angel is a guy—my boss, really," he told her. Doyle carefully grabbed her shoulders. "Look, I can't go out with ye tonight. I've just remembered a very important business meeting I'm late for. I'll give you a call this weekend if that's okay with ye. I swear."

Verna began to question him, but Doyle leaned

forward and gave her a quick peck on the cheek, careful not to stick himself.

"Talk to ya soon," he said, as he turned and ran up the alley. "I'm really sorry. Thanks for being so understandin' and all."

He quickened his pace as he headed toward the street, muttering about Angel wanting to kill him and the likelihood he would be giving up talking to strange women in pubs in the foreseeable future.

The stinking tunnel under the junkyard opened into what appeared to be some kind of Parks Department storage garage.

Angel peered into the darkness. He could make out the shapes of lawn mowers, wheelbarrows and sacks of old grass seed. Rakes, shovels and hedge clippers hung from large hooks in the wall. The filthy aroma of a supernatural beast hung thick and pungent in the air. Angel crawled up from the hole in the center of the garage floor and began his search.

The room was covered in thick layers of dust and dirt; cobwebs hung from the ceiling. It was obvious the garage had not been used in quite some time—at least not by anything remotely human. There were tracks in the dust-covered floor and Angel followed them to the back of the storehouse.

Far off in a corner he saw a flicker of light. He moved carefully toward it and saw that a crude, makeshift curtain separated a small area from the rest of the room. A flame burned on the other side. With great caution, Angel parted the curtain and peered within.

He had found the monster's lair.

A fire burned beneath a large black kettle filled with thick, simmering liquid. To the right of the cooking pot, Angel spotted a heap of discarded clothing and rags. A pathetic whimper drew his attention to the other side of the room.

Six children had been reported missing. Angel had found four of them. They were bound and gagged but appeared healthy enough, their faces and clothes stained with dirt.

They had seen him as well. Their small forms went rigid with a mixture of fear and the anticipation of freedom. He motioned with a finger to his lips for them to be quiet.

Angel parted the curtain further and checked every shadow of the room for potential danger before he moved toward the children.

His foot caught on something, a string or wire strung across the entryway, and he stumbled. A kind of primitive alarm system. The sounds of rattling bones and clanking cans filled the space as the vampire regained his footing. He squatted before the kids.

"Don't worry, I'm usually not this clumsy during a rescue," Angel whispered to the oldest child, as he tugged the gag away from boy's mouth.

"Look out!" the boy screamed.

Angel dove to the right as a blood-encrusted ax blade made its descent, nearly cleaving the vampire's skull in two.

Sparks flew from the blade's edge as it cut into the concrete floor.

Angel was angry, but also embarrassed. What he had believed to be a pile of rags had been in fact the sleeping monster, and he had awakened it with his clumsiness.

"Made it past my puppies, I see," the troll rumbled, pulling the ax out of the concrete with a gurgling laugh. It prepared to strike again. "Bad puppies, didn't do their job. But I shouldn't complain. I like it when fresh meat comes to me."

The troll brought the ax up over its shaggy head and lunged. The creature was about Angel's height, but outweighed him by at least a hundred pounds. It was clothed in tattered, bloodstained rags, and had two, yellowed, tusklike teeth protruding from its mouth.

Angel lashed out with a snap kick, hit the troll in its bulging gut, and sent it sprawling backward into the bubbling cauldron. He quickly turned his attention back to the children and untied the ropes of the oldest child.

"Get the others out of here. Do it."

The child nodded and began to furiously work at the bindings of the girl next to him.

Angel had made a conscious effort to keep his vampiric countenance from surfacing in front of the children. But now, as he turned back toward the troll, he felt his face change for the second time that night. His tongue flicked over the tips of the razor-sharp fangs that now filled his mouth.

The troll had crashed into the pot, knocked it away, and landed on the fire burning beneath it. Now it slapped at the burning hair on its back as it struggled to pick itself off the ground and move toward the ax lying nearby.

Angel could see the contents of the spilled cauldron scattered about the troll's feet and knew the fate of the other two missing children. That and the stench of smoldering troll hair turned his stomach with revulsion.

The troll grinned and shifted the ax from its left hand to its right. "You set my livestock free, vampire, and then you spill my soup? Not a nice thing . . . not a nice thing at all."

It was larger than any troll Angel had previously encountered, definitely a Duergar. Though he knew he shouldn't turn his back on it, he glanced quickly over to see how the kids were faring. The eldest and two others were untying the last and youngest of the captives.

The troll attacked again, swinging the blade with both hands, apparently intent upon cutting the vampire in two. Angel moved out of the way of the swing and felt the displacement of stagnant air as the blade passed by much too close.

"Never had vampire meat, heard it's tough and stringy, but I'm willing to keep an open mind. 'Course, you'll be alive to watch. Otherwise all I'll have is powder."

The kids screamed and ran toward the curtain and freedom beyond. Distracted by their shouts, the troll glanced over at them.

"Come back here, my tasty treats, the only freedom you will have from me is when you pass through my bowels."

Angel took advantage of the distraction and ducked inside the troll's defenses, then slammed a fist into the beast's bulbous midsection. The troll staggered backward and swung out awkwardly with its ax.

"Y'know, I would've figured you for a vegetarian," Angel said as he hit the troll again, a solid blow to the side of its head. The troll pitched forward and dropped its weapon.

"Beans, sprouts . . ." Angel launched a side kick at the creature's dark, boarlike face. "Legumes, tofu. Tofu'd be good for you."

He lashed out again, but the troll grabbed his ankle and twisted, sending him to the floor. The creature loomed over the stunned vampire. It bent down and slashed long, clawed fingers, meant for digging through hard-packed dirt and rock, across Angel's chest.

The pain was excruciating. Angel rolled away before the beast could slash him again. He brought a hand to his chest. His fingers came away a deep red.

Blood dripped from the injured troll's mouth. He spat a large gob of bloody saliva to the floor. "If you live—though I doubt you will—I'd wash them cuts good. Wouldn't want them getting infected." The creature laughed. It was a horribly unpleasant sound, harsh and gurgling.

Then the troll cocked its shaggy head quizzically and pointed a long, black-nailed finger. "I know who you are now—the fearsome Angelus—well, not so fearsome since you got your pretty soul back."

The beast knew his history. Not that it was uncommon for the creatures of darkness to have heard of him.

"You'd be surprised," Angel said as he sprang at the foul beast.

He hit the troll with a vicious punch across the face and felt one of its tusks break away. The creature stumbled back through the curtain and into the main area of the maintenance garage. Angel followed, shaking off the pain in his bleeding knuckles.

"Sorry about the tooth. I'll do the other one if you'd like. Wouldn't want to throw that handsome face off-balance."

Now that they were out in the main area of the garage, Angel spotted the kids. They were struggling with a series of sliding bolts on the door, locks the troll probably installed himself to keep unwelcome visitors away from his den.

"A vampire with a soul," the troll sneered. "Tainted by human weakness—what a freak. It must kill you to remember all you've done. How do you live with yourself?"

The creature laughed again and began to back up toward its tunnel, apparently preparing to flee. "I know how," it went on. "You destroy what reminds you of what you once were." The troll spit blood again. He was almost to the hole.

Angel was annoyed. The creature was actually beginning to get under his skin.

"Troll psychology? Spare me," Angel growled. "You think I'm that easily distracted? You think I'm going to let you just walk out of here?"

"No," the troll replied in a reasonable voice. "Not at all."

Then the creature made its move, but it wasn't what Angel expected.

The children had just gotten the door open, letting in the cool air of the night, when the troll bypassed his hole and went for them. Angel watched in horror as the beast snatched up the youngest child. She was no more than four and began to kick and scream in the hideous monster's clutches.

"You ruined a nice, home-cooked meal," the troll snarled. "So I guess I'll have to have takeout."

The troll put a jagged claw to the soft throat of

the little girl as he again moved toward his tunnel, and Angel. He sniffed at the child's hair. A trail of thick bloody saliva dribbled from his mouth onto the girl's head.

"I go into that hole and I'm sure you're going to follow." He inched closer to the opening. "I can't allow that to happen."

Angel snarled and took a step toward the troll.

The little girl let out a high-pitched yelp as the troll scraped a sharp black nail across her throat and drew a thin line of crimson.

"Come no closer, vampire. I'd have no problem at all opening her up before you killed me. Could your precious soul stand the guilt of knowing you were responsible for her death?"

Angel balled his fists in suppressed anger.

The troll moved closer to his escape route. The little girl whimpered, feet dangling in the creature's grasp.

"What happened, Angel? Why bother with me at all? Way I heard it you used to work with the Slayer to fight the forces of darkness on a much more . . . apocalyptic level. Did you get demoted? Couldn't cut it in the big time, so they sent you off to interrupt a hungry troll's dinner? You've come down in the world, Angel. Far down. Very sad when you think about it."

The troll moved closer to the hole and Angel seethed. The foul creature's words reverberated through his mind. Though he told himself it was just talk meant to unsettle him, he couldn't help wondering if the beast was right. Did the Powers That Be purposely pit him against less universal evils? Worse yet, did he himself somehow choose the more mundane threats? Certainly, he had helped individuals, done a lot of good. But how effective was he really in the larger battle against the forces of darkness?

His thoughts raced.

The troll's clawed toes hung over the lip of the tunnel. The child dangled over the yawning shaft, held in the monster's arms.

"I wonder if they'll demote you even further when word of your failure to stop me gets out? Maybe they'll put you in charge of looking for the smaller evils, the kind that hide beneath rocks or inside old tree stumps."

It tossed its shaggy head back as it laughed, and Angel made up his mind. He knew the child's safety was at risk but he could not allow her to be taken. If she went into that hole, she would not live to see the sun again. For her sake, he had to take the chance.

The creature's skin suddenly turned wet and shiny as lubricating sweat exuded from its pores. The troll was about to go into the tunnel.

"And to think we were afraid of you," it snarled as it bent its legs, preparing to jump.

A hand shot up from the dark tunnel, grabbed the troll's right leg and yanked hard enough to topple the creature. It slammed down onto the concrete on its back and lost its grip on the little girl, who screamed and rolled away.

Doyle popped his head out of the tunnel. *"I'm afraid of him, for pete's sake, and I work for the guy."* A look of revulsion was etched on Doyle's features as he scrambled from the tunnel, wiped something sticky from his sleeves, and picked the weeping child up in his arms.

"That's okay, darlin', I've got ye."

The troll let out an enraged roar and lunged for Doyle. Angel got there first. He kicked the creature in the face, sending its loathsome body back to the concrete floor.

Angel stood over the troll, yellow eyes glaring at the earth dweller with a look beneath contempt. He held something in his hands.

"Take the girl out of here," he told Doyle, his gaze never leaving the troll. "There should be other kids outside."

"Sorry I'm late. I followed yer trail of dead dogs and twisted wreckage from the junkyard. Ye'll never believe why—"

"It's all right," Angel interrupted, "we'll talk later. Go. I've got to finish up here."

Without another word, Doyle turned and took the child out.

The troll tried to rise but Angel's foot kept him pinned against the stone floor of the storage garage. Where were the taunts? Where was the bravado now that an innocent child's life no longer protected it? All gone. There was fear in the Duergar troll's eyes now.

Angel was expressionless as he stared down at the troll, holding a pair of dust-covered hedge clippers out in front of him. He opened the blades with a rusty squeal.

"What do you say," Angel growled, a grim, determined smile snaking across his feral features, "little off the top?"

The blades descended.

CHAPTER TWO

"Look, Daddy!" Aubrey Bentone shrieked happily from the playground swing. "Look how high I can go!" The child pumped with her legs, making herself swing faster and higher. "Daddy!"

David Bentone sat on top of a weather-worn picnic table a short distance away, smoking a cigarette with his back to his daughter. She called his name again and this time he finally turned to look at her. Five-year-old Aubrey was swinging up a storm, letting go of one of the swing's chains for a moment to wave wildly at her father.

Bentone acknowledged with a halfhearted wave. He took a long drag of his cigarette and returned to thoughts of Anton Meskal and his offer.

The day had become slightly overcast, grayish clouds attempting to obscure the warming rays of the sun. Bentone shuddered, an icy chill running up and down the length of his spine. He blamed it on the weather, but in fact he had felt cold ever since meeting Meskal two days ago.

Guy's obviously a nut, Bentone thought. What Meskal wanted . . . Bentone figured it had to be some kind of joke. Though remembering the look on the European's face and those cold, cold eyes, he had a feeling that Meskal was not the joking type.

Bentone watched his daughter. She was giggling, tossing back her head of black curls as she swung. He had never taken the time to notice how beautiful his child was until these last couple of days. Meskal was right; children were full of life and innocence. They were pure.

Meskal had wanted to know everything about Aubrey; her favorite color, what foods she liked and disliked. He said he needed to know the child to receive the full value of his acquisition.

Bentone's hand went to his jacket pocket. He wanted to make sure the thing Meskal had given him had not accidentally fallen out. The pocket felt warm to his touch. Had the item been warm like that when he first got it? He couldn't remember. He tried to picture the moment in his head.

Meskal had carefully removed it from the pocket of his sports coat. It was swathed in plastic bubble wrap. He had slid it across the table toward Bentone, telling him to unwrap it. Bentone had peeled away the plastic and looked at it. The thing had the shape of a gun but it was unlike any gun he had ever seen. It was very delicate and looked more like the skeletal remains of something that had once been alive. He could very easily imagine it scuttling across the ocean floor. He found himself afraid of it.

Now, as he recalled his first look at the thing, Bentone shuddered.

With the giddy sounds of his gleeful child echoing in the air, Bentone slid his hand inside his pocket, carefully examining the object by touch alone. He was sure it was giving off a faint heat. It felt as though it was covered with skin—a thin layer stretched over a delicate bone framework. The thing gave him the creeps and he pulled his hand from his coat pocket.

The collector, Meskal had called it. The name itself gave it an unsettling power.

Bentone finished his cigarette and flicked the filter into the grass. Meskal had explained that David needn't be a good shot to obtain what he wanted. *Just hold it in your hand and aim,* the European had said. *The collector will do the rest.*

The sun broke through the gathering clouds, bathing the park in its warming rays. The light felt good on his face, but it didn't do anything to melt the icy chill he still felt inside.

Bentone couldn't pass up an opportunity like this no matter how uncomfortable it made him feel. Meskal was his only hope of getting out of debt, the only way he could save his own life. The guy was obviously insane—what he asked was ridiculous—but what could it hurt? He would just do what Meskal said and his debt to the Wrench would be taken care of. How could he *not* take advantage of the opportunity?

His daughter jumped from the swing and headed toward him. "Daddy, will you come and play with me?" Aubrey asked, head tilted to one side.

The child was striking, with curly, black hair and deep, soulful brown eyes. She wore baggy little jeans and a pink cardigan sweater with a white Pokémon T-shirt underneath.

"Not right now, Aubrey," he said. "Got a . . . got a lot of thinkin' to do. Why don't you go play on the slide?"

The child didn't listen. Instead, she crawled up onto the picnic table and sat beside her father.

"Go on," said Bentone to the little girl, "go play. Daddy's thinkin'."

She moved closer to her father, pressing her face against his arm. "I'll think too," she said.

He looked down at his daughter and thought about what he had agreed to do. Meskal promised she wouldn't be hurt, that the device would take only what it needed. Then his life would be good again. He'd be free.

I should just do it now and get it over with, he thought, looking around the playground. It was empty; the last group of kids had left with their parents a little while ago.

Just hold it in your hand and aim, Meskal had said.

Bentone got down from the table and faced his daughter. His hand went into his jacket pocket again.

Aubrey smiled sweetly at him.

"You done thinkin', Daddy? Me too. What did you think about?"

The device slid warmly into his hand.

He heard Meskal's accented voice as if he were there. *Hold it in your hand and aim. The collector will do the rest.*

Aubrey rattled on. "I thought about how you use'ta live with me and Mommy. I want you to come back and live in my house again."

Aubrey smiled and her father's heart began to melt. Any chance he had of doing what Meskal wanted was blown away with that smile. He removed his hand from the collector in his pocket.

"I'd like that too—very much," Bentone agreed. He took her small hand in his and helped her down from the picnic table. "But I don't know if I could live with a monkey like you."

Aubrey began to swing on her father's arm, making whooping sounds and scratching her armpit. "Look, Daddy," she said, walking in a crouch. "I'm a monkey. Why wouldn't you want to live with a monkey? Monkeys are nice, aren't they?"

Bentone chuckled as he looked down at the

angelic face of his baby girl. "Yeah," he answered, "I guess monkeys are all right."

They were walking across the playground toward an exit behind a softball diamond. An ice cream truck was parked outside.

"What do you think?" he asked her. "Do monkeys like chocolate or vanilla?"

She looked up and gave him that smile again. He didn't feel quite so cold anymore.

"Vanilla!" she shrieked. She let go of his hand and began running toward the softball field.

Bentone watched his daughter run and began to think that maybe he hadn't put enough thought into this, maybe there *was* something he could do to pay back Giordano. Maybe he didn't need Meskal's deal at all.

"Hey, Aubrey, wait up," he called to her as he stopped in front of an overflowing trash barrel. He took out the collector and prepared to throw it away. He didn't want to carry it anymore. *I run into Meskal again,* Bentone thought, *I'll just tell him I lost it.* Simple as that.

"Good call back there, Mr. Bentone," a voice said from behind.

But the playground had been empty. He had been certain of that. Bentone turned quickly to see two strangely dressed men on the merry-go-round. They both stared at him as the ride spun slowly around.

"You talkin' to me?" he asked, Meskal's property clutched in his hand.

Their faces were hidden in the long afternoon shadows. One of them spoke; he could not be certain which. They wore identical trench coats with the collars turned up and old-style hats, fedoras, like Bentone's grandfather had once worn.

"Mr. Meskal would advise against performing the act in such a public place. Maybe somewhere a little more private, like your apartment or the child's home, would be more appropriate."

Bentone's blood turned to ice. Meskal had people watching him. Tentatively, he slid the device back inside his jacket pocket.

"She's a real beauty, Mr. Bentone," one of them said. "You must be proud."

Bentone could barely move his legs, but he forced himself to turn and walk stiffly away from the overflowing trash can and the men on the merry-go-round. He headed in the direction of his daughter, who waited impatiently at the softball diamond.

"C'mon, Dad," he heard her yell, gesturing for him to hurry.

One of Meskal's men called from the children's ride as Bentone left the play area.

"Better catch up with her, *Dad*. We wouldn't want anything to happen to sweet little Aubrey before you fulfilled your end of the bargain."

Bentone whipped around, face flushed with

anger. He was ready to tell the pair they could both go to hell and their boss was welcome to join them.

But they were gone.

Aubrey called to him again. She was afraid that the ice cream man was going to leave if he didn't hurry.

Bentone searched the park for any sign of the men with the dead eyes.

But there was nothing. The playground was empty, the still slowly spinning merry-go-round the only evidence they had been there at all.

Cordelia Chase sat at her desk in the offices of Angel Investigations and scanned the grocery store circular for bargains. With very little happening in her fledgling acting career and no help forthcoming from her tax-evading parents, Cordelia had no choice but to try to stretch the money she received from working for Angel as far as it would go.

As she clipped a coupon for a breakfast cereal that promised to provide her with all the essential vitamins and minerals she needed to survive the day-to-day rigors of the working woman, she heard the rumble of the elevator coming up from Angel's apartment.

The elevator ground to a halt. She could hear Angel push aside the gate and step into his office.

"Hey," Cordelia called as she flipped to the next page of the grocery store flyer.

"Hey," Angel responded as he walked out to the coffee machine. He picked up the steaming carafe and poured himself a mug.

"How are those troll scratches coming along? All healed up yet?" Cordelia cheerfully inquired. "Running low on Band-Aids?"

Angel sipped his coffee. "The scratches are practically healed and I'm doing all right with Band-Aids. Why?"

"The Save and Shop has them on sale—the ouchless kind for those less than macho, if you're interested." She traced a finger down the page, scissors poised to cut.

"I'll survive."

"Suit yourself. You don't see a bargain like that every day."

Angel shot a confused look at Cordelia. "Can I ask what you're doing?"

Cordy sighed impatiently. "It's called being a smart consumer. I heard you can save all kinds of cash using these coupon thingies, and seeing that I'm two baby steps away from being destitute . . ." She scanned the circular's next page. "What about grape jelly?"

Angel shook his head. "Not really high on my grocery list. I don't actually have much of a grocery list, in case you forgot."

He walked back toward his office and stopped. "Has Doyle been in?"

Cordelia wrinkled her nose disapprovingly at something in the flyer. "Can I get an—eeew!—cocktail weiners? Ewww! And, speaking of weiners, no, he hasn't been in yet."

Angel paced back and forth in front of the doorway to his office, pausing now and then to sip his coffee.

"Hear of anything that might require my attention—anything in the newspaper or on television?"

Cordelia looked up from her circular, setting her scissors down.

"All right, what's going on? You've been running around all give-me-some-Ritalin-boy since that thing with the troll. Spill."

Angel scowled. "Just a little too quiet, that's all." He turned and went into his office.

"Oh, let's see," Cordelia called after him. "In two days you've put the kibosh on a vampire street gang, two slime demons, a nest of harpies and the assorted worshipers of things that would have gone bump in the night if you hadn't killed them all."

Angel came back to the doorway. "I'm just doing my job. You can't exactly fight the forces of darkness part-time."

"Meaning what? You've only got a week to destroy evil? Did the Powers That Be give you some kind of revised schedule or something, because if they did I'm going to be asking for some serious overtime. You can't be everywhere at once, Angel.

51

Can't save everyone. You'll go crazy if you try, and I'd really rather not be around for that."

Angel turned back toward his office, but paused and reached up to scratch his head. He turned to regard Cordelia. "It's just something the troll said."

Cordelia nodded. "Trolls, a very reliable source of information. Go on."

"Well, there's so much evil in the world and what am I really accomplishing? A chaos demon here, a harpy there; it all seems so pointless when you look at the big picture."

Cordelia stared at him. "Okay, is this where I'm supposed to give you the pep talk? Go, Angel, go?" She halfheartedly waved a fist in the air. "Look, you're doing what the Powers That Be want you to do. Every day you sacrifice a great deal for customers who can't pay—and that's okay, kinda."

Angel gazed into his coffee cup as if he were in a trance, or trying to read his fortune there.

Cordelia leaned toward him. "Hey."

He looked up.

"We're all making sacrifices for the good fight," she told him. "Personally, I can't handle any more sacrificing. Hello! It's eight P.M. and I'm not going home soon! And the pay? Witness my cutting of coupons.

"You're doing a good job, Angel. You're helping people."

"But is it enough?" he asked.

An awkward silence filled the space between them, and then it was broken as Doyle came into the office eating French fries from a greasy bag.

"Angel. Cordelia. Didn't know if anybody'd be around."

Cordelia folded the cut-up circular and tossed it into the trash can beside her desk.

"Doing my part in the battle against evil." She held up a coupon and waved it at the man. "Hey, Doyle, how do you feel about beef burgundy in a can? Fifty cents off."

"I don't feel anything. Fry?"

He offered the bag to Cordelia. She turned up her nose and shook her head.

"My body is a temple, not a second-floor walk-up with a shared bathroom and a hot plate, but thanks for asking." She began to gather her things together.

Doyle sat on the windowsill and helped himself to a few more fries. "But ye'll consider beef burgundy in a can?" he asked. He shrugged and had another mouthful of fries. "Suit yerself."

Then he looked at Angel. "So, what's up?"

Angel studied him in silence.

"Look, Angel, if yer still upset over me not gettin' to the junkyard on time, all I can do is say I'm sorry for the hundredth time. How was I ta know that a lovesick demoness would ambush me outside me favorite pub?"

"It's not you, Doyle," Cordelia piped in as she

placed her pocketbook on the desk. She slipped her coupons inside. "Angel's feeling inadequate these days. He's tired of dealing with the piddly evils, yadda, yadda, yadda. Only the mega evils for him, thank you very much. I tried to tell him he's doing a good job but he insists on being tortured-vampire-hero-guy tonight."

Doyle put the greasy bag down and brushed the salt from his hands. He frowned as he looked at Angel more closely.

"I'm sorry, mate, but Cordy's right. Yer doing a fine job, and doing exactly what yer supposed to. Sure, the Powers That Be might need ye to fight some big nasty that threatens the world from time to time, but the real job is right here, on the streets. First time we met I told ye y' needed to get involved with the lives of regular humans. The Powers That Be are killin' two birds with one stone. Y' save lives, and save yerself at the same time. If ye want to be redeemed for yer past, ye have to walk among the average joes, save 'em from the darkness, a life at a time."

They were all silent as Doyle returned to his fries.

"Though I do wish ye white hats would speed things up a mite so I could spend a bit more time at the pub."

As Cordelia slung her bag over her shoulder, preparing to leave, she shot Doyle a withering look. "That's what it's all about, isn't it, Doyle? More quality time three sheets to the wind?"

Doyle talked through a mouthful of fries. "Don't be unfair now. It's got nothin' to do with the alcohol, really. I just happen to find the atmosphere of a pub relaxin'."

Angel and Doyle both watched as Cordelia walked to the door.

"Oh well, that's it for me, kids. I'm going to begin what's left of my exciting evening with a trip to the grocery store and who knows, maybe when I get home Phantom Dennis will have moved my furniture around again. Can you stand the excitement?"

As she pulled open the door Angel called to her. "Cordelia?"

She turned. "Yes, boss?"

He hesitated for a moment, face expressionless. "Thanks."

Cordelia shot him a bright smile. "Glad I could help. Tomorrow we'll talk about my raise."

Doyle took a step toward her. "Y'know, Cordelia, if yer evening is goin' ta be that boring, I could—ah, hell!"

He twitched in absolute agony and threw himself back against the window blinds. His cry of pain was pathetic as he slid to the floor.

Cordelia shouted his name and ran toward him.

The image seared itself into his mind's eye.

A house . . . a ranch-style house in a working-

class neighborhood. A sign on a corner post reads VINE STREET.

Angel was at his side, holding on to his arm as the vision continued to wrack his body.

A child. A little, dark-haired girl no more than five years old. She's in her pajamas, playing in her room.

Cordelia was there as well, on the other side. She slipped a hand behind his head to keep him from banging it on the floor.

A monkey. The little girl is playing with a monkey doll.

Doyle thrashed again, his hands going to his throbbing skull.

Somebody is in the room with her now. She's turned and is smiling. She knows him. She holds the doll up for him to see.

Angel and Cordelia helped him up into a sitting position, but the vision went on, like metal spikes through his head.

What is that? Something is being pointed at the girl. She's still smiling. What is it? A gun? Is it a gun?

The pain was as bad as it had ever been. The agony of the vision itself, and the suffering of what he saw.

The child is hit in the chest by a bolt of snaking blue energy. It knocks her back to the ground. She isn't moving. She lays there, eyes wide, unseeing.

Then the vision was gone, leaving only the pain. Angel helped him to Cordelia's desk chair.

"That seemed like a bad one," Angel said. "You okay? What did you see?"

Cordelia brought him a glass of water. His hands trembled as he brought it to his lips.

"It was a bad one," he confirmed. "They're always worse when there's a child involved." Doyle looked at Angel. "This is what I'm talkin' about, mate. Why I have the visions and ye do whatcha you do. Something horrible's happened to a little girl. Aubrey, her name is. That's all I got, really. That and the street."

Angel grabbed his long, black duster and slipped it on as he headed toward the door, Doyle and Cordelia close behind. At the door, the vampire paused to look at them.

"Like you said. A life at a time."

CHAPTER THREE

Vine Street was a classic working-class neighborhood dotted with tidy, well-maintained ranch homes complete with freshly mowed lawns and swing sets in the backyards.

"This is it?" Cordelia peered out the window from the backseat of Angel's car. "Not exactly on the top ten list of places evil is most likely to pop up."

They were parked on the opposite side of the street, a discreet distance from the house Doyle had seen in his vision. Residents from the other Vine Street homes milled about in small groups, many in bathrobes, wondering in hushed whispers about what might be happening over at number fifteen.

Cordelia tapped on the glass of the rear window with her fingernail. "Wait. Is that a lawn gnome over there? Maybe I was a little too hasty."

The sight of the little ceramic creature on the

grass brought back a memory from her childhood in Sunnydale, when money was no object and life was good. Every day on her way to elementary school, Cordelia would pass an enormous, Victorian manse. In the backyard, over a small fence, among the flowers, she would see them. Lawn gnomes, with their pointy red hats, blue shirts and long white beards. Just decorations, the housekeeper would say in broken English, as the woman escorted her past the house and its sprawling yard. But Cordelia knew better. Every day she studied them, and every day she grew more convinced they were coming closer, moving toward the garden fence, readying for escape.

Then came the day that Cordelia had anticipated, the day they were gone, never to be seen again. That was the day Cordelia Chase decided to take another route to school. They were probably off somewhere with other missing lawn gnomes from all over the planet, planning some horrible fate for the world. *Apocalypse gnome*, she thought.

"There's a threat we haven't faced yet," she said, "but I imagine it's only a matter of time. They're devious, those lawn gnomes."

In the passenger seat, Doyle rubbed at his temple, his head still pounding from his vision. "I been wondering. D'ya think if we ask 'em nice we can get the Powers That Be to skip the visions and just send e-mail? All right, I know maybe they've got a bit of a problem catching up with technology, but I'd be happy with a telegram if it came to that."

"Ah, suck it up there, Brogue Boy," Cordelia chided him gently. "That's the price you pay for fighting the forces of darkness."

"Yeah, easy for you to say," Doyle sighed. "It ain't you with the bloody headaches, is it?"

"I pay the price in other ways," Cordelia replied sweetly. "You have headaches, I have you."

Behind the wheel, Angel ignored their bickering. Cordelia thought he was brooding even more than usual, if that was possible. He stared intensely through the windshield at the seemingly normal suburban house where they knew something horrible had happened. An ambulance and a police car were parked in front of the house.

Cordelia could see that her employer was anxious. She didn't blame him. A little girl was in trouble. They all wanted to move on this as soon as possible, but they had to wait until the authorities had done their jobs. Only when the police and the EMTs were gone could Angel begin to do his.

Two policemen stood outside the entrance to the house. One smoked a cigar while the other did some kind of strange stretching exercises. They were killing time, waiting for the paramedics to finish up inside.

"Describe it to me again, Doyle. What happened to the child?" Angel asked, still staring at the scene up the street.

Doyle shifted in the passenger seat to face his boss. "It was like electricity—some kind of queer energy coming from the barrel of this weird weapon. A kind of gun, like, but not really."

Cordelia watched the impassive face of the house, then shuddered. "Who could do something like that to a little kid?"

Her words echoed in Angel's mind, a bitter reminder. He recalled the countless horrors he had witnessed since regaining his soul, so many of them perpetrated against innocent children. And he recalled some of his own abominable crimes. Whether natural or supernatural, evil seemed drawn to the innocence of youth.

"The really sad part is she knew whoever it was did this to her," Doyle said with a grim shake of his head. "She had a smile on her face when the weapon was used on her, a trusting child. We're dealin' with a cold one here, Angel, I can tell ye that."

Up ahead, the EMTs hurriedly exited the house. They were pushing a gurney, upon which lay a tiny, pajama-clad figure. A frantic woman, obviously the child's mother, ran alongside, holding the little girl's hand. She was crying and stroking the girl's dark hair.

The EMTs opened up the back of the ambulance. They collapsed the legs of the gurney and carefully loaded the girl into the emergency vehicle. One of the paramedics jumped in back to secure the gurney and then helped the mother up so she could ride to the hospital with her daughter. Angel watched the other paramedic exchange words with his partner before closing the back doors. The police officers hurried to the patrol car and its engine roared to life. Lights flashing and sirens wailing, the police car pulled out, closely followed by the ambulance.

The impatient part of Angel rejoiced. With the cops escorting the ambulance, they would be able to investigate the scene sooner than he had hoped. But in his mind and his cold, dead heart, he felt dread extend icy tendrils that chilled him throughout. If the police were willing to leave the scene so quickly, it could only mean the girl's life was in the balance.

The crowd of neighbors continued to mill about. With the police gone, many even wandered over to stand in front of the home, trying to peer inside for some clue as to what had happened.

Cordelia broke the silence. "So, now what?"

Angel turned the key in the ignition and started up the car. "Doyle, I want you to get into the house and look around. See if there's any evidence that can tell us what happened to the child." He put the car in drive. "Cordy and I'll go to the hospital, try to talk to the mother and offer to help."

Angel felt a light tap on his shoulder, and turned to frown at Cordelia.

"Just curious," she said, "but will this be the discount rate for our services or the no-rate rate?"

Angel didn't bother to respond.

Doyle opened the car door and stepped out onto the sidewalk, then leaned back in. "I'll meetcha at the hospital."

He slammed the door and watched as Angel's car banged a U-turn and proceeded up the street following the direction of the police and ambulance.

The excitement over, the Vine Street residents gradually returned to the safety of their homes and the routine of their lives. While many of them were still occupied with their gossip and guesswork, Doyle crossed the street and casually strolled behind another home. From the darkness of a backyard, he waited as the street returned to normal— lights extinguished in some homes, televisions going on in others.

When all seemed quiet, Doyle slunk into the backyard of 15 Vine Street and up three short steps to the back door. Though he would not have minded a chance to work on his rusty breaking-and-entering skills, he found that the back door had been left unlocked and he entered the kitchen. He sniffed the air. It smelled of cooking. Hamburger. His stomach made a strange rumbling, and Doyle pressed a hand against his abdomen. He was hungry. All he'd had to eat in the last twelve hours were the French fries back at the office. He was tempted to check the refrigerator for leftovers, but resisted the urge. Angel would undoubtedly frown upon such behavior.

The light was on over the stove and Doyle moved around the kitchen with ease. It was clean and cheerful, and very yellow. Nope, no shortage of yellow in the kitchen. But it did have the feeling of a happy home. A child's colorful drawings hung from magnets on the door of the yellow refrigerator. He touched what looked to be a brown animal of some kind. In a child's scrawl across the side of the funky paper animal was written her name. Aubrey Bentone is what it looked like.

A little girl with drawings on the fridge. There'd been a time when Doyle had hoped for such wonderfully normal things for himself. Before he had discovered his true nature. Now he doubted such things would ever be within his grasp.

Perhaps if the Powers That Be ever freed him from the obligations that came with his visions? But even as the thought entered his head, Doyle brushed it away. Even without the visions, he still had the obstacle of what he truly was. No matter how they were cut, the cards were pretty much stacked against him.

He shook himself out of his cynical thought pattern and moved farther into the house.

On the wall over a small dinette set was an Elvis

Presley clock. Doyle smiled at the sight of the King's hips swinging back and forth, acting as the clock's pendulum. He might never be free of his demon side, or have the wife, house, dog and the two-point-four kids, but he could definitely get one of those clocks.

Doyle suddenly froze. He could hear the faint sound of voices coming from the next room. It took him a minute to realize that the television had been left on in the living room. It was dark in there, except for the pulsing light thrown from the picture tube. In the strange light he could see that the couch was in disarray. Someone, most likely the little girl's mother, had been relaxing in front of the tube before the incident. In the ensuing excitement an afghan had been thrown on the floor and a glass tipped over, the contents staining the rug beside the couch.

Doyle found Aubrey Bentone's room next. The light had been left on. He stood in the doorway staring into the room and imagined his vision played out. He saw the smiling child holding up the toy to someone she knew, somebody she trusted. And then she was struck down by a bolt of mystical energy.

He stepped farther inside, to the very spot where he imagined the atrocity to have occurred. The monkey doll was lying on its back where it had been dropped after the child fell. Like an afterimage from staring too long at the sun, he could almost see little Aubrey on the floor, eyes wide and vacant. Doyle closed his eyes and pushed the disturbing imagery away.

He looked around the room again. Nothing appeared out of the ordinary. The room looked to be the perfect play place for a five-year-old. There were toys scattered all over, some littering the floor while others spilled out of a green plastic toy box shaped like a frog's head. The child's name was written multiple times in various sizes on a tiny blackboard standing on the other side of the room.

Careful not to step on any of the toys, Doyle approached the child's bed. It was covered in a bedspread decorated with a cheerful-looking purple dinosaur. Doyle scowled. He was familiar with the foul creature, having awakened once after a two-day bender in front of the television. Too hungover the get up and change the channel, he'd endured a half-hour of its inane singing and dancing. He shuddered with the recollection.

Doyle sat down on the corner of the bed across from a little nightstand on which rested a tiny lamp with a bright pink shade and a framed picture of the child and her mother. Doyle picked up the frame and studied the picture. The child was cute and the mom looked like the proudest parent on the face of the earth. But he noticed it didn't quite fit right in the frame. He turned it over, removed the back to get at the photo, and saw that it had been folded on one side.

Doyle unfolded the picture. On the other side of the little girl was a smiling man with a head of dark, curly hair. The child's resemblance to the man was unmistakable. He was the little girl's father. Reasons for him to be cut out of the picture passed through Doyle's mind, the likeliest being that the parents had split and it hadn't been a pleasant experience.

He put the picture back into the frame the way he had found it and replaced it on the nightstand.

Doyle stood up and felt something solid beneath the heel of his shoe. He lifted his foot, quickly taking his full weight off the object so as not to break it. He squatted and picked up what looked like a fancy glass vial lying amongst some colorful building blocks.

"What would a child be doin' with something like this?" he asked himself idly, examining the odd artifact.

It was about three inches long and about an inch and a half wide, the glass opaque. He held it closer and noticed that strange, arcane symbols had been etched into the glass.

A nasty feeling of dread passed over him. Doyle had a sneaking suspicion he knew what this was.

He stood and placed the vial inside his shirt pocket.

He left the child's room, turning out the light as he passed through the doorway. The snaking bolt of mystical energy that seemed to take something from the child, leaving her alive but empty, and now the vial covered with sorcerous etchings, all made a twisted kind of sense to him.

He had to get to the hospital and tell Angel right away. The situation was worse than they expected.

Far worse.

Angel and Cordelia stepped off the elevator in front of the fifth-floor Intensive Care Unit at the USC Medical Center in East Los Angeles. As the elevator door slowly slid closed behind them, they stopped to consider their options. They had been warned at the hospital's patient information desk that no one other than family was allowed to visit the ICU.

"So what now?" Cordelia asked in a stage whisper. Around a corner to their right, she could see three nurses working at their station. One was a young woman and the other two were older, more weathered-looking.

Angel glanced at them, then turned back to Cordelia. "I need to get past them to find the mother and child. I'll need some kind of distraction."

Cordelia threw up her hands and let them fall to her side. "Of course, a distraction. That's me. Distract-O-Girl."

"Listen, if you don't think you're up to it . . ." Angel began.

She glared at him. "I'm an actress, remember."

Cordelia rolled her eyes. "Though my talents are wasted on stuff like this. So what kind of distraction did you have in mind?"

Hands stuffed into his duster pockets, Angel shrugged his shoulders. "You said you're an actress," he said. "Act."

"I don't know why I put up with this," muttered Cordelia as she proceeded around the corner to the nurses' station. As she walked she finger-combed her hair and adjusted her skirt and blouse.

She stopped at the counter smiling, waiting to be noticed. A black woman dressed in mint-green surgical scrubs looked up from some paperwork. She wore a tag that identified her as Dana.

"Can I help you, miss?" she asked.

"Good question," responded Cordelia, pointing at the nurse and punctuating the word *good* with her finger.

The nurse stared.

"Now it's obvious to me why you're the nurse and I'm just the person standing here and—"

"Can I help you?"

The nurse was getting annoyed. She put her hands on her hips in the universal annoyed-authority-figure stance. The other two nurses behind the desk had taken notice of what was happening at the counter.

Cordelia could just make out Angel waiting around the corner. She gave him the evil eye as she continued with her performance.

"Yes. Yes, you can. This is the Intensive Care Unit, isn't it?"

Dana in the mint-green scrubs slowly nodded her head.

"Great. Well, I've been feeling a little out of it lately? There's been this tingling in my fingertips"—she held out her hands—"and I think they've been shaking more than usual, but that could be because I'm trying to knock off the caffeine. Did you know that caffeine makes the body produce insulin and if you're trying to lose weight you should probably switch to decaf?"

Out of the corner of her eye she noticed Angel giving her the hurry-up sign and she scowled.

"So I was wondering if, in your professional opinion, you think this could be the beginning of something bad? A brain tumor, maybe?"

The nurse added the paperwork she was holding to a stack in her arms and moved around the counter. "What I think you might need is a visit to the emergency room. Why don't I walk you down there myself, hon."

Cordelia had to think fast. If the nurse came this way she would notice Angel for sure. She quickly reviewed the best terminal illness performances she could remember: Ali MacGraw in *Love Story,* Julia Roberts in *Steel Magnolias,* and she could never forget Barbara Hershey in *Beaches*.

Dana gently took Cordelia by the elbow. "I'm headed that way now."

Cordelia threw a hand to her brow. "Oh my," she said beginning to sway, "I don't think I feel so good."

She pitched forward onto the desk. Dana caught her under the arms as she began to slide from the counter. It was a good thing, too, thought Cordelia, since she didn't want to lie on the ICU floor. It was a hospital, after all. Who knew what kind of diseases and germs were living there.

The other two nurses came quickly around the desk to assist. Cordelia let her limbs go limp, head lolling from side to side. She spotted Angel sneaking around the corner and heading down the hallway toward the rooms.

Not bad, thought Cordelia. In her mind she saw Brad Pitt standing on the stage of a crowded Hollywood auditorium. He tears open the envelope and reads, *"The award for best portrayal of a woman suffering from some kind of horrible-yet-vague illness goes to . . ."*

The nurses helped her around the reception desk and sat her in one of the chairs. There seemed to be definite concern for her health as they paged the ICU doctor on call. Cordelia only hoped that he was cute.

Angel cautiously moved down the hallway, looking into the rooms he passed in search of the mother and child. Gunshot wounds, heart attacks, car accidents: so much pain and suffering, but not what he was searching for. He paused and tried to look inconspicuous as two doctors emerged from a unit up ahead. Only the fact that their backs were to him saved him, for he knew how out of place he would look in here.

"It's really peculiar. I hope the tests give us some kind of clue as to what's wrong with her," one doctor said to the other.

His companion offered only a tiny shrug. "No elevated temp, no sign of any infection. We'll look at the results of the head CT and keep our fingers crossed. Okay, who's next?"

The first doctor consulted his chart. "Mr. Thomas Stanley, perforated bowel. No mysteries there," he said as they continued with their rounds.

A moment later Angel peered into the room the doctors had just left, and knew he had found the patient he was searching for.

The little girl looked tiny where she lay in the hospital bed. IV bags surrounded her with tubing running from the bags into her arms.

The child's mother stood next to the bed, her hand gently caressing her daughter's brow. She was speaking softly to the child.

"Don't be afraid, Mommy's here. It's all right, baby girl. The doctors are going to make you well. That's it. You rest up and I bet you'll be feeling better in the morning. I really do."

Angel felt self-conscious. The words were not meant for his ears. The last thing he wanted to do was interrupt at such an inappropriate moment, but he didn't know how much time he had. He cleared his throat.

The woman looked up, her cheeks damp with tears. "Can I help you?" She frowned. "Are you a doctor?"

"No." Angel gestured to a room behind him in the hall. "No, I was . . . visiting a friend when they brought your daughter up. How's she doing?"

The woman leaned forward and kissed her child's forehead.

"They don't know what's wrong with her. All the doctors in this place and nobody can tell me what's wrong with my little girl."

The mother began to sob.

Angel slipped into the room.

The woman laid her palm against her daughter's brow. "I'm sorry. I'm a little upset. But I think she's going to be all right—I feel these things." She wiped fresh tears from her cheeks. "Thank you for asking."

Angel stood beside the child's bed. She looked so frail, so helpless. She reminded him of something, chords of a memory being gently stroked.

"They taped her eyes shut so they wouldn't dry out," her mother said, making sure that the surgical tape was still holding the gauze pads in place. "It looks worse than it is."

The woman began to straighten out the sheet and blanket that covered her daughter.

As gently as he could, Angel pressed on. "I don't want to pry, but in a way I can't help it. I'm a private investigator. Do you have any idea what might have happened to cause this?"

She studied Angel's face for a moment, then looked back to her daughter. She resumed stroking the child's hair.

"I had fallen asleep on the couch watching television. I remember waking up knowing that something was wrong. I could feel it in the pit of my stomach." She stared at Angel again. "Have you ever had that feeling—" she stopped. "I'm sorry, I don't know your name."

"Angel," he said. "My name is Angel."

This made the mother smile for a brief moment.

"That's a nice name. My daughter would like it." She leaned close to her child's ear. "Did you hear that, Aubrey? His name is Angel."

"Aubrey is a pretty name also," Angel said.

The mom smiled proudly. "Aubrey Christina Bentone. She's the most important thing in my life." She began to cry again.

"So when you woke up you felt something was wrong. What was it, Mrs. Bentone?" Angel asked, hoping to distract her from her grief.

"Ms.," she corrected through her tears. "Or better yet, just June." She wiped her eyes with a crumpled tissue and then blew her nose.

"June. What did you do then?" Angel prodded.

The woman's eyes became glassy. She was back at her house, reliving the experience.

"I jumped off the couch and ran to her room. I called to her at first, but she didn't answer. I started screaming her name over and over again." June clutched the tissue to her quivering mouth. Her eyes brimmed with emotion. "And this is how I found her. No matter how hard I shook her, she wouldn't wake up. My baby wouldn't wake up."

Angel felt the woman's grief as if it were his own. He studied the child's face, her fragile bone structure, the pale china-doll quality of her skin, her tiny delicate mouth.

Then he remembered. The thing that had been gnawing at the back of his mind surged forward. A painful memory from his past. Another child—another beautiful little girl touched by the unnatural.

With excruciating heartache, he remembered his sister and what he had done to her.

It was after he had been taken by the vampire Darla, after he had died and been buried. After he had risen from the grave as a vampire.

He returned home to his family but found that he could not enter the house without being invited—one of the strange new rules that governed him now that he was undead.

He lured her to the door. His baby sister. He could still see her eyes, red from crying, red from mourning his death three nights previous. She had been so happy to see him. She thought he had come back to her as an angel.

An angel.

The monster he had become told her that he had missed her terribly and asked that she invite him in so he could show her how happy he was to be back. She smiled so innocently as she took his hand and bid him enter.

Angel flinched at the recollection, filled with the self-loathing and guilt that was only part of the curse upon him. He stood in the hospital room and looked down at little Aubrey Bentone, who would now forever remind him of his sweet sister and the horrors he had visited upon her, and he steeled himself against the burden of his past.

He had traded on his sister's innocence and love to gain entry to the family home. That had been just the beginning of seemingly endless depravity and abomination, and yet, of all the things he had done as the monster, Angelus, what he'd done to his sister was probably the worst.

Angel saw his sister lying in the hospital bed, gauze pads covering her eyes, IV tubing leading from clear bags of fluids into needles in her arm. He blinked and the child was Aubrey Bentone again. Someone he *could* save.

Here was a child in desperate need. So much more than Doyle's vision or his own mission for the Powers That Be.

Aubrey's mother was singing her a lullaby when Angel reached out and placed his hand on top of Aubrey's. It was warm. Warm with life. With possibility.

"June, I'd like to help her. I want to help your daughter."

CHAPTER FOUR

The elevator doors parted and Doyle stepped out onto the fifth floor. He had pretended to be an emotionally distraught family member to find out where Aubrey had been taken after being admitted through the emergency room.

Doyle grimaced as he breathed hospital air. He hated hospitals; the smell, the overly bright lighting, the deceptively cheerful pastel-colored walls . . . and there were far too many sick people there.

He casually strolled around the corner toward the reception desk, trying not to look out of place, and saw a bit of a commotion going on. A doctor and some nurses were fussing about a patient out in the hall.

"Thank you. I think I'm feeling much better now," Doyle overheard the woman say as he came a little closer. "So, are you married?"

Doyle knew that voice.

"I just don't know what the problem could be. Maybe the PEZ diet isn't for me, but Gwyneth swears she lost . . ."

Cordelia, Doyle thought. His pulse quickened with sudden concern.

He could not really put into words why Cordelia Chase had this effect on him. There had been lots of women in his life but none, other than his ex, ever had this kind of hold over him. Here was a woman, a tad caustic, a bit shallow, who, at least once a day, made it a point to mention how demons were the most revolting things on the planet. Yet, despite it all, he was smitten by her. *Put a rush order in for a white cane and dark glasses,* he thought, for love had most assuredly struck him blind.

He wanted to help, to let her know that someone who cared was here for her and was just about to call out her name when she caught sight of him.

Doyle smiled and she made a horrible face in reply. It looked as though she were having some kind of seizure until he realized that she was shaking her head *no.* Being the sharp character he was, Doyle guessed that she wanted him to stay away.

He watched as she suddenly went rigid.

"Oh," she exclaimed, as she fell back into the arms of a man Doyle believed was a doctor, though he seemed a bit young.

The commotion began all over again. Doyle noticed that while Cordelia was flailing her arms about, she pointed several times down the hallway behind him.

She caught his eye again and gave him a quick wink. The doctor and nurses were helping her back into a seat. Doogie Howser was checking out her heart rate with a stethoscope and talking about tests.

Doyle headed down the hall in the direction she had pointed. He shook his head and smiled as he peered into various rooms looking for Angel. *How anyone can buy into her act as anything more than a bunch of malarkey is beyond me.*

Doyle found Angel about four rooms down, where he sat with June Bentone next to Aubrey's bed. He tapped on the doorframe to catch their attention. It looked like they were standing watch over the little girl, the mother on one side and Angel on the other. Each held one of the child's hands in theirs.

"Excuse me, Angel?"

Angel gently set the girl's hand down.

"Doyle." Angel motioned him to come closer.

Doyle entered the room and stood at the foot of the hospital bed. The woman looked from Angel to Doyle, back to Angel.

"June Bentone, meet Francis Doyle. He works with me."

Doyle smiled weakly and nodded. He was

uncomfortable with the mother's grief. "I'm sorry about yer girl."

June looked as if she had been through hell but there was something in her eyes—a spark. It was a glimmer of hope. Doyle had seen the look before, in the eyes of others to whom Angel had offered his assistance.

"I'm sure we'll be doin' everything in our power to help her."

"Thank you," June said, as she lovingly stroked her daughter's arm. "Are you a detective also, Mr. Doyle?" she asked.

He shook his head and smiled slightly. "Just think of me as the teenage sidekick without the teen part or the green tights. I help Angel gather information." Doyle took Angel by the shoulder. "Would you excuse us for a moment, Ms. Bentone?"

She nodded and turned her attention back to her daughter as the two men moved into the corridor.

Doyle spoke to his employer in a hushed whisper so the child's mother could not overhear. "I went through the house as you asked."

"Did you find anything?"

Doyle appeared nervous as he reached into his front shirt pocket. "Aye, I found something and I don't like the looks of it one bit." He placed the glass vial in Angel's palm. "Found it on the floor of the girl's room. I seriously doubt it belongs to anybody in the household."

Angel studied the vial.

"The symbols etched into the glass, I think they're demonic in nature." Doyle leaned in close to Angel and gripped his arm. "With all my heart I hope I'm wrong, but I think I know what was done to her."

"What?" Angel asked.

Doyle looked past Angel into the hospital room, at June Bentone and her daughter. June still sat with Aubrey's lifeless hand in hers. Her eyes were closed and her mouth moved silently. Doyle guessed she was praying. He looked back to his boss.

"Girl's life force is missing, Angel." Doyle leaned back against the doorframe and sighed. "I think somebody's taken her soul."

Galway, 1752

"Now I lay me down to sleep, I pray the Lord my soul to keep."

Liam watched his little sister Katherine as she whispered her bedtime prayers. She knelt by her bedside, hands folded, head bowed.

"If I should die before I wake, I pray the Lord my soul to take."

In her white nightgown, she looked like an angel. He watched the young girl bless herself, completing her bedtime ritual. Liam clapped his hands together.

"That's it, then," he said pulling back the covers. "Time fer sleep."

He had been on his way out the door to town when she had asked him to listen to her prayers and tuck her in. It did take valuable time away from his carousing at the pub, but how could he turn the sweet thing down?

She giggled happily, sliding beneath the covers.

"What's a soul, Liam? What is it really?"

He pulled the heavy blanket up under her chin and tried to think of a proper answer. He fumbled with the memory of what he had learned in catechism so long ago. "It's a most wondrous thing, Kathy. A soul makes us who we are. It's what the Almighty saw fit to give to separate us from the beasts."

Katherine's eyes twinkled. "What's it look like?"

Liam put a hand to his chest for dramatic effect. He pretended to be overcome with emotion. "A soul's the loveliest thing you'll ever see. It's made up of all the colors of the rainbow and some that haven't even been thought up yet. To look at one, why, the beauty of the thing'd make you cry with sheer joy."

She sat up, a broad smile on her face. "Is that what my soul looks like? Is it lovely too? Is it?"

He made her lie back and tucked the covers under her chin again.

"Your soul, my sweet darling, puts all the others to shame."

He leaned down and kissed her on the forehead. Her tiny arms shot out from beneath the covers and wrapped themselves tightly about his neck.

"Don't go tonight, brother. I don't want the Devil to take yer soul."

Liam gently pulled away from the child's embrace.

"Now, what makes you think that old Scratch could have the soul of a chaste man like meself?" He ruffled his sister's hair, smiling down at her.

Katherine was deadly serious. She stared up at her big brother with eyes filled with concern. "Da says that yer already on the road to damnation with the way you carry on each night. He said that it's only a matter of time before the Devil takes his due."

Liam's anger flared as it so often did with any topic having to do with his father. He lived life to its fullest and his father disapproved of his only son's carefree lifestyle. The two despised each other. No matter what he did or said, Liam could not elicit from his father the kind of respect he felt he deserved. His father said he was nothing but a layabout and a scoundrel who wouldn't amount to anything. And wanting so to be the perfect son, Liam did everything in his power to live up to his father's expectations.

"Don't you be worryin' about yer big brother now," he said pushing aside the rage he felt over his da's hurtful words. "My soul may be a bit tarnished in places, but I'll be damned if I'll let the Devil have even the tiniest piece of it."

He kissed her on the head again. "Now go to sleep and have only wonderful dreams."

He blew out the flame of a candle by his sister's bedside and walked to the door. "I'll see you in the mornin'," he said, as he gave her a wave and gently shut the door.

Outside his sister's bedroom he adjusted his collar and smoothed his sleeves. Now he was ready to go out into the night and prove his father right yet again. A night of debauchery awaited him, or so he hoped.

Anna, a servant in the household, was walking toward him carrying a stack of fresh linens to his parents' room at the end of the hall.

The pretty young thing looked at the rakish Liam and smiled.

"Goin' out tonight, young sir?"

Liam watched her backside as she passed and a devilish grin spread across his face. "Aye, Anna, I've got an overpowerin' urge to dirty up me soul."

Liam. It was a name no one had called him in over two centuries, but he could still hear it lovingly flow from his sister's lips as if it were yesterday. Angel ran his thumb thoughtfully along the archaic symbols etched into the surface of the vial, the memory painfully fresh.

"There's a rumor on the streets about a drug for demons, supposedly made from human souls," Doyle told him. "Personally I thought it was a load a crap, but now . . ." He stopped, waiting for a reaction.

Angel closed his hand over the small glass vessel. "There was a race of demons that fed on souls, but I was led to believe they died out a long time ago," he replied slowly. "Maybe my information is wrong."

"Possible, but I doubt it's a demon we're lookin' for, Angel. Remember, the child knew who did this to her."

After a long moment in which neither spoke, they returned to the mother and child. June appeared exhausted but still managed to greet them with a faint smile.

"June, is there anyone who might want to hurt you or your daughter?" Angel asked bluntly.

Her eyes widened as the meaning of his question became clear. "What do you mean? Do you think somebody did this to Aubrey, that someone intentionally hurt my baby girl?"

She looked from Angel to Doyle.

"We have to consider every possibility," Doyle said in his most soothing voice. "Is there anyone with access to yer home who you might've had words with . . ." He recalled the folded photograph in the child's room. ". . . someone you work with, a neighbor, or a relative, maybe?"

She twisted a tissue in her hands as she thought.

"Well, my ex, David. We had it out a few weeks back over child support but—" She shook her head emphatically at the two men. "No. No, he's a lowlife but I don't think even he'd sink low enough to hurt his own flesh and blood."

Angel handed June his card. "We're going to continue with the investigation on our end. If you think of anything that might be useful to the case, please don't hesitate to call us at any time."

She took the business card from him. "But we haven't even talked about your rates. I mean, how much does—"

"I want to help," Angel interrupted her. "If you can afford to pay, fine. If not . . . I want to help."

June's mouth opened just slightly, but she had no words to express the gratitude that blossomed on her features. After a moment, she glanced away, overcome with emotion.

Doyle started to make his way out of the hospital room. "Are ye comin', Angel?"

Angel stared at the little girl lying in the hospital bed one last time. He wanted the image burned into his mind, a reminder as to why he did what he did for the Powers That Be.

Angel above all knew the value of the human soul. If the child's soul had been taken, she would soon die—or worse, she could live and become something less than human. He knew what that was like and he wasn't going to let it happen, not to this sweet child.

With a final glance he silently said good-bye to Aubrey and left the hospital room. Doyle was waiting outside in the hall.

"So, what's next?"

They were both distracted by the sound of Cordelia's voice.

"I really don't think this is necessary, Phil. A couple of Advils and a good night's sleep and I should feel daisy-fresh."

She was being pushed in a wheelchair down the hallway by a good-looking young doctor.

"I'm very concerned about these dizzy spells, Miss Chase. We'll have some blood work done and then—"

Cordelia saw Angel and Doyle and smiled. "Hey, guys."

Doyle began to clap. The doctor eyed the pair suspiciously.

"A brilliant performance, girl. I saw a bit of it as I came in."

Beaming, she got up from the chair without so much as a hint of a problem. "You think so? So, what's up?"

The doctor was confused. "Miss Chase? Maybe you should sit down before—"

She turned away from Angel for a moment and smiled radiantly at the doctor. "That's okay, Phil, I think I'm feeling much better now."

She returned her attention to her boss. "Did you find anything out? What's wrong with the little girl?"

"That's something that Doyle and I have to do some more research on. What I'd like you to do is talk to the girl's mother," he pointed to the room down the hall. "See if you can get us anything on the people they have contact with from day to day."

Cordelia nodded. "Check."

"Be sure to ask her about her husband," Doyle added. "I've a sneakin' suspicion she may have more to do with him than she's lettin' on."

The doctor cleared his throat, annoyed. "Miss Chase, the tests?"

Cordelia smiled again at him. "I'm suddenly feeling fine, Phil. Looks like I'm cured."

She proceeded down the hall toward Aubrey Bentone's room.

The three watched her go. Doyle folded his arms and shook his head, fully appreciating the sight of Cordelia walking away from him.

The doctor glared at them.

"It's a miracle!" Doyle exclaimed, throwing up his hands.

Angel and Doyle left Phil standing with his empty wheelchair and walked to the bank of elevators. The look on the young physician's face said he still wasn't sure what had just happened.

On the elevator, Angel turned to Doyle, a grim expression on his face.

"Why don't you head back to the office and see what you can dig up on soul theft," he suggested.

"All right. I can tell by the look in yer eye ye've got another destination in mind, though."

Angel nodded. "The Ninth Level."

Doyle visibly shuddered. "Yer a braver man than I."

CHAPTER FIVE

The sound in Angel's ears was not unlike that of nails on a chalkboard. It took every ounce of self-control he could muster to keep from wincing in pain. He slowly brought his hands up to the headphones, nodding and smiling as if he were enjoying himself. That was the farthest thing from the truth. He was waiting for a polite amount of time to pass before tearing them from his head.

The track ended and Angel saw his opportunity. He quickly removed the headphones before the next song began.

"Well, that was *something*," he said to the man who sat grinning excitedly across the barroom table.

Charlie Nickels reached for the portable CD player and popped the lid to get at the disc inside. With stubby fingers covered in rough, mottled flesh, he carefully removed the CD and returned it to its case.

"I can't believe you never saw *Evita*, never mind not hearing it. It's Webber and Rice's crowning achievement," the ugly little man said. "When I saw it in London back in '78 I thought I'd died and gone to heaven."

Sounds more like cats being strangled, Angel thought. His musical tastes leaned more toward the classical artists from the time in which he lived and the traditional music of Ireland as played by such groups as The Chieftains.

Charlie began to go through stacks of CDs piled on the table in front of him. "I think Patti LuPone is the best, followed by Julie Covington, and then Elaine Paige."

He took a sip of his wine and dabbed at his twisted lips with a cocktail napkin. "If you liked that one you'll really like *Starlight Express*."

He pulled a plastic case from the stack and reached for the player.

Angel's hand came down on the machine, closing its lid. "No more musical theater, Charlie. I need some questions answered."

The disfigured dwarf of a man looked disappointed. He shrugged his shoulders and tossed the CD onto the table. "Whatever you say—just trying to broaden your horizons a bit. What do you need?"

As he reached into his coat pocket for the vial, Angel glanced around The Ninth Level Bar and

Grill at the array of supernatural creatures milling about, sharing drinks and gossip. Many were nervously watching him as he sat with the monstrous Charlie Nickels. It wasn't too often that Angel frequented places like this, and when he did, it usually meant trouble for some of the regulars.

Angel placed the glass container covered in ancient demonic script down on the center of the table.

"Are you sure I can't get you something, Angel?" Charlie asked. "A drink or an appetizer, perhaps?"

Something behind the bar let out a high-pitched squeal as it went into the Fry-o-lator alive.

"What I need, Charlie, is for you to tell me what that is." Angel pointed at the object on the table.

Muttering to himself, Charlie plucked a pair of black framed bifocals from inside his shirt pocket and placed them on his deformed face. Then he reached out a stubby arm and grabbed up the object. He stared at the vial, turning it around, examining it from every angle.

Charles Nickels had once been one of the wealthiest and most handsome men in the United States— one of the first to see the potential in the personal computer phenomenon and the virgin territory known as the Internet. He had made his first hundred million before he was twenty-five. Nickels had it all—brains, fame, looks, money—and he was irresistible to women. But he became bored with the natural world and began to dabble in areas of the supernatural.

The man brought the vial up to his pug nose and sniffed. "Interesting," he said, with a voice that sounded as if he gargled with razor blades, "it hasn't been used."

Nickels had tried to apply the same savvy he had used to amass a fortune in the world of computer technology to the world of the supernatural. He wanted to be a player but soon learned that he was nothing but a little fish in a very big pond. Sorcerers, magicians, necromancers and other wielders of the arcane arts had not taken kindly to his attempts to muscle in on their territory. They joined forces to teach the interloper a lesson.

Nickels went to bed one night wealthy and handsome and awoke the next day a penniless, twisted mockery of a human being. The magic users had taken it all away as punishment for his insolence. His business had collapsed overnight—a rival company released a superchip that rendered his patented technology obsolete—but that was the least of his problems. Something horrible had happened to his body, something that the world's best physicians had no idea how to cure. His bones began to painfully distort and shrink. His skin took on the color and consistency of an old callus. In a matter of days, the Charles Nickels who had once held the world in an iron grip was no more, replaced by the wine-swilling, show-tune–loving creature cursed by the black arts for his arrogance.

Angel leaned closer. "What is it, Charlie? What's it used for?"

The twisted man's glasses had slipped down to the tip of his nose. He looked at Angel over the rims. "Nasty business, Angel. It's used as a receptacle for a soul."

He slid the vessel back across the table to the vampire. "That one hasn't been used yet or it would have a funky smell. Kind of like lilac and cinnamon with a little bit of nail polish remover thrown in for good measure . . . if what I'm told is true."

Angel took the container back. "How big is this, Charlie?"

The disfigured man sipped some more of his wine before answering. "The soul trade? Not very . . . but it does seem to be gaining popularity."

Angel put the vial away. "Educate me. What are the souls used for?"

Charlie scratched at some dry skin on top of his misshapen head with a jagged nail. "Let me see . . ."

After his life had been taken away by the supernatural, the twisted man devoted his time to extensive study of the black arts in hopes of one day curing his paranormal malady. It had been more than fifteen years since he was stricken and he hadn't even come close.

He began to tick off some of the uses for the soul on

his stubby fingers. "Some heavy-duty spells require souls for completion. And, were you aware that at one time there were some demon types that consumed the life essence that is the soul for food? It's true."

Angel looked around the bar again. "What about drugs? Have you heard anything about a drug for demons made with human souls?"

Charlie nodded. He began to neaten his stacks of compact discs. "It's relatively new, called Uforia. Most demons would trade their own mothers for a taste—not that there are many demons out there that even know who their mothers are—but the ones that do, they'd sell 'em cold for this high. Makes 'em feel fearless, I hear. Not a care in the world."

He pulled a disc case from the stack and showed Angel. It was the recording of Andrew Lloyd Webber's *The Phantom of the Opera*. "Ever heard this?" he asked.

Angel shook his head, for the moment confused. He had always believed that *Phantom* had been written by Gaston Leroux.

"Back to the drug—any idea on who's producing or where it's being made?"

Charlie looked disgusted as he put *Phantom* back into one of the stacks. "I can't believe you've never heard *The Phantom of the Opera*. The whole 'Music of the Night' thing? It'd be perfect for somebody like you." He sighed, disappointed.

"Like I said before, Uforia is the latest thing to hit the streets. I have no idea where it's come from, but let me assure you, it's here with a vengeance." Charlie stood up and waved his stubby arms, trying to get the bartender's attention. "Hey, Sol, could I get another Merlot over here? I'm on the verge of losing my buzz."

Sol flipped the ugly man off and continued to dry a beer mug with a filthy rag. Charlie sat back down and grinned at Angel. He leaned forward and spoke in a conspiratorial whisper.

"So, what's the case? Somebody lose their soul or something?"

"You know the score, Charlie. Client confidentiality."

Sol came by and placed a fresh glass of wine on the table. "Should I put it on your tab, sir?" he said mockingly and returned to the bar.

Charlie muttered something beneath his breath and took a slurping sip of his fresh drink. "If I'm right, you're going to be earning your pay on this one. That soul could be anywhere. It could even be in somebody's private collection by now."

Wine dribbled down Charlie's mottled chin. He didn't notice. Angel was going to ask if Sol had any bibs but thought better of it. He still needed information from the twisted creature and didn't want to insult him.

"Souls used for spells, for food and for drugs. And

97

now you're telling me there are soul collectors out there as well?"

Charlie reclined in his chair and put his hands behind his gourd-shaped head. "That's what I'm telling you, Ange. There are freaks out there that collect souls like baseball cards, Beanie Babies and them Hooligan things from a few months back. They're hard to get to begin with and if you should happen to get a special one, like a religious figure or a virgin or, even better, a child? You can name your price in some circles."

He picked up his glass and had some more wine. It ran out the side of his mouth and onto his shirt.

Angel had heard and seen enough. He got up from his chair and removed some money from his pocket. He tossed it down onto the table. "For your time and your tab."

Charlie snatched up the cash and counted it. "Always happy to share the love of my hobbies with friends." He folded the money and put it inside his shirt pocket. "For the next time we meet, how do you feel about *Cats?*"

Angel slid his chair under the table. "I'm more of a dog person."

He turned and began to walk up the aisle toward the exit. Charlie called after him.

"Not real cats, the play! *Cats!* It's based on some famous poem or something. I think you'd really like it."

Angel was just about to ascend the concrete steps to the street when he sensed a presence behind him. And then that presence spoke.

"You've got some nerve coming down here. What's the matter, the good guys don't have a place to drink of their own?"

Angel turned and looked into the face of a blue-skinned Barakkas demon. The demon had a wild look in its three eyes, the pupils narrowed to tiny pinpricks of black surrounded by an ocean of milky white. The creature wasn't in its right mind. It ground its razor-sharp teeth together as it put its face close to Angel's. The vampire stood his ground.

"I'd be more than happy most nights to stay and explain myself to you, but tonight I'm in a bit of a hurry. Why don't you go back to your table, have another drink, a few laughs, and forget you even spoke to me."

The Barakkas didn't move. It clenched its clawed hands into fists and noisily inhaled.

Angel sighed, an image of a frail little girl lying in a hospital bed, soulless, flickered across the screen of his mind's eye. He drove his fist into the demon's face with a sickening crunch. The Barakkas flipped backward, unconscious before it hit the sawdust-covered floor. Angel looked around.

"I really don't have time for a pissing contest, but if there's anybody else who wants me to stay around . . ."

The monster patrons all turned back to their refreshments without so much as a growl.

Charlie, holding a fresh glass of wine, waddled up from the back and stood over the unconscious demon. Angel watched as he bent down, careful not to spill his drink, and pulled back one of its eyelids, examining the orb beneath.

"As I thought. Uforia."

He looked at Angel. "It makes them foolish."

Angel didn't say a word as he climbed the stairs out of The Ninth Level and onto the nighttime streets of Los Angeles.

He couldn't have agreed more.

Cordelia paid for her salad and Diet Coke and stepped away from the cash register. She scanned the hospital cafeteria looking for June Bentone and found her at a table in the back, sipping coffee and staring off into space. She seemed a million miles away, probably in a place where her daughter was safely tucked into her bed, sound asleep and perfectly healthy.

Cordelia approached and set her tray down on the table. "Hope you don't mind, I haven't had anything to eat since some rice cakes this morning and we know how *not* filling they can be."

"What?" June mumbled, startled by the voice. She stared at Cordelia as she sat down. "Oh, no. Don't worry. I don't mind. Please, eat."

Cordelia took a sip of her drink, then began to pick through her salad with a fork. "Some of this lettuce looks as though it could use a jolt from those electric paddles you see on *ER.*"

"I wish I hadn't quit smoking, 'cause I could really use a cigarette right about now. I'm going to jump out of my skin." June bit at a hangnail, nervously looking about the cafeteria.

"Maybe coffee isn't the best thing to be drinking if you're feeling a bit tense?" Cordelia said. She speared a cherry tomato and popped it into her mouth. "Just a thought."

June didn't seem to hear her. "Don't you think I should be talking to the police? You know, since somebody might have done this to her?"

Cordelia continued to pick at her plate, searching for something other than wilted lettuce and bean sprouts. "I don't think the police would know how to deal with this one." She sighed and pushed the salad aside. "Think I've had more than enough of that, thank you. You'd think that a salad from a hospital would be a little healthier, maybe?"

"Why?" June asked. "What makes this different from anything else? If somebody did this to my little girl they have to be caught."

"Let's just say that Angel has a tendency to work on cases that are a bit . . . funny," Cordelia said carefully. "Not *There's Something About Mary* funny, but funny weird, and I'm sorry, I can't see the

LAPD dealing with some of the funny weird stuff I've seen since coming to work for him."

June wrapped both hands around her coffee mug and leaned toward Cordelia. "Are you . . . are you saying Angel handles things that . . . that can't be explained?"

Cordelia took a sip of her Diet Coke, crunching on some ice as she considered her reply. "His cases do have a tendency toward the bizarre."

June was beginning to panic. "Something . . . unnatural has happened to my child? How is that possible?"

"That's what Angel intends to find out."

June put her hands to her face. "I keep telling myself that everything is going to be all right but . . ."

Cordelia shook the ice around in her cup. "Is there anybody that you know into the bizarre stuff? Summoning demons, blood sacrifice, devil worship, the Atkins diet? Any of these ring a bell?"

With a laugh, June took her hands away from her face. She seemed to think Cordelia was joking. "No, none of that. The worst thing I can think of is that my ex is a compulsive gambler. Believe me, that can be pretty bad."

She picked up a sugar packet and began to play with it.

"That guy you met with Angel? Doyle? He likes to gamble—maybe he knows your husband."

Cordelia watched as June tore open the packet and began to spill the contents in a pile on the table.

"I seriously doubt your friend is as bad as David. It's a sickness with him. It's why we split up, really." She looked up from the mess she was making. "I'll never forget the first time I realized how bad it was. We were just coming home from the hospital after Aubrey was born."

June started to move the sugar around with her finger.

"We pulled up in front of the house and there was this man sitting on our steps. David got all nervous when he saw him. I asked who he was and David said he was just somebody he knew."

Cordelia slid the pepper over for the woman to add to her mixture.

June smiled and continued her story. "So we got out of the car and David went over to talk to him. He introduced me and Aubrey. I think his name was Carmen . . ."

June sprinkled some pepper into the sugar and mixed them together.

"Anyway, Carmen didn't give me or the baby a second look. He just started punching David in the face over and over again, screaming that he wanted his money by the end of the week."

"Let me guess, shark, and not the *Jaws* kind," Cordelia said.

June scraped the pile of sugar and pepper into her hand.

"Yep, and that's when I first found out he owed some very bad men an awful lot of money. We paid it off with the savings I had set aside to fix up the baby's room."

She brushed the mixture in her hand into her empty mug. Her eyes began to fill. "And that wasn't the last time we got visits from Carmen, or other guys doing the same job. I was so afraid that I bought a gun to protect myself and Aubrey before I got smart and threw him out."

She wiped the tears from her eyes and sniffed. Then she looked at Cordelia and smiled. "No devil worshipers in my life. Just one big loser."

Cordelia wasn't sure how to respond and began to clean up. "We should get back upstairs. Maybe Aubrey's tests have come back and they can tell us—"

June interrupted. "Is he good?"

Cordelia was taken off guard, not sure of the meaning behind the woman's question. "Excuse me?"

"Your boss. Angel. Is he any good?"

There was a look of desperation in the mother's eyes. Cordelia could see she was losing strength; she needed something to keep her afloat.

Cordelia reached out and grabbed the woman's hand. "Is he any good? Let's put it this way, if there ever comes a time when everybody's given up, when even *you've* given up . . . Angel won't. He's just not built that way."

She gave the woman's hand a reassuring squeeze. "I'd say that's pretty damn good."

Doyle put his feet up onto Cordelia's desk and settled back in the chair. He had a large leather-bound tome from Angel's reference library in his lap and was carefully flipping the yellowed pages. The title of the book was written in some long-forgotten language, but if Doyle's memory served him, the translation was something the equivalent of *Demons for Dummies*.

He curled his nose up in disgust at some of the artist's representations of various demon races. "Nasty lookin' buggers," he muttered, "makes *me* look like George Clooney."

At the sound of the elevator coming up from the basement, Doyle took his feet off the desk and placed the book with some others he had been look-ing through that night. He noticed that the sun was coming up outside.

Doyle stood and stretched as Angel stepped into the office. "So, learn anything from the esteemed Mr. Nickels?"

Angel removed his duster and hung it on the coat-rack. "Three things." He retrieved his coffee mug and poured himself a cup. "First, the soul trade is a growing problem. Second, there's a drug on the streets made from human souls and it's called Uforia."

Angel pulled a chair up to Cordelia's desk and sat down. He took a sip of the hot beverage.

Doyle sat down again. "And third?"

"Third? I don't care for show tunes."

With a grin, Doyle leaned back. "I told ya. The last time I dealt with the ugly little bugger I had to listen to a damn song about some girl who couldn't say no. Had to go to another pub across town when I was through and play the Pogues on the jukebox to get the fool tune out of me head."

Angel set his mug down. "How'd you do tonight? Anything interesting?"

Doyle searched around on the desk for his note pad. "Actually I did find some interestin' bits of info. From what I've gathered, a sorcerous device called a collector is used to extract the soul and it's stored in—"

Angel fished the vial from inside his pocket and placed it on the desk. "In this. I got that much from Nickels. The soul is collected in that and then used in any number of ways, ranging from a demon snack to drug-making."

Doyle picked up the pad and glanced at his notes. "Okay, how about this? Those soul-eating demons you talked about at the hospital? Did you know that they were called the Kurgarru and that after they finished consuming the souls of every livin' thing on their home world they turned on each other for food?"

Angel frowned, and Doyle nodded with self-satisfaction. *Score one for the demon half-breed,* he thought.

"They had developed a foolproof way a stealin' souls and were supposedly the inspiration for some earth sorcerers who tried to duplicate the process." Doyle grabbed a book and began to flip through it. "There's a drawing of one in here. Pretty disgustin'."

"I'll take your word for it," Angel said.

Doyle shut the book and put it aside. "Sucked each other's souls right into extinction. Good thing too; foul eatin' habits aside, it sounds as if they were some pretty tough customers."

Angel nodded. "Have we heard anything from Cordelia?"

Doyle began to straighten out her desk as if the mere mention of her name was enough to spur him into a neatness frenzy. That was all he needed, to leave Cordelia's workplace a mess and have to suffer her wrath. "She called a few hours ago. Said that June was going to stay on a cot in Aubrey's room tonight so she was goin' home to get some sleep."

"How's the girl?"

"She's the same, but Cordy did learn that Daddy Bentone is a compulsive gambler and often owes various loan sharks quite a bit o' coin," Doyle said as he brushed some stray dirt from his shoes onto the floor.

Angel rubbed his chin thoughtfully. "I think we ought to have a talk with him."

Doyle studied the surface of the desk, making certain that everything was perfect before he stood up and returned the chair to where he'd found it. "Mom has supposedly lost track of him, but I'll tell ye what I'll do."

He came around the desk. "Tomorrow, I'll ask around and find out what sharks he still owes money to. I'm sure they'll know where he's hangin' his hat now."

Angel picked up his empty mug and headed for his office. "Good. Go home and get some rest, find out where Bentone is and meet me back here at dusk."

Doyle followed with an armload of books. "Sounds like a plan, then."

He placed the books on the shelves as Angel stepped into the elevator.

"Dusk, Doyle. Did I mention we meet back here at dusk?" he said as he closed the gate.

Doyle stared at Angel through the gate. "You're never goin' ta let me forget that I was late, are ye?"

Angel hit the down button, the slightest hint of a smile on his face.

"I did everything in me power to be there. Really."

"Dusk," Angel said, his final word before descending from view.

Doyle leaned his face against the metal grate and yelled. "I had a poison demon quill stickin' from my neck! The fates conspired against me. Angel?"

There was no response and Doyle, feeling dejected, turned to leave.

"Make one little mistake and yer marked fer life."

CHAPTER SIX

David Bentone lay in his bed fully clothed, deep in thought, staring up at the cracked and water-stained ceiling of his apartment. He clutched both hands against his chest. Oblivious to the early morning sounds that wafted up from the street below, he was lost within himself, recalling the moments in his life that had led him to where he was now . . .

"I'm pregnant," his wife had blurted out, on that long ago night. Not *"Hello, darling,"* not, *"How was your night, sweetheart?"* He had just come home from a high-stakes poker game where he had lost his shirt and this was not the kind of greeting he was eager to hear. They hadn't even been married a year and were too young for kids. There was still so much they hadn't done . . . so much *he* hadn't done. She didn't understand why he was so upset, or more

likely, didn't *want* to understand. June had always been the one who wanted children.

Bentone sat up, throwing his legs over the side of the bed.

When had he finally accepted that he was to be a father? Even though he had seen his wife every day, her belly growing bigger with life, it had not become a reality to him until Aubrey was born. The nurses had cleaned up the slimy, screaming little girl, wrapped her in a pink blanket and placed her in his arms. At that moment everything changed. He wasn't the same David Bentone who had begrudgingly come to the hospital with his wife in the midst of labor. *That* David Bentone went missing the first time he held his daughter close.

But he had come back. God help him, the old David had come back.

Almost tenderly, he lowered his hands and looked at what he held there. The vial glowed with a life all its own. As he had done many times since last night, Bentone stared with awe at the strange phenomena that occurred inside the glass container. The contents of the vial were in constant motion, changing in color, shape and composition; it was quite possibly the most beautiful thing he had ever seen— besides his newborn baby girl.

That first night in the maternity ward, as Bentone held his daughter, he had made a promise. *"I'll never let anybody hurt you. Ever."* He remembered that promise now, and it pained him deeply.

Bentone closed his hand around the vial, feeling the pulsing warmth of what was trapped within. The realization of what he had done to his child didn't seem as painful. Each time he remembered, it hurt a little less.

Maybe this is what they mean by dying in inches, he thought. Perhaps if he kept playing it over and over in his head, eventually he wouldn't feel anything. It would be just like being dead.

Bentone tried to think of something else, something to lift his spirits. He thought of being free of Benny the Wrench. As soon as this was over, he was leaving California. Maybe he'd go to Massachusetts. He had some friends there. *It would be nice to see snow at Christmastime,* he thought.

Aubrey had always asked Santa Claus for snow on Christmas.

Aubrey. The memory of what he had done came back and he began to die all over again.

His slow death was interrupted by the jarring ring of the telephone.

"Who the hell would be calling this early?" Bentone muttered as he glanced at the alarm clock on the nightstand by his bed. It was 8:15.

He leaned over and picked up the receiver. "Yeah?"

"David, how are you this morning?"

The voice on the other end was smooth, with just

a slight hint of an accent. In his mind, Bentone could see Meskal's cold blue eyes as he spoke.

Bentone clutched the crystal vial tighter. "I'm good. I . . . I did what you asked. I used the . . . that collector thing you gave me."

"Excellent," Meskal purred. "Did you have any difficulty?"

Bentone didn't answer. He remembered his daughter holding up her favorite toy, a stuffed monkey doll she called Pip. She had smiled and he had taken the device from his pocket and pointed it at her. And then he had shot her. He saw her falling in slow motion. Her eyes were wide open as she lay on the floor. He had looked into those eyes, normally so vibrant, so full of life. And there was nothing there. Something was missing.

Bentone cleared his throat. "No. No difficulty at all."

He opened his hand again to look at the crystal. He felt but the slightest pang of remorse. Perhaps he was almost done with dying.

"So, when will I be clear with—"

"Your debt with Mr. Giordano has already been taken care of," Meskal interrupted.

Bentone closed his eyes, expecting to feel the weight of the world slip from his shoulders. But he felt nothing and it scared him.

"Let us arrange a time in which you can deliver the item to me."

"Ya know, I've been thinkin'," Bentone said, a tremble in his voice. He held up the vial, letting the muted light from the dirty windows filter through the crystal and its amorphous contents. He wanted to feel something, anything. "What I got here is pretty damn special."

Meskal's voice grew cold. "Yes, David. I'm sure it is."

"What I'm tryin' to say is that, looking at the quality? I think it might be more valuable than what we agreed on."

"We had an agreement, Mr. Bentone."

There was something in Meskal's voice that told him he was treading on very dangerous ground. He should have been afraid—wanted to be afraid, but there was nothing there.

"Yeah, I know. It's just that I didn't really know what I was doing and I think you might have taken advantage of me a little."

"You want more money, is that it?" Meskal asked. There was not the slightest bit of warmth in his voice.

Bentone began to pace, careful not to get tangled in the telephone cord. "Yeah, I think it's definitely worth a lot more."

There was another pause.

"How much more, Mr. Bentone?"

David thought of a figure and then dismissed it. He didn't want to be too greedy. But then again, what did it really matter. He stared at the vessel that contained the soul of his daughter and named his price.

He felt nothing. Inside, he was finally dead.

The two burly men grabbed Doyle by the arms and dragged him across the floor of the meat-packing plant, past the workers in their goggles, hard hats, and bloodstained smocks, past the bloody carcasses of cattle hanging by chains from the high ceiling.

They had roughed him up on the loading dock and he was having a hard time getting the strength back in his legs. The toes of his shoes left furrows in the sawdust that covered the floor as they dragged him into an office. He was dumped into a folding chair before a large metal desk covered with stacks of paperwork and unopened mail.

"Just sit and be quiet," one of the muscular men said, pointing a finger at Doyle. "Mr. Giordano's in a meeting. He'll deal with you shortly."

Doyle rubbed his stomach where he'd been punched. "Thanks, Tony, I really appreciate ya gettin' me in to see yer boss on such short notice. If there's anything I can do fer ye in the future, don't hesitate ta ask."

The man leaned into Doyle's face. His breath smelled of garlic.

"The name's Dominick. That's Tony over there." He motioned to his other half. Both men looked like they spent a good portion of their day at the gym. They were dressed in colorful sweat pants and black muscle shirts that showed off their fabulous physiques.

Probably never met a steroid they didn't like, Doyle thought as he gave Tony a slight nod and a wave.

The sound of a toilet flushing filled the office and Doyle turned to look at the two men. "I think the meeting just wrapped up."

A door at the back of the office swung open and a behemoth that could only be Benny "the Wrench" Giordano lumbered out of a tiny bathroom. Doyle couldn't grasp how someone that large could fit into something that small—but then remembered the circus act with twenty clowns and a little Volkswagen.

Giordano finished buckling a belt around his expansive waistline as he casually returned to his desk, a newspaper rolled beneath his arm. He noticed he wasn't alone and motioned with his chin to his boys. "Who's this?" he asked, as he threw the paper into a wastebasket behind the desk.

"We was warned this morning that somebody's been nosin' around, askin' a lot of questions about our business and such," Dominick explained.

Doyle watched the Wrench watching him. Benny Giordano was a monster of a man. He weighed at least three hundred-fifty pounds and stood six feet two, and try as he might, Doyle couldn't see that the man had any neck to speak of. A wild shock of salt-and-pepper hair sat atop an unusually large head that rested between two massive shoulders.

Tony piped in. "We caught this guy pokin' around the plant and figured him to be that guy. So we brung him to you."

Doyle stood and extended his hand toward Giordano. "Francis Doyle. Pleasure to make yer acquaintance."

The muscle grabbed him by the shoulders and slammed him back into the chair.

Giordano sat down as well, the office chair squealing in protest as he shifted his great bulk. "That'll be all, you two. Get outta here."

He motioned the two out of his office with a ham-size hand.

"You sure, Mr. G?" Dominick asked. "If you want, we could sit in back, you know, just in case."

Giordano pounded his desk with a closed fist. The items covering the surface danced as the shock wave passed across it. "The day I need two punks like you to watch my back is the day they make me Pope. Now get the hell outta here!"

The two left, eyeing Doyle as they went out the door.

"Not the sharpest crayons in the box, I'd wager." He gestured over his shoulder toward the door.

Giordano leaned forward and glared at Doyle

across the desktop. "That isn't too smart, you askin' questions about me. I'm surprised you didn't get yourself whacked."

Doyle studied the fingernails on his left hand for a moment and pretended not to be intimidated by one of the most powerful loan sharks in the California underworld. "Little Don Gervassi, Squid Scarpo, Caesar Conigliaro; they all know I mean business. I'm lookin' for somebody who owes and they said you'd be the man to talk to."

Doyle gave Giordano an emotionless stare. Over the years he had barely escaped having his legs broken by most of those he mentioned. They gave him the information he sought because he was such a good customer.

Giordano leaned his bulk back in his chair. It shrieked like an animal going into a wood chipper. He smiled at Doyle, nodding his enormous head. "I know those guys. You must be pretty well connected."

It wasn't that he was connected so much as it was he had a bit of a gambling problem, though it had become much more manageable since going to work with Angel. "Let's just say we've done some business in the past." He gave Giordano a wink and a smile.

The loan shark pulled open one of his desk drawers. He withdrew a bottle of whiskey and two dirty glasses. "I don't know why, Doyle, but I like you."

He unscrewed the cap and began to pour. "Anybody else come in here askin' questions that I didn't know from friggin' Adam? You know what I woulda done?"

Doyle leaned forward and took one of the glasses from Giordano. "What would ye've done?"

Doyle sipped his drink and winced. It had been some time since he had straight whiskey before lunch.

Giordano put the bottle back and slammed the drawer closed. "You know why they call me the Wrench?"

Doyle casually crossed his legs, turning the question over in his mind. "Could it have anything to do with yer love of tools?"

Giordano let out a barking laugh and slapped the top of the desk. "If I only had a buck for every time I heard that answer I'd be a freakin' millionaire." He took a big gulp of his drink and set the glass down on a small stack of paperwork. "It's got nothin' to do with tools."

"You don't say," Doyle responded, feigning interest. The whiskey was burning a hole in his gut.

"Ya see, when I first started in this business they'd bring me these guys that was late on their payments." Giordano picked up his glass and downed some more. "I needed to teach 'em a lesson so I'd grab 'em by the wrists and give their arms a yank, wrenching 'em right out of the sockets. You get it—

wrenching? The Wrench? Boy, did they scream." Giordano let loose with another laugh and shook his head. "Them were the days."

A chill went up and down Doyle's spine as he realized he was in the presence of a monster. Not the kind that howled at the moon or drank blood, but the human kind, the ones who didn't realize there was something disturbingly not right about their behavior. It was moments such as these that Doyle didn't feel quite so bad about his demon side.

Giordano sighed. "So, Doyle," he said, a twinkle dancing in his dark, primitive eyes, "what's your story? Tell me why I like you when I don't even friggin' know you."

Doyle leaned forward and set the glass of whiskey on the desk. "Well, it's like this, Benny." He paused. "Can I call you Benny?"

The Wrench threw his hairy arms up. "Hey, we're friggin' pals!"

Doyle had begun to feel very uncomfortable. This was going far too easily, and a bonding experience with a vicious loan shark was the last thing he wanted.

"I work for a guy who's lookin' for a guy who—"

"Who? Who you work for?" The Wrench leaned across the desk, a look of curiosity on his overly tanned face.

Doyle thought fast. "Uh, he's new in the business.

I don't know if you've heard a him. Angelo . . . Angelo the Saint is what they call 'im."

The Wrench stroked one of his double chins. "Angelo the Saint. I think I heard a him."

Doyle pulled the folding chair closer to the desk. "Well, the Saint is lookin' fer a guy that I believe owes you quite a bit o' dough."

Benny's face grew grim. "What's he want him for? If you guys kill him he can't pay me back. I hope there won't be a problem—"

"No, no we're not lookin' to kill anyone. We just need to know where he is so's we can ask him some questions," Doyle reassured the shark.

Giordano smiled. "Good. I'd hate for there to be a problem with my new friend. I have so few these days."

He opened another drawer and removed a book—a ledger—and placed it on the desk, in front of him. From somewhere on the desk, Giordano produced a pair of dark-rimmed glasses and put them on. He opened the book and began to flip the pages. "Gimme the name and I'll see what I can do."

"Bentone," Doyle said. "His name's David Bentone."

Giordano closed the book and plucked the glasses from his face. "Don't even have to look that one up. It was taken care of yesterday, paid in full by some guy with a funny accent." He looked at Doyle apologetically. "Not that there's anything funny about *your* accent."

Doyle sat back. "So, somebody paid off Bentone's debt?"

The Wrench nodded. "Every last nickel plus interest. And this wasn't chump change, if you know what I'm sayin'."

Doyle stood, prepared to leave. "Hate to be a bother, Benny, but can ye give me an address for 'im? We still need to ask 'im some questions."

Giordano replaced his glasses and opened the ledger. He grabbed a pen and scrawled an address on a piece of scrap paper. "I don't care what you do to the bum now—I got my money." He handed Doyle the paper. "Here you go, my friend."

Doyle took the scrap, glanced at it and slipped it into his shirt pocket. "Thanks, Benny. Guess I owe ye one," he said reluctantly.

Giordano suddenly surged out of his seat and came around the desk. Doyle stared at the wall of flesh coming toward him and thought he was about to die.

The Wrench grabbed Doyle in a loving embrace. "I don't know what it is," he said into Doyle's neck. "I just got the feelin' that me and you are very much alike. Like family or somethin'."

Doyle backed away and tried not to show how freaked he was by the loan shark's bizarre affection for him.

Benny smiled at Doyle, pointing to himself. "You come across as a nice guy, quiet and calm with that accent a yours. Wouldn't hurt a fly. But I got a gift, see, I can sense somethin' . . . inside you're an awful lot like me. Am I right?"

Doyle was horrified. Was it possible that this human monster could somehow sense his *own* monstrous side? "You got me there, Benny," he laughed nervously as he backed toward the door.

Benny followed him. "You come by again, friend. I think me and you will be like brothers."

Doyle grabbed the doorknob and turned. "Brothers. Now wouldn't that be somethin'?"

Bentone tossed the olive-green duffel bag onto the mattress and stuffed some underwear and socks inside. He glanced at his watch. Only three more hours before he was supposed to meet Meskal at the bus station to make the exchange, and then it was out of L.A. for good.

The crystal vial was resting in the center of his pillow next to the bag. Gently he picked it up, again marveling at the transcendent beauty of its ever-changing contents. He stroked the cool glass with the tips of his fingers and watched the silver, mercurial liquid inside transform to a billowing mist of the deepest red.

Red was Aubrey's favorite color.

A slight hint of emotion stirred within him, but he

wanted nothing to do with it. Bentone went to the bathroom, unspooled a large wad of toilet tissue and began to wrap the crystal. All he needed was to deliver damaged goods to Meskal. Confident that it was protected, he carefully placed the fragile package inside his bag between the layers of underwear.

Bentone was startled by a sudden knock at his apartment door, but then remembered he had called for takeout earlier.

"Come on in, door's open," he called out as he fished a ten-dollar bill from his wallet and headed for the door. "Hope you remembered the chips!"

He swung open the door, expecting to see an acne-faced teen with his sandwich, but instead found himself looking at two men, one of whom appeared to be very angry.

"No chips, just questions," the larger of the two snarled as he pushed Bentone back into the apartment. The man had dark hair, blazing eyes and wore a long, black coat.

Bentone stumbled backward, tripped and fell. From the floor he watched as the second man closed the door behind them.

"Easy there, Angel," the second guy said to the first. "We don't want him broke before we get the answers we're lookin' for."

Who are these two? Bentone thought in a panic. His mind raced. *Did Meskal lie? Are they from the Wrench?*

He scrambled to his feet and lunged for his night-stand. He withdrew a nasty looking knife from the drawer and brandished it at the one called Angel. "Who the hell are you? What do you want?"

Angel glared. "We've got some questions about your daughter."

Bentone held the knife tighter. *They know,* he thought. He could feel his guilt spread across his face like a mask.

Angel stepped toward him and Bentone lashed out with the knife.

"Keep away from me!" he threatened.

Angel grabbed his wrist in a vice-like grip, bent his arm back painfully and forced him to drop the blade.

"That wasn't too smart, was it, David?" the man with the brogue said, as he watched from across the room.

Bentone cried out as Angel kicked the knife blade out of reach and drove him to his knees.

"I'll let you go if you promise to answer our questions. Do we have a deal?" Angel asked him.

Bentone shook his head. "I don't know what you're talking about," he gasped. "I haven't seen my daughter in—"

Angel pulled his arm back farther and empha-sized each word. "Do we have a deal?"

"Yes, yes, yes!" Bentone screamed as the pain intensified.

Angel let go of his wrist.

Bentone slowly stood, massaging his aching arm. "Who . . . who are you two? Who sent you?" he asked as he walked to his bed and sat down.

"I'm Angel, that's Doyle," he pointed to the other man. "We're working for your wife and daughter. I think you know why."

Bentone stared at Angel. There was something about him, something that told him it was no use denying his involvement. Maybe it was Angel's eyes, like the wrath of God staring down on him. Or maybe the promise of something else . . . something far removed from heaven.

"I . . . just ran outta choices. I owed so much they probably woulda killed me just to make an example to others."

Bentone buried his face in his hands. "I was gonna leave town. But this guy just kinda dropped into my life, said he had a way I could clear my debt."

Bentone looked up, a mixture of fear and shame in his gaze.

Doyle moved to stand beside Angel. "Let me guess, a guy with a funny accent?"

Bentone blinked in surprise and nodded. "Rich guy named Anton Meskal."

"And how did he say you could pay off your debt?" Angel asked.

Bentone averted his eyes. "At first, I thought he

was some kinda nut with a lot of cash, so I went along with it." He turned, picked something up off the bed and tossed it to Angel. "Then he gave me this and I didn't know what to think anymore."

Angel caught the object wrapped in plastic. As he peeled away the bubble wrap an empty glass vial fell to the floor. Angel gazed with revulsion at the soul collector in his hands.

Doyle bent down and retrieved the fallen vial. "Found another one a these at yer wife's the other night."

Bentone nodded. "Meskal gave me extras—in case I screwed up."

He was beginning to feel the shame of what he had done all over again. Maybe he wasn't quite so dead after all. He only wished he was. "He . . . Meskal said all I had to do was point it at her . . . and I'd be free and clear."

He glanced up and recoiled in horror. Something had happened to Angel's face; his brow had grown thicker, his eyes had taken on a yellowish, bestial hue and his teeth . . .

"You pointed this thing at your own daughter?" Angel snarled.

"He said she wouldn't be hurt . . . that the collector would just take her soul," Bentone stammered, heart racing with terror. He began to cry, furious, ashamed and very afraid of this man who had become a monster.

"Her *soul*. I don't believe in God, and I sure as hell don't believe in the idea of souls. I thought he was crazy. I'd give him something I didn't even believe in and my problems would be solved."

Bentone looked pleadingly at Angel. "You gotta believe me. I didn't want to hurt my girl. I just had to get out from underneath what I owed."

Angel's features softened as he slid the collector into his coat pocket. Suddenly, he looked like a man again. "Aubrey's soul. Do you still have it?"

Bentone stood and shifted from one foot to the other. "I'm supposed to meet Meskal tonight at ten at the bus station—to make the exchange."

Angel leaned forward to glare at him. "Give it to me."

Bentone backed away and pointed at the bag on the bed. "It's in there . . . in the bag," he said hurriedly.

Doyle went to the duffel bag and rummaged through its contents. Carefully he removed something wrapped in layers of toilet tissue. He removed the paper and stared with wonder at the glass vessel. "Mother a God, it's . . . beautiful."

Angel went to his side. Both seemed overcome by the beauty of the vial's contents. Bentone watched them, and felt the guilt in his heart continue to grow. Perhaps, he thought, with the help of these two men, he could set things right with his daughter.

A tremendous explosion shook him from his

reverie as the door to his apartment splintered and crashed open with the force of a tremendous kick.

Three powerful figures in trench coats strode in, features hidden by upturned collars, fedoras atop their heads. Bentone had seen at least two of the invaders before, at the park. They worked for Meskal.

"Bentone," one of them said, his voice cold and dead. "We've come for Mr. Meskal's property."

CHAPTER SEVEN

Silence and the crackle of impending violence hung in the air in David Bentone's apartment. Angel studied the three intruders who had broken down the door.

The invaders were featureless, their fleshy pink countenances blank. There were indentations where eyes should have been, a bump where the nose would normally protrude, and a lipless gash instead of a mouth. Yet they were not identical. One wore black metal hoops through the misshapen lumps of flesh on the sides of its head that might have been ears. Another had a small red teardrop drawn beneath the indentation where its left eye would be. On the right cheek of the one that had spoken was tattooed the circular image of a snake consuming its own tail.

The one with the snake tattoo pointed a gloved finger at Doyle. "The vessel, give it to us now."

"They don't have any faces. Can you see that?

They don't have faces!" Bentone cried, on the verge of panic.

Angel motioned for the man to stay calm.

The faceless leader held out its hand. "Give it to me."

Intensity roiled in the air like a powerful storm building.

Angel gave Doyle a slight push. "Take the soul and get out of here."

The storm broke and the faceless creatures advanced. Angel's vampiric visage emerged and he snarled savagely as he attacked.

"Move. Now!" he yelled to Doyle.

Snakeface moved toward Angel with unbelievable speed and swatted aside his attack with a powerful backhand. Angel was hurled across the room, barely missed Bentone, and crashed into the nightstand beside the bed, smashing it to pieces.

The clock from the nightstand fell to the floor and set off the alarm. It filled the room with its annoying ring.

Doyle yanked the door open, but a gloved hand slammed it shut. He looked up to see the creature with the earrings looming beside him. Earrings headbutted Doyle, who stumbled back, clutching his nose, momentarily blinded by pain.

"You're going nowhere. Not until you give up Mr. Meskal's property," the creature intoned.

"Not fair," Doyle said through his hand, "you coulda broke my nose."

He lunged at Earrings and leaned into a sucker punch that snapped his attacker's head violently to the left. Doyle glowered at him. "Seeing as ye have no face and I can't tell fer meself, yer gonna have to let me know if I'm hurtin' ye or not."

Earrings recovered remarkably fast. He grabbed Doyle by the throat and lifted him off the floor.

"Not."

Teardrop threw a jackhammer punch at Angel, who ducked beneath the creature's fist and grabbed hold of its arm. He twisted the limb viciously. It would have been gratifying to hear the thing cry out in pain, but Angel had a feeling these things felt nothing at all. They looked alive, but that might be a matter for debate, he thought.

Angel felt something tear in Teardrop's arm but was pulled away by Snakeface, who grabbed him from behind. Angel rammed his head back into the creature's face and escaped its grip. He spun around and delivered a kick to Snakeface's midsection that knocked him to the floor. Teardrop pounded on Angel's back with clenched fists. The vampire fell to his knees as the intruder prepared to deliver a kick of its own. Angel knocked Teardrop's legs out from under with a sweep of his leg, then, fangs bared, he pounced as the creature hit the floor.

✻   ✻   ✻

Doyle struggled for breath in Earrings's grip as the faceless creature tore open the pocket of his coat with its free hand. Spots danced before his eyes as he watched the ball of tissue containing Aubrey's soul fall to the ground.

The creature viciously slammed him back against the apartment wall. Through a thick haze of pain, Doyle saw Earrings hold aloft its prize.

"I have it," it cried.

Bentone cowered in the corner by the bed, clutching the still-ringing alarm clock in both hands. He watched in terror as Angel wrestled the creature with the teardrop tattoo.

Suddenly, he realized that the one with the snake adorning its face was coming toward him. Bentone pressed himself against the wall. He waved the ringing alarm clock at the horrifying creature, as if it were some kind of protective ward against evil.

Snakeface gripped him by the hair and gave his head a violent shake. "You should never have played games with Mr. Meskal, David."

Bentone stared up into the blank face, his eyes drawn to the image of the snake consuming itself. "I'm sorry. Tell him . . . tell him that I'm very, very sorry. Please, don't . . . Do what you want with those other two . . . they mean nothing to me . . . but please leave me alone."

The grip on the back of his head grew tighter and

Bentone inhaled sharply. Snakeface took the alarm clock from his hand and crushed it. The alarm stopped abruptly, the pieces raining to the floor.

"Mr. Meskal told us to make sure you understand how disappointed he is."

Bentone closed his eyes tightly. Tears ran down his face. "I understand . . . really, I do." His voice trembled with fear.

Snakeface brutally slammed his head against the wall. Bentone sagged with the force of the impact, but Snakeface still gripped his hair, holding him up.

"I'll be sure to tell him that you were sorry . . ."

The creature slammed his head into the wall again. Bentone felt blood beginning to run down his face as his head hit the wall a third time.

". . . and that you took your punishment like a man."

Angel rained a succession of blows down onto the featureless face of the creature with the blood-red teardrop. He heard a series of thuds behind him and glanced quickly over his shoulder to see Snakeface drive Bentone's head into the wall.

"Dammit," he muttered. Then he grabbed Teardrop by the front of its coat, pulled it up and hurled it into the kitchen area where the creature landed on the table and flipped onto the floor.

Earrings seemingly appeared out of nowhere, grabbed Angel in a bear hug and picked him up off the ground. As the creature spun him around, Angel saw Doyle climbing shakily to his feet in the corner of the room by the door.

"Doyle," he barked, using what little air was left in his lungs. "Bentone. Get to Bentone."

Angel drove his heel down into Earrings's knee. The creature pitched to the side. Angel spun around, grabbed the back of its head and brought it down onto his ascending knee, the force of the blow so great that both earrings flew off its head.

The creature stumbled back as Angel prepared for the next attack.

It didn't come.

Something was wrong with the creature. It seemed confused. It touched the sides of its head where the black metal hoops had been attached, then fell to its knees in a frenzied search for its earrings.

Angel turned to see that Doyle had reached Bentone and was trying to pull him away from his attacker.

"Doyle, the tattoo," Angel shouted as he charged forward. "Destroy the tattoo!"

Doyle reached out and raked his fingernails across the creature's cheek, tearing away thick, rubbery flesh, defacing the circular serpent mark.

Snakeface began to scream and let go of the bloodied, battered Bentone. Angel tackled the hysterical creature and drove it to the ground. It didn't attempt to defend itself, but curled into a quivering ball, its gloved hand covering the torn flesh on its face.

Teardrop stared at Angel for a moment—if a creature without eyes could be said to stare at anything—then went to the aid of its sobbing comrades.

Angel joined Doyle, who was on his knees examining Bentone's wounds. There was a dent in the wall behind his head and bloodstained plaster chunks littered the floor.

"How bad is he?" Angel asked.

Doyle frowned. "Pretty bad. Better call an ambulance."

Angel stood to find the phone and saw that it had been smashed in the scuffle. He also saw Teardrop helping its sobbing brothers toward the door.

"Going somewhere, guys?" Angel asked.

"The one with the jewelry," Doyle said. "That's the one with the vial."

Angel extended his hand. "Give it back."

The creatures withdrew another step toward the door.

"Our master will destroy us if we fail to return with the vessel," Snakeface said, hand still covering its mangled tattoo.

Angel stepped menacingly closer. "*I'll* destroy you if you don't hand it over. No matter what, the soul stays with me."

Earrings took the wrapped vial from inside its coat.

"Don't do it," Teardrop hissed, glancing at Snakeface, but the wounded creature only dabbed at the patch of skin dangling from its face.

"Give it to him," Doyle ordered.

Earrings placed the vial in Angel's outstretched hand. Angel felt a sense of calm with the soul back in his possession. Now he just had to figure out what to do with the three creatures before him. They weren't human, yet they were sentient. To just destroy them . . .

June Bentone suddenly appeared behind the three creatures, outlined in the shattered apartment door. An expression of horror was seared into her features.

"D-d-david?" June stammered.

"June, get out of here," Angel yelled as he ran at the creatures, who had all turned to face the woman.

She had seen the hulking figures in their coats, but didn't understand the threat. Instead, June's gaze settled on Angel's face, the blazing eyes and ridged forehead, the gleaming fangs . . . the countenance of a vampire. And she screamed.

Snakeface let go of its injured cheek and grabbed June about the throat. The creature spun her toward Angel. "I'll rip her head off if you come any closer."

Angel froze. He could feel June's eyes upon him, see her fear growing more intense.

"Your face . . . what . . . who are these people? Oh my God, what's going on!"

"It seems the ball is back in our yard," Snakeface said, voice flat and dead. It squeezed June's throat and she gasped for air.

"Court, you stupid git," Doyle snapped. "Ball's in your *court!*"

"Yes. It is," Snakeface agreed. It glared at Angel.

Earrings—with jewelry restored—strode confidently forward and tore the wrapped package from Angel's hand.

"I'll be getting that back very soon," Angel threatened. "You can count on it."

The creature smashed him across the face hard enough to make him stumble backward. With the sleeve of his coat, Angel dabbed at the trickle of blood that leaked from the corner of his mouth.

"Let 'em go, Angel. Don't risk the woman's life," Doyle said from across the room. "There'll be another chance."

Angel turned to Doyle with a snarl. He knew the demon halfling was right, but he couldn't bear to lose the child's soul.

Teardrop opened the door and the creatures began to back out, June in tow. With a sudden display of strength, Snakeface picked up its struggling prisoner, raised her over its head and hurled her across the room.

Angel reacted instantly. He threw himself in her

way and their bodies collided. He could hear the air explode from the woman's lungs as they tumbled to the floor in a tangle of arms and legs.

"Are you all right?" he asked, as he helped her to stand.

June looked at him, scrutinizing his appearance, but his features had returned to normal. She only frowned and shook her head.

"I-I'm . . . fine," she said as she looked past him, to where Doyle knelt by the bloody body of her ex-husband.

"What happened to him?" June pushed past Angel and cradled her former husband in her arms. "David? David, it's June. Can you hear me?"

Angel stood over her as the man's eyes fluttered open. The pupil of Bentone's left eye was extremely large, while the right pupil seemed normal in size. He blinked repeatedly as if trying to clear his vision.

"Juney?" His voice was slurred. "Juney, honey . . . I . . . I screwed up again."

June held him close, his bloody head resting against her chest. The mournful sound of a police siren wailed in the distance. She stroked her ex-husband's head and her hand came away stained with blood. She held him closer and began to rock.

"It's all right. You rest. We'll talk about this later."

Bentone's body was wracked with a coughing fit that made him squirm in agony. "No. Gotta talk . . . now. Not much time left," he rasped.

June looked into David's mismatched eyes. "What is it?"

Bentone coughed again, his face twisted in pain. "Aubrey . . . I . . . did it, Juney. I did it."

The woman seemed confused. She was still not aware of what had befallen her daughter. "I don't understand, how could you have anything to do with—"

He gripped her arm with a blood-covered hand. "Thought . . . thought it was gonna be . . . big break. Never believed it would . . . I took her soul . . . I took our baby's soul, June. I sold it."

June glanced up at Angel and then back to her mortally wounded husband. "You're talking crazy, David. You rest now."

He coughed again, a wet sound. His mouth opened in a silent scream of agony, and then he was still. The police were closer, only moments away now. Angel squatted beside the woman who held the unmoving form of her ex-husband in a motherly embrace.

"June?"

At first she didn't respond, but then slowly she turned her gaze to him. Angel saw fear in her eyes.

"Cordelia said you were different. That you deal with things most people wouldn't understand," she said to him.

Angel nodded.

"My husband . . . my husband sold Aubrey's soul?"

"And if I'm going to get it back I'm going to need you to be strong. You have to trust us. You have to let us do our job, June."

The sirens were close, pulling up in front of the building.

"Angel, we have to leave," Doyle prodded. He glanced nervously out the window at the street below.

Angel gently touched June's shoulder and she flinched.

"I'll stay with Dave," she said, gazing at the blood-spattered face of her husband. "Leave. I'll tell the police what happened."

He stood and with Doyle walked to the door. He turned back to the woman. "I'll find Aubrey's soul," he said. "I promise."

June looked at him, eyes dulled with pain. "You see that you do."

She rested her cheek against David's blood-matted hair, slowly rocking from side to side.

Cordelia sat at her desk and held a note pad at arm's length. She squinted as she attempted to decipher the writing. She knew Doyle had awful penmanship, but never imagined it was this bad.

Maybe if I turn it upside down, she thought, turning the pad around to see if anything became clearer. It didn't.

She had spent most of the day sleeping after

arriving home from the hospital in the early hours of the morning. Without any prospects for the evening, Cordelia had decided to pay a visit to the office to see how the Bentone case was progressing.

She had been pleased to find the office empty. That meant some uninterrupted time to get things organized and to put together a file on their latest case. She had gone to her desk ready to work and then stared at its surface with horror.

Her desk had been defiled. The mess had Doyle written all over it: pencils in the pen drawer, paper clips linked together, creepy books from Angel's reference library in a stack on the corner, note pads covered in a scrawl that not even Giles could decipher. But no one had been in the office to bear the brunt of her wrath, so she had been forced to use her frustrations constructively, returned her desk to its proper order and attempted to organize Doyle's research.

Finally she settled down to examine the marked sections in a reference volume and to translate fragments of the notes scrawled by Doyle. It wasn't long before she managed to piece things together and learn the truth of what had actually happened to Aubrey Bentone.

The little girl's soul had been stolen.

What would it be like, she wondered, goose-bumps erupting across her skin, *to have something like that taken away?*

She tried to find experiences from her own past that might compare. Cordelia recalled a time that she left a very expensive designer handbag in the dressing room of an exclusive dress shop in Sunnydale. By the time she returned to retrieve it, the bag was gone. That had been painful, she remembered. She had loved that bag—but it was still just a handbag.

Worse was the realization that she and her family were suddenly penniless when the government took everything to pay the taxes her father had neglected for years. She had been mortified; gone were the wealth and some of the arrogance that went along with it.

But Aubrey Bentone had lost her soul.

Her soul.

That was so much more than anything Cordelia had ever endured. She knew the pain for those who loved Aubrey must be unbearable. She couldn't imagine the magnitude of such a loss.

Then again, she wondered if, deep down, she just didn't want to.

Cordelia pushed thoughts of loss and pain out of her mind and picked up another of the heavy leather volumes. She began to flip through the ancient text searching for more information.

The door to the office swung open. Cordelia looked up as Angel strode in with Doyle behind him.

She was about to greet them with the usual haranguing, but then caught a glimpse of Angel's face. He wore an expression she had seen before, a look that said if she was a force for evil, she should seriously consider a change of careers. Maybe something in food services.

Cordelia watched him hang his duster and remove something from the pocket. There was some bruising around the vampire's mouth.

Doyle stepped up beside her desk. He too appeared rather banged up.

"Rough night?" she asked, in an attempt to break the oppressive silence.

"Very," Angel grumbled, not bothering to turn around as he went into his office.

Doyle started to speak, but she held up her hand to silence him.

"If you ever leave my desk in such a mess again I will be forced to hurt you in ways that would make even the most hardy masochist say 'ouch.' Do I make myself clear?"

Doyle was stunned. "How . . . did you know? It's not . . . I didn't even . . ."

Cordelia ignored him. Instead, she glanced toward Angel's inner office. He hadn't turned on the light.

"So what's got tall, dark and brooding even moodier than usual?"

Doyle carefully sat on the corner of the desk and

leaned in. "We found Aubrey's father, and her missing soul," he said softly.

"So he's the one who took it? You're telling me a petty thief with a big time gambling problem somehow mastered the black arts and stole his daughter's soul? I'm going to need the instruction manual on this one."

Doyle brought her up to speed on Bentone's debts, and the deal he made to square the balance. Cordelia thought she was going to throw up.

She picked up a paper clip and began to bend it out of shape. "Suddenly I'm understanding why the marriage didn't last."

Doyle rubbed his eyes. "We figure Meskal to be some kinda sorcerer. He gave Bentone the means to collect the soul and Bentone was supposed to drop it off tonight at the bus station."

Cordelia had begun to jot down a few notes. "So I'm guessing with grimmest man in the world sitting in his office in the dark, Aubrey's soul wasn't rescued?"

Doyle sighed and slid from the corner of the desk. He shuffled around the office. "I think Bentone mighta tried to change the deal. Meskal sent some faceless goons to get the soul and take care of him. But they didn't count on us bein' there. Situation turned ugly. Bentone was killed."

"Not good," Cordelia said, thinking of yet another tragedy for June to cope with.

"Worst part is, we had the soul but then the girl's mother came in and wound up a hostage. We had to trade it for her life," Doyle sighed.

"June showed up at her ex's place? She told me she didn't know where he was living," Cordelia said, annoyed. She added to her notes, speaking aloud. "Note to self, take all information from client's mouth with a grain of salt." She looked at Doyle. "So now what?"

"We find Anton Meskal and I bet we find Aubrey's soul," he replied.

Angel called to them from his office. Cordelia went in first and flicked on the light switch. She let out a little shriek as she saw what was laid out on top of Angel's desk.

"Tell me you didn't find that crawling up the wall in here."

She watched with disgust as Angel picked up the fragile device and examined it more closely.

"No. It came in with me. This is what was used to steal Aubrey's soul. It's called a collector."

"I call it gross," Cordelia retorted.

Angel picked up one of the glass vials and attached it to the bottom of the device. "If it wasn't broken in the scuffle it would be capable of stealing the soul from your body and storing it inside this vessel." He set it back on the desk.

Doyle had taken the seat alongside Angel's desk. He leaned forward, studying the collector. "Certainly doesn't look like it was built. I'd guess the ugly thing was grown."

Angel fingered one of the bony protrusions on the side of the weapon. "You're probably right. Grown, just like the faceless trio we fought tonight. I didn't make the connection at first, but looking at this, I'd guess those creatures were homunculi—artificial life forms created with magic and a mixture of flesh, blood and, if you can believe it, horse manure."

Cordy held her nose. "All together now, ewww."

Angel leaned back, his dark eyes never leaving the device. He appeared tired, worn out.

"We're going to need every bit of information we can gather about the mysterious Anton Meskal." He looked at Cordelia. "Cordy, I need you to search the magic user databases to see if Meskal is—"

Cordelia interrupted him with a yawn. She tried to stifle it, but couldn't. "I'm sorry, Angel, what was that again?"

Angel pressed his palms against his eyes. "We're not doing anyone any good in this condition. I think we all need to get some rest."

Doyle had his head down on Angel's desk. He didn't even bother to open his eyes. "I think that's a perfectly brilliant idea. Remember, I was up early rubbin' elbows with organized crime. We can start fresh in the A.M."

Angel wore a deep frown. "We were so close tonight."

"We'll get there again," Cordelia promised him. "Get some rest and I'll hit the Internet first thing tomorrow."

In the outer office, she got her things together and said good night to Doyle as he slunk out the door. Angel had not yet left his office. She strolled back to the doorway to say good night.

Angel had turned off the light again and was sitting in darkness.

"It's going to be dawn soon. Are you going downstairs?" Cordelia asked.

"No," he answered at length. "I haven't been sleeping too well. Think I'll stay here until I'm good and tired."

The collector was still laid out on the desk.

"Not to go all *Oprah* or anything but . . . anything you want to talk about?" she asked.

Again there was a lengthy pause before he responded.

"Good night, Cordelia."

She sensed his need to be alone. "Good night, Angel," she said quietly, leaving him to the darkness.

It wasn't long after Cordelia left that Angel went down to his apartment. He thought a cup of tea might help him to unwind. He fixed himself an Earl Grey, took a book of poetry from his library, Blake's *Songs of Innocence and Experience*, and reclined on his bed, trying to relax. He was distracted; all he could think of was Aubrey's soul and how lovely it was. He wondered if his own tarnished soul could ever be as beautiful.

An hour passed and still Angel did not sleep. He set the book on the nightstand beside his empty tea mug and closed his eyes.

Splashes of color played across the insides of his eyelids: bright reds and greens, muted yellows and explosions of silvery white similar to the colors he had seen manifest within the crystal soul receptacle. But nothing could compare. He had been correct those many years ago when he answered his baby sister's question about the appearance of the soul.

". . . *the most lovely thing you'll ever see*," he had told her.

He saw the vessel now, floating in the darkness. He felt himself begin to unwind.

"It's made up of all the colors of the rainbow and some that haven't even been thought up yet."

It appeared as a gas, billowing white. Tiny explosions of color erupted within the body of wafting mist.

"To look at one, it would make you cry with sheer joy, it's so beautiful."

And then the mist and the blooming colors began to coalesce. The contents of the vessel became like liquid.

Like blood.

And the soul trapped within screamed to be free.

❖   ❖   ❖

Angel couldn't remember how he came to be in the ancient cemetery, but he knew well enough where he was.

It was where his family had been laid to rest two centuries before.

His bare feet crushed dry leaves beneath them as he walked between the headstones. A cool fall breeze blew across the burial ground, causing prickly goose-flesh to erupt across the naked skin of his chest.

Why am I here? *he thought. He tried to read the names on the grave markers as he passed but couldn't. It was unusually dark and many of the names had become obscured by thick, leafy vines that grew across the surfaces of the headstones.*

At first he believed it to be the sighing of the wind, but then he listened more carefully. It wasn't the wind but a child's voice he heard.

"Hello?" he called. "Is somebody there?"

A thick bank of clouds slid across the face of the moon, allowing the cold rays of the midnight sun to shine, illuminating this place of the dead.

He saw her then, across the yard, a tiny figure kneeling before a grave. The child was speaking, but he could not understand the words. He drew closer.

She was busily ripping away the green, leafy plant life from the headstone. Her back was to him, but Angel could see that she wore a pink hospital gown.

He could suddenly hear what she was saying and realized the child was speaking to him. "I been here awhile and she's been tellin' me stuff. She was really mad when you got dead, you know."

The child dug her tiny fingers beneath a band of vines across the front of the stone and pulled them away.

Angel moved closer. Before he even read the newly exposed name, he knew whose grave he stood before.

The little girl droned on. "And then you came back and she was happy. She thought you was an angel, did you know that? That's what she told me." She leaned back to survey her work. "But you wasn't no angel."

The wind blew and ruffled the child's long, curly black hair.

Angel read the name on the stone over and over again, the date she had been born and the date she had died. He remembered her birth. At his mother's urgings, he had reluctantly held the newborn. From that moment on a special bond formed between him and his little sister Katherine.

"You was a monster and you killed her," the child said.

Angel fell to his knees, overcome by the excruciating flood of memories, of the day that bond was torn to bloody shreds. He remembered killing her, the look of terror twisting her innocent face as what she believed to be an angel bore down upon her.

She had struggled briefly as he sank his fangs into

the soft flesh of her throat. With sickening clarity he remembered the disappointment that the monster he had become felt when she had not lasted longer.

"She wants you to help me, Angel," the child said as she rested her hand upon the cool face of the weathered stone.

Angel lifted his head, the agony of the past dissipating but the recollection still painfully tender.

"Who are you?" He reached a trembling hand out to the child.

She began to turn. No more than five years old, the child's pale skin was stark in contrast to the blackness of her hair. Thick gauze pads had been taped over her eyes, to prevent them from drying out. An IV tube ran from her arm to the ground, snaking beneath a cover of dried leaves.

Aubrey Bentone looked toward Angel and spoke.

"You took your sister's soul and now you're gonna help find mine."

He watched as she began to sink into the earth of his sister's grave.

"I gotta go now but you got a lotta work to do."

Aubrey was up to her neck now in the rich black earth.

"I'll tell your sister you said hello."

And with that, she was gone, swallowed up by the hungry grave.

CHAPTER EIGHT

Meskal sat in a high-backed, black leather chair behind a desk of chrome and glass. Its surface was vacant except for a sleek phone and an old wooden box that seemed entirely out of place on top of the stark, modern piece of furniture. Dressed in a robe of scarlet silk, he stroked his chin in contemplation.

The homunculus with the circular snake tattoo hanging from its face removed its fedora. It bowed its head as it spoke, in respect to its creator. "He was a vampire. They called him Angel. He was there with another." Snakeface's hand went to the flesh that dangled from the wound on its face.

The other homunculi said nothing. They stood apart from Snakeface, letting it explain what had happened at Bentone's apartment. They too had removed their hats and lowered their gazes.

"And this vampire . . . Angel . . . tried to prevent

you from collecting my property? This disturbs me greatly."

When Snakeface looked up, the piece of skin that hung from its face flapped obscenely. "He wanted the vessel, Master."

Meskal leaned forward in the chair, caressing the cold surface of the desk with the palm of his hand. He had heard of the vampire Angel but always considered him to be nothing more than an urban myth, the demon equivalent of the bogeyman. He imagined demon mothers wagging clawed fingers at their young. *Eat up all your flesh or Angel will get you.*

"Why? Why this sudden interest in my business? No one has ever attempted to interfere with my practices before. Now, out of the blue, we have this Angel sticking his nose where it doesn't belong."

Snakeface did not respond. It was attempting to stick the skin back into place on its ravaged face with one gloved hand.

Meskal, his ire on the rise, took notice. "What are you doing?"

Snakeface quickly dropped its hand. "My . . . my face was damaged in the battle and I was trying to—"

Meskal scoffed. "I know exactly what you were doing. You were attempting to reattach your ridiculous *identity*. I know what that foolish mark means to you. I know all about your little attempts at individuality." He pointed to the homunculi behind

Snakeface. "You with your silly earrings and you . . . you with your teardrop of blood."

Meskal rapped the glass top of the desk with a knuckle.

"There is nothing you do that I do not know about. Must I remind you? You are of my blood, my flesh. I am the one who made you what you are." He leaned back in the chair and began to swivel from side to side. "Servants, slaves, enforcers of my will—you are what I tell you to be. Nothing more, nothing less."

The homunculi cowered beneath their master's harsh words.

"The ancients warned of those created by sorcery becoming overconfident in their gift of life. Let them live too long and they forget their place, is what the old ones claimed."

Meskal closed his eyes and sighed. "Of all my homunculi you three have served me best and longest. I saw no real harm in letting you dabble with the concept of self. Jewelry and tattoos. What did it really mean to the scheme of things? Nothing."

Meskal's eyes snapped open and he glared at them. "Until now. Until it began to interfere with my business. I'm beginning to think the ancients might have been correct in their assumptions."

Snakeface nearly crushed his fedora in his nervous grip. "But, Master, we did achieve our goal."

Snakeface turned to Earrings and held out its hand. The jewelry-wearing homunculus dug into its coat pocket, produced the vial containing Aubrey's soul, and placed it in Snakeface's palm. Snakeface held the vial out to his master, an offering to appease the god who had made them.

"You see? We have the vessel and David Bentone is dead. I smashed his skull like the shell of an egg."

Meskal didn't move. He stared at the homunculus with his intense blue eyes. Snakeface came tentatively forward and gently placed the vial on the desk. Then it quickly stepped back into place with the others.

Meskal stared at the vial for a moment. "A valuable piece. The purity of a child's soul makes it very attractive. But it still doesn't explain why Angel would attempt to steal it from me."

His anger abated, he smiled at his servants. "Since I got rid of Kabbarat, I'm the only soul trader in town. What was he going to do, steal it from me and then try to sell it back? Not even a vampire is that stupid." He laughed softly. "Give me the collector and get out of my sight. I'm suddenly feeling merciful."

Snakeface turned to its brothers. Earrings shook its head while Teardrop covered its face with a gloved hand. Snakeface turned back to Meskal.

"We . . . we do not have the collector, oh merciful Master. We did not even see the device when we entered and—"

The sorcerer went rigid, as if a hundred thousand volts had passed through his body. "Tell me this is an attempt at a character trait. The practical joker? The funny man?"

Snakeface wrung the hat in its grip. "No, sir, it is not a joke. We did not retrieve the collector. Perhaps if we were to return to the dwelling we could still locate it among the man's belongings."

Meskal rose and moved around the desk. His icy blue gaze had turned even lighter—colder. "Do you know how long it takes to grow a proper collector? Do you?"

The homunculi did not answer, their gaze trained on the floor.

"Ten times as long as it takes to grow the likes of worthless pieces of filth like yourselves."

Meskal stood before Snakeface, his body seeming to crackle with repressed energy. The homunculus slowly lifted its eyes.

"We retrieved the soul. Is that not worth something?"

Meskal shuddered as though he had been spat upon. He raised his right hand and began to mutter in an ancient, long-forgotten tongue. It sounded like the angry buzzing of a wasp trapped behind a windowpane.

His hand began to glow and then to burn. Bright orange flames leaped from his fingertips and danced in the air as if alive.

Meskal reached out and tore the flap of skin from Snakeface's cheek. The creature let out a pitiful squeal; its hands flew to the exposed wound.

The sorcerer held the piece of tattooed skin in his flaming palm and watched it shrivel and burn. It was as if the snake were truly consuming itself now. The oily aroma of frying homunculus flesh mixed with the heady smell of overturned earth wafted through the sorcerer's living area.

"Let me show you what your impertinence is worth."

He reached out and grabbed the homunculus' face. The flames hungrily leaped onto the creature's head as though it had been doused with an accelerant. Meskal let go and stepped away from his creation.

The creature screamed, its hands beating at the unnatural fire. They too began to burn and the fire spread down the arms to its upper body. Snakeface fell to its knees, its pathetic struggle becoming more feeble.

The other homunculi watched silently as the supernatural fire consumed their brother.

"I gave it life and now I have taken that life away." Meskal watched the black ash that had once been Snakeface drift across the hardwood floor. "It is my right as creator."

His hand still aflame, the sorcerer turned his attention to Earrings and Teardrop. "If I were to conjure the spirits of the ancients for guidance, they would most certainly advise that the two of you share your brother's fate."

Meskal brought the hand up to Earrings's face. The homunculus recoiled. "And I would have to agree. But seeing as business is booming, and I'm already short-staffed, I'm going to allow the two of you to live."

He reached out and cupped the metal hoop hanging from the homunculus' ear in his burning hand. The creature screamed as the jewelry melted into the side of its head. Meskal turned to Teardrop. He pressed a flaming finger against the red tear mark and watched the flesh sizzle.

"Now you each wear a mark that sets you apart as individuals, but also binds you together as one. You each wear a mark that shows you have displeased me. Disappoint me again and I won't give a second thought to snuffing out your worthless lives."

Meskal blew on his hand and the magical flame was extinguished.

"Now, you have work to do. Go to the club and collect the night's Uforia receipts." He dismissed them with a wave of his hand as he walked toward a bar set up in the corner of the room.

The two homunculi ran for the stairs, eager to be gone in case their angry creator should suddenly change his mind.

Meskal placed a glass tumbler on the bar and

picked up a pair of gold tongs to remove ice from the bucket for his drink. But they fell from his grasp as an excruciating spasm of pain shot through his right hand.

Breathless with agony, he raised the hand to examine it. It had become like a claw. Furiously, he massaged the appendage in an attempt to relieve the throbbing hurt. He had felt this pain before but its intensity was on the rise.

He stared with horror at the top of his hand and watched dark brown liver spots blossom. The skin was growing thinner, almost translucent, the blueness of the veins beneath the flesh more obvious.

"Dammit," he cursed, lurching toward his desk. "There was a time I would scarcely break a sweat with the burning hand spell." The other hand began to stiffen as he grabbed the old wooden box from the corner of the desk. "Now it's nearly killing me," he said through clenched teeth.

He struggled with the box's lid, finally managing to get it open. *When was the last time I needed an injection?* he asked himself. *Not long ago, maybe a week at the most.*

He moved around the desk and fell into the leather seat, the joints in his legs growing more rigid by the minute. Desperately the sorcerer tipped the case and spilled multiple ampules of glowing, green liquid and a hypodermic needle onto the glass desktop.

He snatched up one of the ampules and the hypodermic in his newly gnarled hands. Carefully he slid the needle tip inside the ampule and drew the colorful fluid up into the syringe.

He tasted blood in his mouth as his gums began to recede.

Meskal extended his arm. The flesh had become pasty white and loose. Looking carefully, he found a spot along the track marks left by previous injections.

The needle sank beneath the aging skin and he gently pushed down on the plunger. The glowing contents of the syringe coursed through his bloodstream like wildfire. He withdrew the needle and tossed it onto the desk, already beginning to feel the effects of the injection. His breath came in short gasps, his body wracked by painful convulsions.

Meskal leaned back and watched as the age spots slowly faded from his hands. He flexed the stiffness from his fingers. "Like a charm," he said.

The frequency of the attacks worried him. He had always known that his body would eventually grow more resistant to the effects of the longevity drug, but it seemed to be happening very quickly.

Meskal counted four ampules left. He would need to increase his production of the drug and that was something he was not looking forward to. To distill the drug was a painstaking and time-consuming process. The number of fresh souls needed to fill only one of the ampules with the life-sustaining juice was astounding. He would have to cut down on his day-to-day spellcasting to buy himself more time.

He returned the ampules and the hypodermic to the old wooden box and closed the lid. The agonizing effects of the drug had begun to fade so he returned to the bar for the Scotch the deteriorating attack had interrupted.

Meskal sipped his drink as he strolled over to one of the smoked glass, floor-to-ceiling windows that looked out onto the city of Los Angeles. He remembered when the place had been nothing more than desert—and now this. It all seemed to happen in a mere blink of the eye.

His reverie was suddenly invaded by thoughts of his business and the vampire who had tried to steal his property.

Drink in hand, Meskal returned to his desk. The vial was still there. He set his drink down and examined the quality of the child's soul trapped within. *Why this particular soul?* he wondered as he turned it around in his hand, admiring its beauty.

He picked up the telephone and punched in a series of numbers.

The call was answered on the third ring.

"Julien? It's Anton." Meskal took a quick sip from his drink. "I need some information." He paused before he continued, to stress the importance of his request.

"Get me everything you can on the vampire called Angel."

Steven Doherty was so overcome with emotion, he thought for sure he would cry. He stepped from the thick copse of shrubs and stared at the high, wrought-iron gates, the only things separating him from the place he had always dreamed of seeing.

Horror House stood at the top of the winding road that led from the iron gates, and Steven could barely contain his excitement.

Built in the early 1930s by the great horror-film star Graham Sunderland, the sprawling mansion was constructed high in the Hollywood hills away from the prying eyes of a curious public. The Gothic-style manse was designed to resemble the medieval castle from Sunderland's first studio hit, *Castle of Night*. Stone turrets, a great, iron gate that could be raised to allow visitors access to an underground garage, gargoyles hanging from the gutters; these were only a few of the many details insisted upon by the actor.

The inside of the house was rumored to be just as impressive. Where the outside resembled a stronghold from the past, the inside contained every modern convenience. For a time after its completion, Sunderland's Horror House, as it came to be known, was the architectural wonder of the Hollywood Hills.

He looked around again to be sure that no one was watching, then began to scale the fence.

Steven had been fascinated with the horror legend since he was ten years old, when he first saw the film *Dead Men Tell No Tales* on late-night television. Over the next twenty years, he watched all of the actor's fifty-nine films repeatedly and read everything written about Horror House and the infamous star who had lived there. To be so close to his obsession was like a dream come true.

He clung to the shadows on the side of the road as he made his way toward the house.

He had made the decision to go to Horror House on his thirtieth birthday while he watched his special edition DVD of the Graham Sunderland shocker *Cloak of Shadows*. At the end of the disc was a documentary about Sunderland and the house he built in the Hollywood Hills. As he watched the piece for the fiftieth time, it hit him like a bolt out of the blue. He had to go there, had to see where the legend lived and died.

Elvis fans had Graceland; Steven had Horror House.

As he reached the top of the road, a grin spread across his face as he looked upon the dark beauty that was Horror House. It was all he expected and then some.

There had always been rumors of wild parties and strange goings-on at Sunderland's Horror House; it was what the public expected. Most chalked it up to the life of a celebrity and left it at that.

But it wasn't long after the release of *Night of a Thousand Screams* in 1942 that a lead in the whereabouts of a missing teenage girl brought the police to Sunderland's home. What the police found that fateful night established the actor as one of the most notorious figures in the pantheon of old Hollywood.

Steven absorbed every detail of the building's front and headed around back. It was there, in the pool house, where *it* had happened.

Steven entered the enclosed backyard of Horror House through an elaborately carved wooden gate with a broken latch. A marble walkway led through what was once a beautiful garden. Tufts of grass grew up from between the cracked, white rock, and the garden now resembled a jungle of weeds with an occasional wildflower thrown in for color. Steven was disgusted. *How could anyone let such a treasure as this fall so far into disrepair?* He shook his head and followed the path to an elaborate structure that protruded from the back of the mansion. The pool house.

Steven felt giddy. *Maybe I'll stay here the entire day,* he thought as he reached for the ornate knob on a side door.

It was like an answer to his prayers. The doorknob turned. He pushed the door open and stepped into murky darkness. It was humid and a damp, musty aroma hung heavy and thick in the air. He looked around and up, and noticed that tarps covered the skylights.

Maybe somebody is about to do some work around here after all, he mused as he approached the Olympic-size swimming pool. *They filled the pool,* he noticed, though the water was now stagnant and murky. He stood at the pool's edge, taking in the room's every detail.

This is where it all came crashing down, he thought, imagining how fabulous the room must have been back in 1942.

The Hollywood police had raided the house during one of Sunderland's frequent parties to find a bizarre satanic ritual going on and the missing girl about to be sacrificed by a dagger-wielding Sunderland.

Police later said he looked like something right out of one of his movies: decked out in blood-red silk, face painted with strange markings, wearing a headdress of ram horns and holding a knife with a blade over a foot long.

This was much more than a night of drunken rowdiness or a scuffle with paparazzi. He must have known there was no chance of the studio getting him out of it. So he fled, the police in pursuit.

At the edge of the pool, Steven closed his eyes. This was where they said he had stood before . . .

The police had cornered Sunderland in the pool

house. He had dropped the knife but had picked up a pistol from somewhere. The police were closing in, their weapons drawn. They ordered him to drop the gun. But with a smile on his face, Sunderland placed the gun beneath his chin, pulled the trigger and blew his brains out.

Steven imagined his idol tumbling backward into the pool.

"Tragic," he muttered as he gazed down into the water.

A cluster of bubbles broke the surface of the filthy water and startled him. Steven jumped back from the pool's edge.

In a deeper patch of shadow, something moved. It made a rustling sound like the flapping of wings.

He squinted into the darkness.

Probably a bird, he thought.

At the far end of the room, something else flew from one shadowy corner to another. Steven could hear its claws scrabble across the tile floor as it landed.

Something told him it wasn't a bird.

Carefully he began to back toward the door.

From multiple areas at the back of the pool house came the sounds of hissing and things scraping across the ground.

He lunged for the doorknob.

Something blocked his way.

Steven let out a squeal of surprise as his eyes took

in the details of a large figure in a fedora and trench coat standing in front of the door.

He doesn't have a face, he thought, his mind beginning to race as he stumbled back. *He doesn't have any face.*

Steven didn't know whether he should laugh or cry. He had always wondered about this as he sat before his thirty-five-inch television screen. *What would I do?*

"I'm . . . I'm a fan . . . a fan of Graham Sunderland . . . the biggest," he stammered.

The faceless man said nothing.

Something brushed his face and Steven screamed. He flailed his arms and stumbled back. His foot landed on something that thrashed beneath his sneaker and he let out a blood-curdling shriek that filled the pool house.

Needle-sharp teeth sank into his ankle. Steven yelled and reached down to slap at the thing. The flesh of the animal was cold and leathery. It growled as he touched it.

Another of the animals landed on his back; its claws raked his flesh through the *Night of the Blood Monster* T-shirt.

He felt the animal at his ankle began to climb up his pants leg.

Steven turned to the man in the doorway and screamed. "Help me, for Christ's sake! Call the police! Do something!"

The thing did not respond.

Two more of the animals landed on his back. One sank its teeth into the top of his spine. Steven screamed some more and thrashed around. He slipped and fell to the ground on his side. One of the creatures let out a yelp of pain as he fell upon it.

He could feel the blood running in tickling rivulets all over his body.

Leathery wings beat the air above him. He tried to swat them away but they kept coming. *What are these things?* his brain screamed. *God, they're eating me!*

Then he remembered the pool, the filthy, disgusting pool that now smelled of sewage and who knew what else.

Steven turned on his belly and began to crawl to the pool's edge. One of the animals was on his head. It bit at his scalp. Blood ran down his face into his eyes. He slapped at his head and the animal . . . *was it a bat?* . . . snapped at his fingers. Steven crawled faster.

It seemed like his only hope. Submerge in the pool and the things would let go. He wasn't sure what he would do after that but his main concern was to get the biting things off him and stop the excruciating pain.

He squirmed feebly to the pool's edge, pulled his pain-wracked body over the side, and slid into the stagnant water. It was surprisingly warm and he thrashed beneath it to loosen his attackers. He opened his eyes in the dark waters and watched them float toward the surface.

The bites and scratches that covered his body stung unmercifully in the polluted water. He'd need antibiotics for sure when he got out, maybe even a rabies shot.

Steven's lungs felt as if they were about to burst and he knew he had to surface, whether the things were gone or not.

He began to rise but something caught his ankle from below in a vise-like grip. He peered down into the darkness but could see nothing but his foot disappearing into the inky black.

Explosions of color blossomed before his eyes as his brain began to experience the effects of oxygen deprivation. He struggled but to no avail. He couldn't free his foot.

As the foul water rushed in to fill his lungs and his struggles ceased, Steven's gaze again fell upon the shadows that held him tight.

This time he saw that the darkness at the bottom of the swimming pool had two circular yellow eyes and an enormous smile of razor-sharp teeth.

It reminded him of a monster he had seen in a movie once.

The difference, of course, was that this was real.

The Kurgarru demon called Shugg gracefully slid his great mass beneath the water of the pool. His large hand still clung to the ankle of Steven Doherty. Like a child holding onto the string of a balloon, he pulled the body along behind him as he made his way to the shallow end.

The demon broke the surface. His dark, oily skin glistened like a rainbow in the faint light creeping around the edges of the tarp-covered skylights.

Shugg blinked his large, bulbous eyes as he adjusted to the surface light of the room. The homunculus by the door had been joined by four others and all slowly approached the pool.

The water erupted as Shugg threw the dead man's body out of the pool as if it were a toy. It landed in a grotesque, broken heap behind the homunculi, near a stack of rusty patio furniture.

"For my babies," Shugg grumbled as he waded closer to the pool's edge and began to haul his enormous mass from the water. The homunculi bustled about the demon as they attempted to help him out; water cascaded off his body.

The demon seemed uneasy on land. He swayed on his thick legs, and the homunculi had to be careful not to let him fall as they began to dry his vast bulk with thick white towels. Shugg let himself be tended to and paid the faceless servants no mind. His attention was drawn to the corner where he had thrown the intruder's body.

Shugg spoke to the darkness. "There you go, my precious ones; a special treat, all for you."

From out of the shadows the creatures that had driven the human into the pool began to emerge. Some crawled, others glided down from hiding places in the ceiling. At first they sniffed and nipped at the body and when they sensed no resistance, they began to eat voraciously.

The demon watched his precious pets feed as he lifted his arms so the faceless servants could dry beneath them.

"They were hungry babies, yes they were," the demon cooed lovingly at the hairless, bat-like beasts that noisily feasted upon the corpse in the corner of the pool house. The horrendous sounds of flesh gulped and bones crushed in powerful jaws drifted through the air. The Durge, as the animals were called, brought the demon immense pleasure. *It is good for them to receive special treats now and again,* Shugg thought. It reminded the Durge of how much he loved and appreciated them.

Shugg felt his sense of calm disturbed as he recalled the troublesome situation that had arisen earlier that morning. He had gone into the water to relax after a distressing call from his business partner, Anton Meskal.

Angel had taken an interest in their business.

Shugg had always known that as the soul trade continued to grow and prosper, the vampire who fought on the side of light might eventually take notice of them.

Two homunculi helped the demon into an enormous terry-cloth robe.

The Durge still crawled about in the blood and viscera they had spilled in their frantic consumption of Doherty's body. They had left little more than shredded cloth and slivers of bone. Shugg held his robe open to expose the broad shiny skin of his enormous chest and stomach. The Durge began to move toward him, spreading their blood-covered wings and leaping into the air one right after the other.

The demon's eyes closed with pleasure as the Durge collided with his flesh and attached themselves to his body with their mouths.

"Ahhhhh, that's it, my lovelies," Shugg said as the creatures latched on, furled their wings and hung from his massive body.

Like some species of fish that cling to the underbellies of larger sea creatures for food, the Durge latched onto Shugg's body, feeding off the impurities that polluted the demon's bloodstream. The two races had a symbiotic relationship; Shugg kept the Durge fed and the Durge served as living dialysis machines and as a swarm of voracious bodyguards, protecting the demon's privacy and property.

The demon gently stroked the hairless backs of the creatures.

"Welcome home," he purred.

Shugg shifted his weight from one foot to the other. "Bring me my canes," he said to the homunculi.

Two hurried toward the demon; each hefted an intricately carved, enormous cane of dark polished wood.

Shugg took the canes and shambled toward the double doors that would take him inside the house. His mind was clearer after a swim and a bit of murder. He felt more at ease with the predicament that faced him.

"I'm hungry," he said. "Bring me something to eat in the den."

"But, Master," said a homunculus, eyebrows drawn onto its face with Magic Marker, "you have already fed twice this morning and Master Meskal said that you must curb your appetite or—"

The demon slammed one of his canes onto the floor with tremendous force.

"Meskal does not dictate when I feed," the demon seethed. "Now bring me sustenance or I'll set the Durge upon you." They flapped their leathery wings and growled low and menacing.

Shugg continued into the house, his breath coming in short, wet gulps. As if the situation with Angel wasn't enough, now he had Meskal attempting to dictate when he could eat.

His den was a dark, cave-like room with a gigantic

fireplace on one side built to resemble the visage of a roaring lion. A small fire still smoldered within the mouth of the giant cat. On the other side, against the wall, sat the demon's pride and joy, a fifty-five-inch, big-screen television.

But not even that would bring him release from his troubles this day. The demon approached a large chair across from the television. It had been specially constructed to hold someone of his immense size and weight. He lowered himself down with a sigh and leaned his canes against the chair.

"Can you sense it, my darlings? Can you feel that something upsets me?"

The Durge stirred as he touched them.

"Angel will try to ruin everything that I have worked so hard over the centuries to build."

A strange trill came from the Durge as he petted them, like the purr of a contented house cat.

"And of course, there is Meskal. There is always Meskal."

Shugg felt himself grow tense again. His stomach rumbled. "Where is my food!" he bellowed in a rage.

A homunculus bustled into the room, carrying a silver tray piled high with soul vials.

"Maybe it's time I had Meskal grow me some new help," the demon growled.

The glass tinkled merrily as the homunculus gently set the tray down on a small table next to Shugg's chair.

"Careful, you faceless idiot. Those vials are extremely delicate and their contents worth more than a thousand of you."

"Do you require anything else, Master Shugg?" it asked with a slight bow of the head.

The demon snarled as he reached down to pluck a vial from the top of the heap. "You'll know when I do."

The faceless servant retreated.

Shugg tossed the vial into his enormous maw and bit down. The glass shattered and his mouth was filled with the delicious essence of soul. The demon was careful to keep his mouth closed; he didn't want any of the precious life energy to escape.

The great folds of the demon's throat and chest glowed as the soul slid down his gullet with the shards of glass.

Shugg moaned in ecstasy as the Durge began to rhythmically suck out the impurities of the soul. It was growing more difficult to find pure souls, and if allowed to build up, the poisons of tainted souls could kill him.

Hungrier than he thought, Shugg grabbed a handful of the vials and tossed them into his mouth. He chewed greedily, the explosion of soul energies into his body almost overwhelming. He had to be careful not to overdo it; too much of the ethereal fruit could prove dangerous—and he didn't want to cut into Meskal's profits.

The Kurgarru tossed back his head and let the soul energies pulse through his body. As he often did in stressful times, the demon recalled the times in his life when he had triumphed over great adversity.

Shugg remembered his home dimension, the sprawling cities, the great Kurgarru empire, so proud before their kind evolved into soul-eaters. Even then, they might have survived, had they not begun to feast on one another. Shugg had been the first to do so . . . and the only one to survive.

He ate more of the souls and ran a finger around the inside of his mouth to loosen pieces of glass stuck there. He swallowed the fragments, sated for the moment. The Durge continued to suckle, their sleek bodies growing larger, fatter. They had begun to trill again, satisfied with their sustenance as well.

For the moment.

CHAPTER NINE

"You've got a lot of nerve coming here," Verna snarled.

Venom-coated quills started to poke through her skin as she glared at Doyle, who sat on a stool at the counter of the Cup O' Joe Diner. Doyle put on his best *I don't want any trouble* face.

"Can't a guy come in for a cup o' coffee and maybe a doughnut and not be lookin' to give you a hard time?"

She began to furiously scrub at a coffee stain on the counter with a cleaning rag. "You know I work here. Common courtesy would have you stay away."

Doyle knew this wasn't the most sensitive thing he had ever done. He knew how Verna felt about him and how he had treated her.

"You didn't even ask for my number before you were taking off for a date with . . . Angel or somebody." She tossed the filthy rag down onto the countertop and put her hands on her blue uniformed hips.

"What, it didn't work out with her so you think you might give me a second chance? Well, let me tell you something, Doyle, you can—"

Doyle held up his hand to silence her, not sure that it would work. Verna was on a roll.

"Not a date, darlin'. Angel is my boss, really."

She crossed her arms.

Doyle continued. "I'd lost track of time and left him in a spot of trouble. I'm sorry about your number, it's just I was in such a rush—"

She turned, pulled a mug from the rack behind her and began to fill it. "Keep your excuses," she said as she placed it in front of him. "I'm over you."

Momentarily at a loss for words, Doyle picked up the mug and took a sip. He set it down, still feeling her eyes upon him. "I really am sorry if I hurt yer feelings. I didn't mean to lead you on or anything."

Verna scowled but slowly let it turn to a begrudging smile.

"It's all right. Like I said. I'm over you."

"Right. Good, then. Cheers." He toasted her with his coffee.

"What brings you here, Doyle?" she asked as she walked to a serving tray laden with doughnuts. "I know you didn't come in here just to apologize for hurting my feelings." She lifted the glass lid and took one.

Doyle smiled as she slid the doughnut on a small plate in front of him. "I've been looking for an acquaintance of mine, used to haunt this part a town. Tall demonic-type with a complexion like pepperoni pizza. He goes by the name of Margus. Have ye seen him?"

She frowned and went back to wiping the counter. "I want nothing to do with anyone who hangs out with that waste of life. Maybe you should think about getting some new friends."

"An acquaintance, not a friend. He's given me some information in the past. And that's what I'm looking for now."

Verna brought the rag to the sink and rinsed it. "I don't know the last time you saw your buddy Margus, but I'd be surprised if he could give you anything of value now." She tossed the cloth to the side of the sink and turned her attention back to him.

Doyle finished his doughnut and brushed the crumbs from his hands into his coffee mug. "You've seen him?"

Verna looked thoughtful for a moment, then grabbed the coffeepot and refilled his cup. "I see him almost every night, but I wish I didn't. If I owned this place I'd ban him."

"When does he come in?"

"After the bars close. He's a real piece of work, usually strung out on who knows what. The skin's bad enough but he's also obnoxious as hell."

Doyle picked up his mug thoughtfully. He knew Margus to enjoy an occasional drink, but drug use was something altogether different.

"Well, at least I know he's not dead," Doyle said as he slid off the stool. He reached into his pocket, counted out some bills and tossed them onto the counter. "I'll be back tonight, if you don't mind."

The demoness shook her head as she picked up the money. "Not at all. Long as you don't wreck the joint."

Doyle continued to stand at the counter. "So I might see you later, then."

Verna nodded and smiled. "It's too bad about us," she said. "I could have made you really happy."

Doyle walked backward toward the door. "Yer wrong there, darlin'," he said, pushing it open with his back. "I'd only break yer heart."

Doyle returned to the Cup O' Joe Diner a little past two in the morning. Verna was serving some cabbies their infusion of energy as he came through the door. She gestured with the steaming pot to the back.

Doyle saw Margus there hunched over a cup of coffee. Dressed in dark pants and a hooded sweatshirt, the demon seemed to be nodding off to sleep. Doyle pulled out the chair across from him and sat down. Margus lifted his head, gold-flecked eyes blinking away the need for sleep.

"Margus," Doyle said cheerfully, "long time no speak."

Recognition gradually crept across the demon's mottled features.

"Doyle," he slurred. He found his coffee cup and brought it to his mouth.

Doyle noticed the tremble in Margus's hand as he slurped his coffee.

"Go away," the demon said as he hunched lower over his cup. He pulled his hood up over his head. "I've got nothin' to talk about."

Doyle crossed his legs and leaned casually back in the chair.

"I think ye do. Rumor has it ye've started indulgin' in drugs. Is that a fact, Margus?"

The demon lifted his head and glared at Doyle. There was something wrong with the look. Something hungry, wild and reckless. "If you don't leave now, things are gonna get ugly."

Doyle turned to glance at Verna at the front of the diner.

"Remember what I said about wreckin' the place," she called.

Doyle reassured her with a wink and turned his attention back to Margus. "Where were we?"

Margus was breathing harder. The flesh of his face had started to bubble and tiny rivulets of a milky fluid were running down his face. This was actually common when his species became upset, but that didn't make it any less disgusting.

Doyle pulled some napkins from the holder and

tossed them across to the dripping demon. "Wipe yerself off, man, before ye make a mess of yer clothes."

Margus stood abruptly. His chair crashed to the floor.

"Where do ye buy yer drugs, Margus?" Doyle asked calmly. "Where do ye get yer Uforia?"

"I don't have to tell you nothin'," Margus snarled.

The demon glared at Doyle another moment, then turned to leave, only to find his path blocked.

"It's about time ye got here," Doyle said as he glanced at his watch and then to Angel.

Angel pushed Margus gently back toward the table. "Pick up your chair and sit down. We haven't finished talking."

Margus did as he was told. He grabbed his coffee cup in fiercely trembling hands and began to nervously slurp the contents.

Doyle glanced at the vampire as he pulled up a chair.

"Sorry I'm late," Angel said. "The demons around here don't care to discuss where they buy their drugs." The vampire glared at Margus. "Things had to get a little rough."

Margus looked as though he wanted to cry as he stared at Angel and then back to Doyle.

"Yer just in time," Doyle said to Angel. "Margus was just about to tell me all about his Uforia dealer, weren't ye, Margus?"

The demon seemed to deflate, his ferocity leaking away as fast as his bodily secretions. "Don't think I'm gonna give this up for free."

Doyle uncrossed his legs and leaned forward with his elbows on the table. "You'll get something for yer troubles. Now, where do ye get it?"

The demon squirmed. "I score out back of this club on Danforth—Night School." He drained the last drop of his coffee. "Trendy place for magic user wannabes. Don't take kindly to my kind of clientele. They make us wait in the alley for the stuff."

The demon grew more agitated and his face started to drip even harder. Margus grabbed some napkins from the holder and dabbed at his face. "The club's manager has the stuff. Supposedly he works for some big-time sorcerer."

Doyle was about to ask the obvious question but Angel got there first.

"What's the sorcerer's name?"

Margus flinched away from Angel's attention.

"Masztal . . . no, Meskal. That's it. The dude's name is Meskal but I don't deal with him. The guy I talk with is named Julien."

Doyle looked to Angel. "Meskal again. What a coincidence."

Angel reached into his coat pocket and withdrew some folded cash and a business card. He tossed it down in front of Margus. "For your time," he said. "And if you hear anything else, give us a call."

The demon snatched up the card, read it, and stuffed it inside his sweatshirt pocket. Then he turned his attention to the money and grinned greedily as he began to count it.

Angel got up and walked from the diner.

Doyle stood watching the demon. He couldn't help but feel a slight twinge of pity for Margus. "A word to the wise," he said.

Margus stopped counting and looked up, smiling.

"I'd stay away from that club if I were you." He nodded at the money. "Use it fer a fresh start."

He turned and started to leave.

"Hey, Doyle," Margus called. "You don't know what it's like . . . being me. Sure, you're part demon, but look at you—and then look at me. The Uforia . . . it helps me deal with what I am. You know what I mean?"

Doyle said nothing. He knew exactly what Margus was talking about. There had been many a day he spent at the bottom of a bottle as he tried to deal with the reality of what he was.

Margus began talking again. "That Meskal guy? The sorcerer? I hear he has a business partner. A demon. Real old and nasty. Just thought you'd like to know."

He held up the money to Doyle and then put it into his pocket. "Thanks for the fresh start."

Angel was waiting outside.

"Our rather moist friend just gave me some

bonus information," he gestured with his thumb behind him. "He says this Meskal fella has a demon partner. A very old demon partner. Are ye thinkin' what I'm thinkin'?"

Angel stared off into space, his expression grim. "That reference you looked up. What were they called, the soul-eaters?"

Doyle nodded. "Kurgarru. But the book implied they're extinct."

"Then again, they might not be. We'll have Cordelia do a computer search on Meskal and his nightclub, but we're going to need some more extensive information on the Kurgarru."

Doyle nodded. "Couldn't agree more. Maybe you could give that English gent back in Sunnydale a call—what was his name? Jeeves?"

"Giles," Angel corrected. "But I don't want to call anybody up there unless it's absolutely necessary. Besides, there's someone closer with just as much expertise who I'd like you to talk to."

Doyle was confused. Who did they know who could possibly have information about an ancient demon race that fed on human souls?

And then it dawned on him.

"Ya want me to get in touch with Harry, don'tcha?"

His ex-wife was as good as one could get when it came down to information about demon races. It was her specialty. In truth, her fascination with and acceptance of demons was part of the reason why their marriage had failed.

"I think she's our best bet right now," Angel said.

Doyle didn't like it but knew Angel was right. Harry would be the person to talk to.

"Are you all right with this?" Angel asked.

He reached into his pocket for some change.

"Sure," he said, looking through the money in his hand. "Let me give her a call."

Meskal watched with revulsion as Julien cracked the peanut shell and popped the contents into his mouth. He brushed the remnants of the shell from his black silk shirt and reached for yet another handful from the brown paper sack in his lap.

"What time is it, anyway? I hadn't even been to bed yet when you called. The club was hopping last night."

Meskal glanced out the tinted windows of the limousine as it made its way through the early morning streets of downtown Los Angeles. They were on their way to the Hollywood Hills, to the home of his business partner, Shugg.

"It's early, Julien," he said. "Now tell me what you have learned."

Meskal bristled as Julien spit peanut shell onto the floor of the car before he answered.

"I really wish I had better news for you, Anton. This Angel character? Worst case scenario? He's it, my man."

Meskal stared out the window. The man sickened him, but he did serve a purpose. "Just tell me, please."

Julien Cresh was the manager of the sorcerer's trendy, downtown club, Night School. Meskal first met the youth when Cresh had attempted to rob him late one night as he was leaving the club. There was something about the skinny street kid, a wild look in his eyes that said this was someone who could learn to understand the world in which the sorcerer operated. So, Meskal took a chance, allowed him to live and offered him a job. His instincts had not been wrong. Within two months, Cresh was the manager of Meskal's largest club and had more than doubled its profits.

"The guy's a vampire," Julien said through a mouthful of nuts. "But what makes this Angel different from all the other bloodsuckers is that he thinks of himself as one of the good guys."

Cresh also proved to be quite good at another very important function. People liked the gangly youth with the blond hair and the devil-may-care attitude. And when people liked someone, they talked, and Anton Meskal heard every word.

Julien casually picked peanut shells from his tongue and continued his report. "From what I hear, this guy's a real force of nature, if you know what I mean."

Meskal pulled his attention away from the passing city. "No, I don't know what you mean."

Julien raised his butt off the seat and attempted to brush away the debris that had accumulated there. "Sheesh, I'm makin' a mess here."

Meskal made a mental note to have the vehicle thoroughly cleaned that afternoon.

"Let's see," Julien continued. He ran his index finger along the inside of his mouth and sucked away what he found there. "Okay, there was this nest of Drakkazi demons over on Fairfax? They were hiring themselves out as muscle to some of the other demon gangs."

Julien fished through the bag between his legs and brought out yet another handful of nuts.

"Well, before the Drakkazi even know what's hit 'em, this Angel comes out of nowhere and kills them all dead. No hellos, good-byes or kiss my scaly butt. Bang. Deader'n a silent actor's career." He shoved more peanuts into his open maw. "That's what I mean by force of nature."

Meskal closed his eyes and pinched the bridge of his nose hard. He felt a headache coming on.

"Why now," he wondered aloud. "Why has he decided to plague me now?"

Julien had an answer. "He hasn't been in L.A. all that long. Came in a little over a year ago from some podunk town called Sunnydale. Rumor has it he was romantically linked to the current Slayer there." He made a face as he brushed broken shells back into the bag. "Not too sure I believe that press. A vampire and a Slayer? Yeah, right."

Meskal opened his eyes as Julien closed up the bag of nuts and placed them on the seat next to him. The club manager suddenly got very serious and leaned closer to him. "Y'know, if he's after you, you might want to consider laying low for a while."

With a sniff of disapproval, Meskal crossed his legs and adjusted the crease in his dark dress slacks. "Laying low is not an option."

"You're the boss," Julien said. He shrugged his shoulders and looked out his window. Then he reached for the bag of nuts. "These things are friggin' addictive."

Meskal opened a small compartment on the padded armrest beside him and withdrew a bottle of mineral water and a glass. "I'll meet with Shugg and then decide how we should proceed." He unscrewed the bottle top and poured the bubbling water into the glass.

Julien snickered and shook his head. "Shugg. What exactly does he do for you again?"

Meskal sipped from his glass. The bubbles tickled his upper lip. He held Julien in his gaze. "Mr. Shugg and I go back many years."

"Yeah, I got all that, but what does he do for the partnership now? What exactly does he contribute? I'm curious."

Meskal was silent. He could not believe this insolent wretch had the audacity to question him in such a familiar way.

A hand in the bag of peanuts, Julien went on. "He's a recluse now, isn't he? Holed up in that creep-show mansion of his in the Hills? I understand loyalty and all that, but it seems to me we're talkin' about some serious dead weight."

Julien gestured toward Meskal's drink. "Could I have some of that? Peanuts are making me awful dry."

The sorcerer reached into the still open compartment and handed the man a bottle. Julien unscrewed the cap and drank.

"It's totally obvious that you're the brains of this operation." He stifled a belch.

Meskal watched as Julien set the bottle down between his feet and leaned forward in his seat. He rubbed his hands together as if sitting down to a delicious meal. *Like a hungry fly atop a heap of dung,* Meskal thought.

"Think about it. Who's responsible for the club? The Uforia? Would I be lying if I said it was all you?" Julien smiled a conspirator's grin. He sat back in the seat and slouched down with his eyes closed.

"Man, I'm beat," he said as he yawned loudly. "Tell you the truth, Anton, I'm kind of surprised you're taking this thing to Shugg. That you don't try to handle it all by your lonesome."

The sorcerer set his glass down. He looked at the floor of his limousine. Peanut shells littered the dark gray carpet about Julien's feet.

"Y'know what I'd do if I was you?" Julien asked. "I'd find a way to get rid of Shugg and take over the whole ball a wax."

He wrinkled the top of the peanut bag closed again and held it out to Meskal. "I'm through with these, want any?"

Meskal mouthed the word "no" and waved it away with a slight movement of a perfectly manicured hand. "You have no problem with betrayal, then?" he inquired.

"Betrayal is kind of a harsh word, don't you think? It's business. And if what I said strikes a chord with you, and you do decide to off Shuggy? I wouldn't mind one bit if you made me your number two man." Julien laughed and nodded, a big idiot grin on his scruffy, yet handsome features. He gave the sorcerer the thumbs-up sign. "Me and you, Anton. We'd rock this town."

"I don't think so," Meskal said as he waved his hand in the air and spoke in a language that sounded as if he were attempting to clear his throat.

Cresh was puzzled. "What's that all—" he began. And then started to choke.

The manager of Night School pitched forward in his seat, grabbed at his neck and coughed violently. He coughed and coughed until his face began to turn a scarlet red. Meskal moved to the edge of his seat. Julien held out his hand in a silent plea for his employer's assistance.

"Kill my partner of seven hundred years? For you?" Meskal asked.

Julien's body convulsed and something mixed with frothy yellow saliva spewed into his hands.

Peanuts. Whole peanuts still in the shells.

Julien gazed at Meskal and then back to his hands before another spasm of coughing wracked his body. He slid from the seat onto the floor.

Meskal loomed over him. Watching.

"Do you have any idea what Shugg and I have been through together?"

Julien had curled into a little ball as he coughed up even more whole peanuts from somewhere in his body.

"The Black Death, two world wars . . . disco."

The choking man was in convulsions now as his body screamed for oxygen and the peanuts continued to surge up from deep within to clog his windpipe.

Meskal leaned back in his seat and listened to the final death rattle of Julien Cresh. He picked up his drink and had a little sip.

The sorcerer felt satisfied, if a little tired. He knew he should conserve his power, but he couldn't resist snuffing out the life of the traitorous employee. He would need to be careful with his use of magic or pay a hefty price for his fun.

The panel that separated the backseat from the driver's area slid down to reveal a homunculus behind the wheel of the luxury vehicle.

"Is everything all right, Master Meskal?" the faceless driver asked.

Julien's body gave one last shudder, then was still.

"Everything is fine," he said, "but there has been a slight change of plans. Mr. Cresh will not be going with us. We'll need to drop him off."

Meskal paused as he stared down at the corpse.

"Preferably someplace secluded where a body could go unnoticed for quite some time," he snarled.

"Very good, sir," the homunculus said as the panel slid back into place and returned his master to privacy.

Meskal balanced his drink on his knee and turned his gaze to the window. Traffic was picking up on the freeway as the everyday people scurried off to their daily drudgery.

He thought of Julien's treacherous words.

Business without Shugg. He would be a liar if he said the thought hadn't crossed his mind on more than one occasion, especially of late.

Meskal gazed at his Rolex. It was a little past seven in the morning.

He closed his tired eyes with a sigh. Of all the demons he could have partnered with, he had to be stuck with an early riser.

The catacombs beneath Rome, 1214

Meskal slid the simple glass-and-leather goggles down over his watery eyes and stared directly into the swirling vortex of the dimensional doorway he had conjured.

The entrance to a universe beyond pulsed and puckered like the mouth of some great toothless beast, spewing multicolored sparks of unearthly light into the damp confines of the catacomb chamber. Anchored by a framework of human bones and opened with the spilled blood of an innocent and an ancient Sumerian spell of summoning, the entryway yawned hungrily in the center of the secret laboratory.

"Heave, you pathetic beasts," the sorcerer screamed to three primitive homunculi. They were attempting to withdraw a great net that had been cast into the void of the other dimension. Each of the malformed creatures was anchored to the catacomb floor by thick leather belts attached to metal links so as not to be sucked into the supernatural maelstrom.

"Fail me and it's back to the vats with you," the withered, aging sorcerer threatened.

The pitiful creatures were dressed in robes of brown burlap. They were the first of his sorcerous attempts to create life, but he knew they would not be the last. The homunculi tugged at the net, working hard against the powerful currents of interdimensional space.

This was the fourth such portal into the beyond that he had conjured for trawling this week. He hoped the results of this latest encroachment into the beyond were more fruitful than the previous efforts had been.

Since the moment the emperor Constantine the First had accepted Christianity, the spellcaster had hidden himself away beneath the great city of Rome to escape persecution from those who would interpret his brand of science as a force against the one true God. The catacombs lying deep in the underbelly of the ancient city provided him with the perfect environment in which to perform his experimentation.

A whimper of fear from behind distracted him from the beauty of the doorway. He turned and glared at three children huddled together in the straw-strewn cage behind him.

"Do not fear this, children of God. You look upon a true miracle." Meskal pointed one of his long, twisted fingers at the dimensional whirlpool. "This is God, little ones."

He studied their fear-filled expressions through the emerald tint of his goggles. It had been one of their brethren whose untainted blood had been spilled to open the portal this day. Three others had already been sacrificed. They had to know it was only a matter of time before their own lives would be called for.

Meskal had purchased the seven children from an Egyptian slaver on the black market, the remnants of a children's crusade to drive the infidels from the Holy Land. They believed that God had told them to leave their homes and families and march across the countryside to Jerusalem. As he gazed at them in the cage, the oldest no more than ten years, the sorcerer almost pitied them.

What kind of God would allow mere babes to fall into my hands? he thought, amused. *Perhaps the Christian God is on my side after all.*

He laughed out loud at the idea and turned his attention back to the doorway where his homunculi continued to work the net. The sorcerer could barely contain his excitement. For the last four years, he had trawled the myriad dimensions for anything that could feed his voracious appetite for unearthly knowledge. Evidence of races that existed beyond the veil, plant and animal life the likes of which this world had never witnessed; this was the priceless treasure Meskal claimed as he tossed his nets into the dimensional oceans of the beyond.

The artificial men struggled; something was definitely caught in the netting on the other side of the pulsing rift.

On legs bowed with age, Meskal moved across his lab toward an ornate metal box on a table across from the bone threshold, eager to share his excitement. The sorcerer bent down and flipped back the locks. The box slid open to reveal the mummified head of a man. The head's rough skin was the color and texture of cured leather, with sporadic tufts of snow-white hair dappling the top of its rounded head. The thin-lipped mouth was sunken in, void of teeth.

Meskal slammed his hand down on top of the box. "Wake up, Dommicus. This is not the time for rest."

The head that was Dommicus slowly opened its milky green eyes and looked about the room, its gaze falling on the latest incursion into the ether.

"Oh, this again," it groaned.

"This is it, Dommicus, I can feel it in my bones," said the sorcerer happily.

Dommicus closed his eyes sadly and pursed his leathery lips. "You feel nothing, upstart, except the dampness of these damnable catacombs."

The homunculi seemed to be making progress. Meskal eagerly listened to their grunts of exertion as they drew his prize closer.

"How long did you try to breach the void, Dommicus? Could jealousy over my superior skills be tainting your words?"

"You continue the same errors you made as my apprentice. You dabble with forces you could not hope to understand. Let whatever you have snared go, it does not belong here," Dommicus warned him.

Meskal pounded his fist upon the top of the metal box. "Never!"

His gaze turned back to the doorway. "You taught me much, Dommicus. I thank you, but I have surpassed you. I need to know more."

"You have already learned too much," Dommicus said, his voice trembling with anger.

Meskal laughed at the head's emotion. He reached inside the cage and stroked his former master's tufts of downy white hair. Dommicus opened his ancient maw and attempted to bite him. The sorcerer withdrew his hand with an insane giggle.

"You're still angry that I managed to bring you back from death with my potions and magics."

Dommicus did not respond, and Meskal looked to see what held the head's attention. The homunculi were hauling the catch into this world.

"What shall it be this time, Dommicus? Animal? Vegetable? Mineral? Something that will change my life forever, I suspect."

With a final heave, the homunculi dragged something from the dimensional rift. It was quite large, its skin as black as pitch. It lay curled upon the chamber floor still wrapped inside the netting.

The portal sputtered to a close behind Meskal's prize, the magical spell spent. The sorcerer slid the goggles from his eyes. *What gift has the beyond seen fit to bestow upon me?* he thought. *What wonders will the great sorcerer-alchemist, Meskal, have as his this day?*

Without warning, the prize reared up, tearing free of the net. With a ferocious roar, it lashed out with razor-sharp claws, tearing the head off one of the homunculi servants with a single swipe.

Meskal watched in stunned silence. The other homunculi leaped away from the savage monster, trying desperately to unhook themselves from the floor tethers. After a moment, they succeeded and snatched up weaponry hanging from a wall nearby in an attempt to hold the great beast at bay.

"What is it, Dommicus?" Meskal asked in a whisper. "It . . . it's beautiful in its savagery."

Meskal watched with horror as the monstrous invader disposed of another of the homunculi. The poor faceless wretch had jabbed at the monster with a spear in an attempt to protect its master. With a savage snarl, the creature tore the spear from its grasp and thrust it through the homunculus, pinning it to the catacomb wall.

"It is as I feared," Dommicus said to the sorcerer.

The creature grabbed the last of Meskal's servants and tore the arms and legs from its body. The black-skinned monster's horrible yellow eyes darted about the chamber, studying its new environment. The creature was remarkably thin, its bones visible beneath its loose-fitting flesh. Strange, shriveled growths dangled from its torso.

"What is it, Dommicus?" Meskal asked. "Tell me or I shall make what remains of your existence upon this world seem an eternity of pain and suffering."

Dommicus laughed. "As if what I have already endured were pleasurable."

The monster turned its attention to the homunculus that had been pinned to the wall. It extended its arm and pointed something at the helpless creature. A bolt of blue energy erupted from the end of the device.

"I believe it is a Kurgarru," the mummified head whispered. "A soul-taker. I had thought them all dead."

The energy bolt burrowed inside the chest cavity of the impaled homunculus. It tried desperately to pull itself from the spear, its body spasmodically shivering as if being torn apart from within. It let out a mournful wail and exploded in flames.

Meskal was in a panic. "Soul-taker? Explain yourself."

"They were a vile species of demon that learned to harvest the power of the soul and survived by consuming the life forces of living things. The Kurgarru use what is called a collector to extract the souls from their prey. Your artificial servants are not truly alive, they have no souls to collect and, as we have just seen, are thusly destroyed."

Suddenly, the demon turned toward Meskal. It studied him just as he studied it. It swayed uneasily. A low moan escaped it.

"What is wrong with it, Dommicus?"

"From the looks of this one, I'd say it's starving."

Meskal began to approach the Kurgarru demon, hands held high to show that he meant it no harm.

"A race of demons that has learned to harness the power of the soul. Fascinating. Think of what it could teach me, Dommicus."

"The only thing the Kurgarru will teach you, old man, is that your time upon this world has come to an end," the ancient head spat after him.

The demon cautiously watched him as he hobbled closer. It raised its arm and pointed its soul-stealing device at him. The tip of the obscene object glowed as if white hot.

"Nonsense. Look at its eyes, Dommicus. There is a savagery there but also a spark of intelligence. It knows that it would not be in its best interest to destroy me."

"The Kurgarru were responsible for their own extinction. They consumed each other's souls until they were no more. There is no intelligence to be found in this one and if you were wise, you would attempt to destroy it before it makes a meal of your soul," warned Dommicus.

Meskal cackled. "It would choke upon the foulness that is my soul."

The sorcerer stood before the great demon and

looked up into its dark, toadlike face. The creature stood near eight feet. It blinked its eyes repeatedly and swayed upon unsure legs.

"See, it does not strike. It knows I can help it to live."

"Just as you helped me, Meskal?" the head asked. "I'm sure it will be as thankful as I to be in your debt."

The Kurgarru let out an ear-piercing shriek and fell to its knobby knees. It was practically eye level with the sorcerer now. It still limply pointed the soul collector at him.

"Step away from it, fool," Dommicus warned from his box. "It is weak from hunger, vulnerable. Strike it down and be done with it. Surely its corpse will provide you with some of the perverse knowledge you crave."

Meskal reached out and laid his hand on the collector. It was warm to his touch as he gently pushed it down.

"No, Dommicus. This fine specimen will not be destroyed this day."

The Kurgarru could barely keep its head aloft.

Meskal smiled and took the demon's large face in his ancient hands. "You know that I mean you no harm."

The Kurgarru gurgled; the things that hung from its body writhed and unfurled their leathery wings. Meskal gasped as he saw that they were not growths at all but some kind of parasitic life-form.

"Glorious, absolutely glorious," he muttered, his excitement growing.

"Kill it, Meskal," Dommicus shrieked, "kill it now or it shall make of this world its dinner table."

Meskal turned his head to glare at his former teacher. "Quiet, Dommicus. I care as much for this world as I do for talking heads in a box. This creature has knowledge that I want and it shall give it to me."

The sorcerer looked back at the Kurgarru.

"And you shall have it," the demon said.

Meskal gasped, a crooked smile spreading across his ancient face. "You know my tongue?"

The creature nodded. "I know it now."

The sorcerer's icy blue eyes glistened wetly as he stared at the magnificent sight before him and clasped his hands to his chest in reverence. "You shall teach me everything you know about the power of the soul."

The Kurgarru shut its bulbous eyes and swallowed. "Everything I know shall be yours, but for a price."

Meskal stepped back. "You are in no position to make demands here, demon. You will teach me what I desire and I will see what can be done to keep you alive. That should be payment enough."

The great demon smiled, an enormous grin exposing slimy black gums riddled with rows of needle sharp teeth. The sorcerer felt a twinge of fear.

The Kurgarru unexpectedly leaped to its feet and

lunged at him. Before Meskal was even aware of what had transpired, the creature grabbed him about the throat, the warm tip of the soul collector pressed beneath his sagging chin.

"You will do for me and I will do for you . . . or I will take your soul here and now and you will have learned nothing. The decision is yours."

Meskal squirmed.

"Are you suggesting a partnership?" he rasped.

"If you wish to call it that, yes. A partnership."

"Don't do it, Meskal," Dommicus screamed.

"Tell me," Meskal croaked, staring at the soul collector. "What do you want?"

The Kurgarru looked hungrily about the underground laboratory. His eyes fell upon the cage containing the three child crusaders. An enormous black tongue snaked from its mouth and slid across its lips. He pointed at them with a thick, clawed finger. "The babies . . . give them to me."

The children began to wail pitifully as they realized their time had finally come and the God they had left their homes for and sworn their undying allegiance to had abandoned them to the darkest of evils.

"Take them."

"Excellent," the demon growled as he released the sorcerer. "And then you shall teach me of your world. There is much I should know if I am to live here."

Meskal watched as the demon cautiously moved

away from him and approached the metal box lying atop the table.

"And this noisy little . . . head. What is it to you?"

Meskal shrugged his shoulders. "Once it was attached to the body of a great sorcerer, but now, I'm sorry to say, it is nothing more than what you called it. A noisy little head."

The Kurgarru laughed, reached into the metal box, grabbing the head.

"I thought your kind extinct," Dommicus whispered.

"All but me," the demon said as he dropped the ancient head into his cavernous mouth.

"All but Shugg," the Kurgarru repeated, as he began to chew, his powerful jaws reducing the skull to digestible splinters.

Meskal awoke with a start, the grotesque sound of Dommicus's skull being pulverized still ringing in his ears. The memory of that fateful day when their partnership was sealed resonated through his mind. He had kept his part of the bargain and so had the Kurgarru.

Such things the demon Shugg had shown him through the centuries: the perfection of his homunculi servants, how to grow soul collectors, the distillation of the human soul into a drug that kept him safe from the ravages of time as well as a narcotic highly addictive to demons.

The limousine began to slow, and Meskal peered out the window to see that he had finally arrived at his destination. He listened to the whine of hydraulics as the gates guarding Shugg's mansion slowly parted to allow him entrance.

The sorcerer glanced about the back of the car and noticed that Julien's body had been removed while he dozed. The aroma of peanuts and sudden death still clung to the air.

His driver came around to the side of the car and opened the door for its master. Meskal emerged, donning sunglasses in the early morning sunshine. The demon had taught him much, and in return, the sorcerer had provided him with a plentiful source of souls to satisfy an almost insatiable hunger, and allowed him the anonymity he needed to exist upon this world.

Now Angel wanted to change all that. A partnership that began close to eight hundred years before sundered by the meddling of a vampire with delusions of goodness.

Maybe something of use could come from this predicament, after all, he thought as he walked toward the front entrance of Horror House.

CHAPTER TEN

"I couldn't find much on the elusive Anton Meskal," Cordelia said as she manipulated the mouse on her computer and called up the file she had created for Angel. "But I did find a rather interesting skeleton dangling in his closet."

She looked to see if Angel was sitting on the edge of his seat, anticipating the information she had unearthed.

He wasn't.

The vampire sat across from her desk, slumped in a chair, sharpening a nasty-looking dagger with a whetstone.

"What did you find?" Angel asked, as he ran his finger along the blade's edge to test its sharpness.

So much for suspense, she thought, as she looked back to her monitor.

"I guess Anton's daddy, Clive, was the business

manager for—drum roll, please—Graham Sunderland."

Again she looked at him expectantly. The vampire just stared.

"Graham Sunderland?" she prodded. "The 1940s horror-movie actor? Don't tell me you never watch scary movies."

Angel squirmed. "I don't really enjoy the horror stuff, a good comedy is—"

Cordelia began to tick off film titles on her fingers. "*Castle of Night, Dead Men Tell No Tales, A Coffin for Two,* which, incidentally, I hear Wes Craven is remaking with that guy who looks like Johnny Depp, but isn't. Personally, I would have gone with the real Johnny Depp—"

Angel held up a hand. "The skeleton, Cordy?"

She shrugged her shoulders apologetically. "Sorry, sometimes I get a little carried away with the biz."

Cordelia looked back to her computer screen.

"Okay, since you're not up on your *Hollywood Babylon,* Graham Sunderland became an 'E True Hollywood Story' when the police figured out he was involved with some kind of Satan-worshiping cult thing and was sacrificing runaway teenagers at his Hollywood Hills mansion. He shot himself before he could be arrested. Anton's daddy, Clive, was believed to be part of the whole thing."

Angel wiped the blade with a cloth. "Was it ever proven?"

Cordelia shook her head. "Nope. Lots of suspicion, but they could never pin anything on the guy. He left California for Europe in 1945, never to return."

She studied the expression on her boss's face and could practically hear the gears turning.

"And Anton showed up when?"

Cordelia checked her screen. "Sonny boy showed up in 1996 and turned the club scene on its collective ear. Supposedly he has more money than God and isn't afraid to use it."

She sighed, leaning back in her chair, hands behind her head. "How come all the good catches are either married, gay, or evil soul-stealing sorcerers?"

Angel ignored her question. "Doyle's snitch said that Meskal could probably be found at the club he opened. What's it called? Night School?"

Codelia stood and moved around to sit on the corner of her desk in front of her boss.

"Yep, Night School, and it's got that kind of bad reputation in a good way. You know, like the Viper Room?"

Angel got up from his chair and went to his coat. He put the newly sharpened dagger in an inside pocket.

"I'm going to need you to go there tonight and check it out, see if you can draw Meskal out into the open."

She made a face and plucked at her clothes. "Love to, boss, but Night School is pretty exclusive. On the salary you're barely paying me I can't afford the kind of wardrobe I'd need to get through the door, never mind coax an evil magic guy out of hiding."

"So you're saying you need some new clothes before you'll go."

She scampered over to him excitedly. "And a makeover if you want me to turn heads, and I should probably be relaxed so a massage wouldn't hurt, either."

"How much is this going to cost me?" he asked, withdrawing a wad of bills from his pants pocket.

She plucked the money from his hand. "How bad do you want me to snare Anton Meskal?"

Harry answered Doyle's gentle knock on her door dressed in a terry-cloth robe. She was drying her dirty-blond, shoulder-length hair with a fluffy white bath towel.

"Hello, Francis," she said.

Doyle stood in the doorway and drank in the sight of her. He'd forced himself to believe he no longer had feelings for his ex. *Water under the bridge,* he'd thought.

He was wrong.

"Are you coming in or are you going to pick my brain about the Kurgarru from out there?"

Doyle nervously entered the apartment. He caught a whiff of her shampoo as he passed and practically lost his breath, the smell was so fine.

"Sorry to call ye so early," he said. "It's just that Angel and I are workin' on this case and—"

She shut the door and padded past him on her way back to the bathroom. "It's okay. I planned on getting up early today, anyway. I have a pretty full day ahead of me."

Doyle looked around the apartment, tastefully decorated except for the demonic masks that hung on the wall beside a very organized, yet cluttered-looking desk. He stepped closer and studied one in particular. The face was familiar and he believed the demon owed him money.

"So, the ethnodemonology business is doin' well by you?"

Harry came out of the bathroom wearing black sweatpants and a big T-shirt. "It's all right. I'm working on a book about the Namarrgon demon tribe from Australia. Pretty interesting once you get into it."

"I'm sure it must be," Doyle said politely as he glanced at some of the ancient texts laid out on the desktop.

He turned. "Nice place you got here. Live alone, do ye?"

Harry smirked and rolled her eyes as she went past him to her desk. "I'm not seeing anyone at the moment if that's where this line of small talk is headed."

Doyle followed her to the desk. "So ye never managed to fix things between you and that Ano-Movic demon? What was his name—Richard?"

Harry sat and began to straighten a stack of notes. "No chance of that happening, unless you've changed your mind about the Eating of the First Husband's Brain ritual?" She looked up at Doyle. "Have you?"

Doyle shook his head. "Nope. Sorry, contrary to popular opinion, I'm still usin' it at the moment."

She went back to straightening her desk. "No problem. It wasn't meant to be. Besides, I'm too busy right now for anything serious."

Harry glanced up at him again and Doyle was captivated by her eyes. Here was everything he ever wanted in a woman. She didn't even care about his demonic heritage. In actual fact, she found it of great interest.

If only *he* were so understanding of his true nature.

"That's too bad," he said, looking deeply into her eyes.

Harry broke the gaze and abruptly changed the subject. "Okay, let's get to work, shall we?"

She hefted a large, black leather tome. "I think what you're looking for is in here. It's the Kurgarru you were asking about, right?" She began to flip carefully through the yellowed pages of the ancient text.

Doyle watched her throw herself into the work she loved. *If she can accept my demon side, why can't I?* he thought. He couldn't help it, though. He despised what he was.

"Did you know the Kurgarru are supposedly extinct?" She continued to flip through the book.

Doyle felt an old familiar anger return. The anger he had felt when he realized what he was, the anger he felt when he knew his marriage couldn't possibly last.

"We suspect there might be one still left alive."

She turned in her chair with excitement in her eyes. "That would be amazing. There's so little known about the Kurgarru. We know they were one of the older demon races and that over time they developed a mystical technology that enabled them to extract life energies—the soul—from living things. They developed a real fondness for the taste of souls and it became a major part of their diet."

Doyle's frustration continued to grow. How could she find such enthusiasm for something so vile?

"They wiped out all life on their world and then eventually themselves. Ate each other's souls into extinction," Harry explained. "But now you say there might be one still alive? Do you know how exciting this is? Just think of what it could teach us about itself and the world it lived in. I could—"

"Ya could tell me how to kill it fer starters," Doyle snapped, the anger bubbling up to escape from his mouth.

Harry looked stunned by his callous words.

Doyle fumbled to explain. "I'm . . . I'm sorry I barked at ye like that. It's just that this case is gettin' on me nerves. We think the demon is responsible for stealin' a child's soul and—"

Harry interrupted, her expression dark. "Is that how you deal with it now, Francis? Kill a demon and it makes you feel that much more human?"

"It's not like that at all," he said, backing toward the door. "It's about saving lives, Harry. These things ain't sharks, ye know. Not dumb beasts that don't know any better. Study 'em all you want, but don't try to make 'em pretty."

She stood up from the desk and halfheartedly stepped toward him. "Doyle, I—"

"Thanks for the information," he said as he opened the door. "Sorry to have bothered ye."

He shut the door on her, as he had done years before. It hadn't gotten any easier.

Meskal slid his breakfast plate away from him. "These eggs are cold," he yelled. "How do you expect me to eat cold eggs?"

The homunculus dressed as a waiter bowed before the petulant sorcerer. "I could have the kitchen make you more, Master Meskal?"

Meskal glared at the faceless servant. "I would have preferred it done correctly the first time while I still had an appetite."

He stood abruptly and tossed his white linen napkin onto the tabletop. "I'm sick of waiting. Where is Shugg?"

The homunculus began to clear away Meskal's breakfast plates. "Master Shugg has finished his bath and is waiting for you in the den."

Meskal stormed past the artificial being. He descended three steps into the sprawling living room and turned right toward a rounded door of dark wood. It looked like the entrance to a medieval torture chamber.

Meskal rapped on the door and pushed it open. "Shugg, we have to talk."

The beast sat naked in his great chair; a bowl of soul vials rested on the great expanse of his lap. He was mesmerized by a game show on the big-screen television before him.

"Quiet, Anton," the demon grumbled. "I find this particular program most fascinating. Have you seen it?"

"No, I haven't seen it. I have a business to run. I don't have time for television."

The demon laughed, a horrible barking sound, and reached into the bowl for a handful of vials. "I have them on tape. I will let you borrow them sometime if you like."

He dropped the vials into his maw and began to chew. The skin of the demon's face glowed as the powerful soul energies were released into his body.

"I'd be careful with those," Meskal cautioned. "Remember, soul energies can be quite lethal when mixed."

Shugg tore his attention away from his program. Slivers of glass fell from his mouth as he began to speak. "You talk to me as if I were a child, Anton. I am well aware of the souls' dangerous power. Remember, it was I who taught you."

The Durge stirred, lazily flapping their wings as they fed on the impurities of the souls Shugg had just ingested. The sorcerer took a step back. He found the animals filthy and preferred as little contact with them as possible.

"We have to talk about Angel," Meskal said as he moved to stand between the demon and the television screen.

The demon grabbed the remote that rested on the arm of the chair, leaned around him and turned the television and VCR off. "Why do you torment me so today, Anton? Angel is merely a minor annoyance. We will deal with the vampire the same way we have dealt with others who have attempted to interfere with our trade through the centuries— with death."

Meskal paced in front of the blank television screen. "Intuition tells me this one will not be so easily eliminated. From what I hear he is quite a formidable foe."

Shugg smiled. "Look at it as a challenge, then. When was the last time you truly had to exert yourself to protect what was yours?"

"The same could be said for you, demon," Meskal snarled.

The Kurgarru laughed. "Then we will face this challenge together." Meskal removed the wrapped vessel containing Aubrey Bentone's soul from his pants pocket. He undid the wrapping and held it out to the demon. "This is what he's after. The soul of a little girl."

Shugg licked his chops with an obscenely muscular, black tongue.

"What I don't understand is why? Of all the acquisitions we've made throughout the centuries, why now? Why this soul?"

Shugg held out his hand. "There is nothing more precious, more pure and intoxicating, than the soul of a child."

Meskal gave the vial to Shugg. "But we've taken countless children's souls. What makes this one so special as to garner his attention?"

Shugg admired the soul held within the containment vessel, watched with glee as the contents turned from a vibrant yellow to an oily brown. "Perhaps the child from which this soul came is destined for future greatness," the demon suggested.

"Or perhaps it is simply that our luck has run its course."

"Luck has little to do with it. It's called being careful," Meskal chided him.

"But not careful enough," Shugg added. He sniffed the vial as if smelling a fine cigar. "There is nothing more profitable than the souls of babies, but I think it wise to refrain from selling this acquisition."

"An excellent idea," Meskal said. "We should keep it until after we've dealt with Angel. In case we have need of a bargaining chip."

The sorcerer clasped his hands behind his back and began to pace again. "If Angel is as cunning as I am led to believe, he is most likely already fast on my trail."

"A trap with you as bait, perhaps? Let the vampire come to you . . . let him think that he has you." Shugg smiled. "And then the trap is sprung and he learns why we have existed unopposed for centuries."

Meskal thought about the demon's words. A slight smile played across his face. Sometimes the Kurgarru still had the spark of his former, vicious self.

A thick stream of drool began to ooze from the demon's wide mouth. "Rumor has it this Angel has a soul."

Meskal watched as a thick rivulet of drool

streamed down the demon's multiple chins. The Durge flapped their wings in annoyance as they were drenched in saliva. "Yes, a one-of-a-kind item. Think of the value."

"Never mind the value," the soul-eater mused. His eyes had taken on a glassy stare. "Think of the taste."

CHAPTER ELEVEN

Cordelia plucked the lime wedge from the side of her glass and squeezed more of its juice into the soda water. She felt the eyes on her as she sat coolly at the bar of the Night School dance club.

Not that I can blame them, really, she thought. *Just look at me.*

Hair and nails done by the Veronique Boutique, the Versace party dress: all bought and paid for by her favorite, sun-sensitive boss. If it weren't such a cliché, she'd admit that she was a vision of absolute loveliness.

She sipped at her drink, and a tiny piece of lime pulp lodged itself between her teeth.

Oh, what the hell, she resigned herself to the obvious facts, *I am a vision of absolute loveliness.* She pried the piece of pulp from between her teeth with a maroon nail.

Cordelia casually glanced about the bar. She pretended to be completely disinterested in the controlled chaos that went on around her. She had long since figured out that Night School was not a typical dance club. There were some pretty unusual things on the dance floor. And a techno beat, no less.

As expected, the dateless predator types had caught wind of her scent and emerged from their darkened corners in an attempt to score. They began to hungrily converge, sidling up to the bar on either side of her. It took all the willpower she could muster not to reach into her designer purse for the Mace and blind them all just on principle.

But she behaved. It was important to the case that she did.

A tall, skinny guy with more styling gel on his head than hair was the first to speak to her. He was dressed in black leather pants and a white silk shirt. She could feel his eyes as they moved over every inch of her.

Cordelia stifled the urge to poke out his eyes. She didn't want to risk getting eye goo on her new dress.

She stirred her drink and brought it to her mouth, careful to avoid any more pulp. Out of the corner of her eye she noticed the bartender watching her. Gel Head reached out and quickly touched her hand.

"Just wanted to make sure you were real," he said with a lopsided smile as he leaned in to speak over the pulsing beat of the dance music.

She could see the other predators study her reaction to Gel Head, already formulating their follow-up lines if he should crash and burn. She looked the man in the eyes. It was time to begin. Acting as though she really wanted to waste valuable time pretending to be friendly to this slug was probably going to be even harder than her terminal illness performance at the hospital the other night.

Cordelia forced herself to smile. This was but one of the sacrifices she would have to make for her art—and her boss, who had said she could keep the dress if she agreed to do this.

The predator smiled back. She noticed his teeth were unusually small.

Like little pieces of niblet corn, she thought as she stared at his mouth.

He leaned in again. "I've been watching you since you came in and I notice you're alone."

Internally she practiced her mantra: *Be nice, Cordy. Be nice, Cordy.*

"Wow, noticed that all by your lonesome. You're pretty observant."

Gel Head smiled uneasily.

Had she said something inappropriate? She would need to be more careful.

He shook off the look of unease and moved on to something he probably thought was much more sensitive.

"Somebody as ravishing as you? It's just not right that you're here by yourself." He smiled again, confident that this heavy artillery pickup line would have her melting into his arms—or at least the backseat of his car, in no time.

"Did you know your teeth are unusually small?" she asked.

A collective gasp went out among the dateless predators.

"Is it a medical condition or some kind of genetic trait?"

It was the first noninsulting thing she could think of to say. The look on his face told her the teeth were probably a touchy subject. She'd seen staked vampires look less pained.

"It's not as if they look bad or anything—just kind of freakish," she said quickly.

The man stepped back, self-consciously bringing his hand to his mouth. He gave her a nervous wave as he stumbled away and became lost in the undulating masses on the dance floor. She looked around to see if any others would care to make small talk, maybe give her some information.

They too were gone.

That's the problem with dateless predators these days, she thought, *they have no concept of the simple art of conversation.*

The bartender who had been watching the exchange placed another drink in front of her.

"From an admirer who worships me from afar?" she asked, looking around.

He shook his head. "From me. I've never seen Larry taken down so quickly and easily. Right for the soft underbelly—you're a real pro."

Cordelia smiled, genuinely flattered. "Why, thank you."

The bartender extended his hand. "I'm Nick. A pleasure to meet you . . ."

She took his hand in hers. Her mind raced as she attempted to come up with an alluring alias. "Vickie," she blurted out, "Vickie Vale."

"Pleased to meet you, Vickie," Nick said as he let her hand go.

Vickie Vale? Cordelia thought, horrified by her lack of creativity.

"So, what brings you to Night School, Vickie Vale?"

Cordelia glanced around and took in more of the unusual sights. *Did that guy just light a girl's cigarette with his fingertip?*

"I heard this was the place to come to find out more about . . ."

She paused for dramatic effect.

". . . you know, things of a bizarre nature?"

Nick's face was blank, as if he had no idea what she was talking about. "Bizarre how? I'm not sure I get where you're coming from."

She took a sip from her old drink. "Bizarre, as in abracadabra."

Nick laughed. "Oh that. Looks like you did come to the right place. We get quite a few curious people in here every night. Most don't stay around too long, though." He held her in his gaze. "Exactly how curious are you, Ms. Vale?"

It was obvious Nick was trying to scare her. She had dated Xander Harris; it would take a lot more than a creepy bartender to get goosebumps out of her.

"Curious enough to want to meet Anton Meskal."

Nick's face went deadly serious. "Who?" he asked, doing his best dumb-guy imitation. "Is he a regular?"

Cordelia pushed aside her old drink and started on the new.

"C'mon, I know all about Anton and I know he owns this place. From what I hear he is one pretty fascinating fella."

She squeezed more lime into her fresh drink, recalling what she'd read on the Meskals and their sordid past.

His look told her he still wasn't convinced.

"An acquaintance of mine? I think his name is Margus? He said I could meet Anton here. What do you think, Nick?" She sipped at her drink seductively. "Do I have a chance?"

She could see that he was sizing her up. Then he walked to a phone at the end of the bar and made a call, his back to her.

The music had grown louder and her ears started to ring. It seemed that the more carefully she looked, the stranger the crowd became. She wasn't a hundred percent sure, but she thought there might be some very nonhuman types down on the dance floor kicking up their hooves.

She glanced at Nick. He had finished his call and was talking to some bald chick with a dragon tattooed on top of her skull. Cordelia tried to get his attention, but it was obvious he wanted nothing more to do with her.

It looked as if she had driven off another one.

Good job, Cordelia, she thought. *If you didn't already know you're exceptionally attractive and have a fascinating personality, you might start to develop a complex.*

She glanced at her watch. It was getting late. Seemed as though Angel had sprung for the high-priced items for nothing. She wondered if he would buy her another ensemble for tomorrow night. She hoped he didn't think she could wear the same thing twice.

"Ms. Vale?" a voice said from behind.

She didn't respond.

"Ms. Vickie Vale?"

Cordelia suddenly remembered that she was in fact Vickie Vale tonight. "That's me," she exclaimed as she spun around on the barstool and made eye contact with the handsome older man who stood behind her.

He was the spitting image of his father. The man reached for her hand and gently kissed it.

"I am Anton Meskal. I hear you've been asking for me?"

He has the strangest blue eyes, Cordelia thought as she slowly drew back her hand.

"News sure travels fast in this place," she said with a polite laugh. She rubbed the top of her hand where he had kissed it. "Has anyone ever told you how much you look like your father?"

Bad choice of small talk, Cordelia realized as she watched the man's expression grow cold.

"My father?" he asked, the hint of an accent now more evident. "How, may I ask, do you know him?"

His eyes seem to grow paler, like frozen lake-water.

Cordelia thought fast. "I'm a really big movie buff. I've seen some pictures of him rubbing elbows with celebrities in the movie books I read."

Meskal smiled. "Of course. How perceptive of you. I never realized . . . Dad had achieved a level of celebrity."

She smiled back at him. "That's me, Little Miss Perceptive. The resemblance is amazing."

"May I buy you another drink?"

She reached behind her to retrieve her glass. "Thanks anyway, and please, call me Vickie."

Call me nauseous is more like it, she thought.

Cordelia watched as he glanced about the club.

His eyes seemed to take in every detail. She noticed that the music had grown softer since his arrival, as though they knew he would be trying to have a conversation and didn't want him to strain his voice.

She was nervous. Here was the guy responsible for stealing and selling human souls. Not someone you want suspecting you work for the good guys.

He returned his attention to her. "What did this Margus tell you?"

Nick came down the bar and gave him a drink. It looked like a Scotch on the rocks. "Here you go, Mr. Meskal."

"Thank you, Nicky," he said. He placed his drink on a napkin and waited for her response.

Cordelia put on her serious face. "That you were the guy to see in matters concerning the soul."

Meskal picked up his drink and took a sip. "The soul?" he asked. "I think he might have me mixed up with a parish priest."

"I can't think of any priests who would sell Uforia to demons. But, then again, this is a pretty rough neighborhood," Cordelia said, never taking her eyes from him.

He started to squirm just a bit. "I think this friend of yours has a very big mouth."

Even though he said it in a joking way, Cordelia could feel a sense of menace in the man's words. She suddenly felt bad for Margus.

"Don't be too hard on him," she said quickly, "I

used my feminine wiles to get the information from him."

Her feminine wiles and a demon. Cordy tried not to be sick.

"How do you know Margus?" the sorcerer asked. "I doubt you two come from the same side of the tracks."

"He drinks at a bar I sometimes go to. The Ninth Level? We started talking one night. He told me all about you."

She gave him her best I'm-a-great-big-tramp look to see where it would get her.

He placed his drink precisely in the center of the napkin. "So you're interested in the business of souls, are you?"

"I think souls are hot." It sounded insipid but it seemed to evoke the right response from the sorcerer.

"How would you like to go somewhere more private?" Meskal asked. "I promise I am even more interesting than your friend Margus can imagine."

His smile would have been quite charming had it not come from someone who stole souls from little girls. All Cordelia could think of now were sharks.

"I'd like that." She placed her glass on the bar and slid off the stool.

Meskal gestured to Nick. "Call the car," he said, "and have it brought around back."

The bartender went right to the phone.

Meskal took her arm and began to escort her around the periphery of the dance floor toward a red door marked Private. Cordelia was momentarily distracted as they passed by a young woman dressed entirely in snakeskin on her way to the bar. They entered a storage area filled with extra chairs.

"We will go to my place—if that's all right with you?" He put his arm around her and gave her another sharky grin. She heard the theme music from *Jaws* play in her head.

"That would be . . . great," she said with a nervous laugh.

He steered her across the room to another door that opened onto the alley.

Cordelia saw the limousine slowly coming toward them. She looked about nervously for her savior. He was supposed to be watching the club—watching her.

Meskal noticed her sudden agitation. "Is everything all right, Vickie?"

The way he said her name, the way he looked at her. She was beginning to think he was on to her. She tried to step back, but he held her arm in a firm grip.

The limousine glided to a stop in front of them.

"We'll have a nice chat, you and I. Who knows what we will learn about each other."

The jig is up, she thought. Cordelia was preparing to tell him about how she got violently ill in limos when she heard the voice she had been waiting for.

"Hey, Anton."

It's about time, she thought with relief.

Angel strolled down the alley, his hands shoved into his duster's pockets.

Meskal's grip tightened on her arm and she winced. *There will most definitely be a bruise on my bicep tomorrow.*

"Do I know you?" the sorcerer sneered.

The vampire stepped into a patch of light thrown by the naked bulb over the nightclub's back door.

Not yet, Cordelia thought, not even remotely feeling sorry for the sorcerer and what he had coming to him, *but you will.*

So this is the guy who paid a father to steal his daughter's soul, Angel thought, studying the man standing beside the limousine with Cordelia. He felt his face begin to change as he allowed his vampiric nature to emerge.

"There's something you and I need to discuss," Angel said. He made sure to show how nasty his teeth had become.

The soul trader seemed completely unfazed. "I guess we'll have to have our little chat some other time," he said to Cordelia as he let go of her.

Angel made eye contact with her and nodded. She carefully backed away from the man and made her way up the other end of the alley. He wanted to be certain she was out of harm's way before devoting his full attention to Meskal.

"Lovely girl," Meskal said. "Said her name was Vickie Vale." He laughed and flashed a cruel grin. "We both know that's probably not true."

Angel wasn't sure what Cordelia had said, but seeing the man in front of him only inflamed his anger. "You took a little girl's soul, Meskal, and I've come to get it back."

Meskal tilted his head to one side as if confused. "A little girl's soul? Let me see. . . ." He tapped his cheek with a finger. "There was a teenage boy's soul from Chicago a few weeks back and a saintly granny's I received from a man in Louisiana just the other day." The sorcerer shrugged his shoulders and threw up his hands. "You see, so many souls are sold to me, I can't possibly recall them all."

Angel snarled and stalked closer. "Maybe I can help you remember."

Meskal examined his nails. "That will never do." He looked back to Angel. "Why don't we behave like reasonable men? You name your price to go away. Much more civilized than threats and violence, don't you agree?"

Angel reached out and grabbed the front of Meskal's jacket. "I want the child's soul and I want you out of business."

Meskal sighed and removed the vampire's hand. He seemed disappointed. "Now how did I know you would say something foolish like that?"

The sorcerer clapped his hands together and two homunculi began to climb from the limousine. Angel recognized both from the attack at Bentone's apartment. Earrings and Teardrop.

Earrings was the closest of the two and Angel decided that he would be the first to go down. He kicked the driver's door closed, and pinned the jewelry-wearing homunculus. The creature thrashed as Angel leaned in.

Angel put everything into the first punch. The homunculus' head snapped to the right with the savagery of the blow. Not giving it an opportunity to recover, the vampire rained a rapid-fire series of hits upon the stunned supernatural-construct's face. He felt what passed for bone begin to crumble beneath the creature's artificial flesh.

Earrings went limp. Angel stepped back and let the unconscious homunculus slide to the ground.

"I should have destroyed you with your brother. You're useless," Meskal grumbled from nearby.

Teardrop came up from behind and grabbed Angel in a grip meant to crush the life from his body. He picked the vampire up off the ground and spun him around. Angel twisted and slammed an elbow back into Teardrop's face and then did it again for good measure.

The homunculus' grip loosened enough for the vampire to break free. He spun around just as Teardrop let fly with an unexpected punch. Angel wasn't fast enough. The punch connected with the side of his head and he stumbled back, dazed.

"That's it," Meskal cheered. "Destroy the vampire and I might consider giving you a face of your own."

The promise of an even more defined identity seemed to spur the artificial man into furious action. Teardrop screamed a high-pitched shriek of rage and threw itself at Angel. Its gloved hands gripped the vampire's face and began to squeeze and twist.

"Maybe the master will give me *your* face," the homunculus said to him through its wet gash of a mouth.

Angel had had enough. From the inside of his coat pocket he withdrew his equalizer. He suspected he might have to deal with these creatures again if he went after their master and had brought a weapon from his armory to even the odds.

The knife was called the Fang of Turdakus and it was said to possess the ability to disrupt magical spells of animation. He hoped whatever sorcery had brought the homunculi to life would fail when interrupted by the blade. Angel thrust the dagger into Teardrop's stomach and gave it a vicious twist.

"Sorry about the face," he said, as he pushed the blade even deeper, "but I'm still using it."

The creature stumbled back, hands feebly clutching at the sudden spray of fluids streaming from its belly. The smell of rot wafted about the alley.

His research paid off. Angel pulled the blade back and watched with fascination as the homunculus fell to its knees and began to decompose.

Instinctively he leaped to one side as a sudden blast of intense heat shot past his face. It seared the shoulder of his jacket and part of his cheek as he half turned to see Meskal standing behind him, one of his hands engulfed in mystical fire.

"What's the old adage? If you want something done right—"

Another bolt of searing flame shot from the sorcerer's outstretched hand and enveloped the spot where Angel had just been standing. What was left of Teardrop caught fire and began to sizzle and burn.

As Meskal prepared for another blast, the unholy blaze surrounding his hand growing brighter, Angel took aim and let the knife fly. The blade spun through the air, whistling on a course across the alley.

The pommel of the Fang of Turdakus connected with Meskal's forehead, just above his nose. Stunned, he fell to the ground beside the limousine.

Angel crossed the alley and hauled Meskal to his feet. He had retrieved the knife and now he held it against the sorcerer's throat.

"Why don't we behave like reasonable men. You tell me what I want to know and I won't have to resort to violence." Angel leaned in closer to the man. "And in case you didn't know? I'm very good with violence."

Meskal brought his hand, no longer aflame, up to his forehead and gently touched the lump growing between his eyebrows. Angel pressed the blade firmly to his throat.

"An amazing throw," Meskal commented. "You show remarkable skill."

"Don't let me fool you. I was aiming for your cold, black heart." He grabbed Meskal by the front of his shirt and pulled him in close, the blade's tip beneath the sorcerer's chin. "And it might end up there yet if you don't take me to the child's soul."

As Angel studied the sorcerer, he noticed that the man's appearance seemed to be changing. Heavy bags had appeared beneath his eyes and there was gray in his hair. He didn't recall the sorcerer looking quite this aged when he had first laid eyes on him.

Meskal sighed. "Even if I wanted to, it is very unlikely that I could locate the specific soul you seek."

There was a scuffling sound behind him and on pure instinct Angel whirled. He thrust out with the blade. The Fang buried itself deep into Earrings's face where the left eye would have been if the homunculus had had one.

The creature let out a scream of surprise, fingers scrabbling at the knife blade protruding from its face. It began to rot away before their eyes.

Angel wiped the foulness that covered the blade on the front of the sorcerer's suit jacket. Meskal gazed down at the stain and the knife that was now poised directly above his heart.

"I'm sorry. You were saying?" Angel asked.

Meskal waved at the foul vapors rising up from the decaying homunculus. "I said I doubt I can locate the soul you want." The sorcerer smiled a smile void of humor. "But it's not completely impossible."

Angel pushed the man toward the limousine. "Now that's what I call being a reasonable man."

June Bentone watched the conflict from the shadows of the alley. She was concealed by a Dumpster filled to overflowing with cardboard boxes and bags of garbage.

She recalled the conversation she'd had with Cordelia in the hospital cafeteria. *"His cases do have a tendency to lean a bit toward the bizarre,"* the girl had said. And bizarre this was, with faceless men dressed in trench coats, a detective who was really a monster and a man who could throw flames from his hands. She still could not wrap her mind around it all.

June peered over a box sticking from the Dumpster to see Angel hold a knife to the throat of the man who had picked up Cordelia. Was he the one who hired David to steal their child's soul?

With a surprising wave of sadness she suddenly remembered that her ex-husband was dead. She had remained with David's body until the police arrived. The detectives asked her all kinds of questions that she had no idea how to answer. June had had no choice but to lie, for she knew that to tell the truth would probably buy her a trip to the psychiatric ward.

She stayed as close to the truth as she was able, talking about her husband's gambling problem and his involvement with a criminal element. The police seemed satisfied that David's death was mob-related and they allowed her to leave.

She had gone directly to the hospital to be with her daughter. It was concern for Aubrey's health that kept her anchored in sanity.

June had come to the disturbing realization that something unnatural had happened to her daughter. And, if Aubrey was to be saved, unnatural means would need to be taken.

At knifepoint, Angel forced the man into the limousine and June ran to her car, parked outside the alley.

Angel wanted her to let him do his job, but she couldn't stand the waiting. Aubrey was growing weaker each day and if she could do anything to help her little girl, she was determined not to miss the chance.

The limousine rolled out of the alley and turned right. She waited for a short time, keeping the taillights in sight, then banged a U-turn to follow.

Earlier in the evening she had followed Angel and Cordelia from their office to the Night School club. She had watched as Cordelia got out at the entrance and Angel drove away. She had been torn. Who should she watch? Intuition had told her to keep an eye on Cordelia and that was exactly what she did.

Inside the club, June had watched from a safe distance as the pretty young woman attracted men like flies. June had been close to giving up, convinced she should have followed Angel, when the well-dressed man approached Cordelia.

There was something about him that told her he was somehow involved with what happened to her baby girl. She had watched as the two talked and then moved toward a back doorway that she guessed would take them to the alley.

June had run to her car, ready to follow the couple, when she saw Angel head into the alley. A chill ran up her spine as she recalled the carnage that had unfolded.

June stayed a safe distance behind the limousine, just as she had seen them do on TV and in the movies. This area of L.A. was unfamiliar to her, thick with burned-out shells of buildings and what looked to be warehouses.

The limo's brake lights flashed up ahead as it pulled up in front of one of the warehouses, and she pulled her own vehicle over to the side of the road.

She had the urge to confront the man, but she restrained herself. She waited and watched from the darkness of her car, her little girl lying sick in a hospital bed never far from her thoughts.

June would allow Angel to deal with it. This was what he did.

Doyle lay draped across Cordelia's desk, atop an assortment of ancient texts on demonology and sorcery. He had been trying to gather more information when lack of sleep caught up with him.

"Francis?" a voice called.

Doyle's body shuddered and he let out a piggish snort.

"Hey, Doyle," the voice yelled.

He came awake, disoriented, his mind still awash with images of ancient demons with insatiable hungers for depravity and violence . . . and of an enraged Cordelia Chase discovering that he had again made a mess of her desk. In his disorientation, Doyle's own blue, prickly skinned demon persona appeared for a brief instant and then was gone.

"No, Cordelia. I'll clean it up, I swear," Doyle mumbled as he struggled to be fully awake.

Doyle emerged from the fog of sleep and looked about the office. Harry was standing in front of the desk, travel bag slung over her shoulder. She stared at him, surprise on her face.

"She rattles you that much, huh?"

Doyle rubbed sleep from his eyes. "It's not a pretty sight when ye mess up her desk."

Harry walked over to her ex. "She doesn't know?"

Doyle looked up at the woman who, no matter how much he wanted to deny it, still held on to a good portion of his heart. "Waitin' fer the right time."

She affectionately rubbed his head. "I wanted to apologize for what I said to you at the apartment."

Doyle shrugged. "Don't worry yerself. There's probably a bit o' truth somewhere in what ye said."

"When are you going to let up on yourself, Francis?" she asked. "When are you finally going to realize that you're a good person despite what you think of your heritage?"

He looked away. "I wish it were that easy, darlin'. It's the first thing I think about when I wake up in the mornin' and the last thing when I close my eyes at night."

Doyle gazed up at her again. "I hate that part o' me and I would do just about anything to be rid of it."

Harry started to rub his back.

"But that ain't an option . . . so I'm gonna have to get used to it."

She squeezed the tension-filled muscles near his neck. "Maybe working with Angel . . . maybe it'll help . . . maybe it will help you get used to it and then you'll see . . ."

Harry stepped away and moved toward the bag she had left in the middle of the office. She squatted down next to it. "After you left this morning I felt guilty and did some more research on the Kurgarru."

Doyle watched her search the bag. "Goin' somewhere?"

She removed a notepad and rezipped the bag. "Red-eye out of LAX to Sydney in about two hours. I've got some bushmen to interview for that book I was telling you about."

Doyle nodded. "I knew a Ronny Bushman once; terrible cardplayer. Always knew when he had a winnin' hand 'cause—"

"Ha, ha, very funny," she interrupted. "You should have your own act in Vegas. Really. All right, it's amazing how little we know about this particular species and even that seems to have come from a single source."

She glanced at him to be sure he was paying attention, which he was.

"Some writings were discovered in an archaeological dig inside the Roman catacombs that date back to about 1200." Harry handed Doyle the notepad. "We have no idea who the writer was, but he sure seemed familiar with the Kurgarru, as though he were getting the information from the demons themselves."

Doyle scanned Harry's notes, but as usual they were nearly illegible.

"The writings talk about how hundreds of the Kurgarru perished from starvation before it occurred to them to break their most holy law—that Kurgarru did not feed upon Kurgarru."

She pointed to the bottom of the page. "The later notes seem to be talking about one demon in particular, a warrior of the highest order, trained to survive no matter what the cost. He was the first to indulge in the forbidden act. On the verge of death, he consumed the life energies of his mate and then their children."

"Nice fella. So is there anything in these mystery writings that can help us against 'em?" he asked.

"There is a statement from the writer that says something along the lines of 'the Kurgarru is the most ferocious of demon beasts I have encountered and its hunger shall be its undoing.'"

Doyle repeated what his ex had just said, rolling it around in his brain and off his tongue. "Any idea what it means?" he asked her.

Harry shrugged her shoulders. "That its hunger will be its undoing. I really don't know much more than that." She glanced at her watch. "Hey, sorry I couldn't be more help, but I have a plane to catch."

Doyle came around the desk as Harry picked up her bag. "You were a big help. I'll show yer notes to Angel and maybe something'll make sense to him."

Harry slung the bag over her shoulder. "I'll give

you a call when I get back, see how things worked out. Okay?"

Doyle moved past her and opened the door. "You do that."

She walked out into the hall and turned to her ex. "You take care of yourself, Francis."

"You know me, always lookin' out fer number one."

She smiled, turned and walked toward the stairs.

"Hey, Harry," he called after her.

She turned to look at him.

"Thanks . . . for everything," Doyle said.

She gave him a wave and continued on her way down.

Doyle strolled back into the office. He picked up Harry's notes and tried to read what she had written. "You are a nasty fella, ain't ya, Mr. Kurgarru."

Doyle heard something behind him and turned to see Cordelia enter the office. She looked absolutely amazing and Doyle couldn't help but tell her so. "Cordelia, ye look wonderful."

She glanced down at herself. "Not bad for a decoy. I can't believe that Angel, buying me all these pretty things knowing full well I can't resist them. Then he makes me sit in a sleazy dance club getting hit on all night hoping some creepy sorcerer guy will try and pick me up so—"

Then she saw her desk. "Look at my desk!"

"Where is Angel anyway?" he asked quickly, hoping to distract her.

It seemed to work, halting her escalating rage for a moment. "We found our baddie and I think Angel's having a little talk with him."

"Meskal?" Doyle asked. "You found Meskal?"

She had been staring at her desktop again. "Yup. He tried to pick me up at his club. Wanted me to go for a ride with him to his place. He had a limo and everything." She moved closer to her desk and Doyle attempted to block her way.

Cordelia pushed him roughly aside. "Look at this. It was perfect when I left."

Doyle snatched up the notes Harry had left, hoping the desk wouldn't look so messy with something removed. "Harry was by. Brought us some info that might help with the Kurgarru demon if that's what Meskal is working with."

Cordy looked away from the chaos of her desk. "Harry was here?"

Doyle nodded. Could that be a hint of jealousy in Cordelia's voice? "Yep, she came by to drop off that information and say good-bye. She's goin' to Australia to work on a book."

"Harry's Guide to the International Demon Dating Scene, perhaps?" she asked with a wry smile.

Doyle scowled, the illusion of Cordelia's jealousy swatted aside by her barbed wit. "Such a pretty thing," he said to her, "but ye have the sharpest of tongues."

"How sweet of you to notice," she responded as

she moved around the desk to her seat. "Now do me a favor and don't think about my tongue ever again." Cordelia stared at her desk and sighed. "If I'm going to get this back to some semblance of order I'd better get to work."

Doyle simply stood, not sure what he should do. "So, Angel is with Meskal then?"

"Uh-huh," Cordelia said, furiously straightening.

"Did he happen to mention what we could be doin' to help?"

She stopped her organizing and glared at Doyle. "He said that if he caught up with Meskal, I was to go back to the office and wait."

"So we're gonna wait till he gets back?"

Cordy didn't answer; instead she began to stack the ancient tomes from Angel's reference library on the corner of her desk.

Doyle strolled over to help. He picked up a few of the smaller books and attempted to place them on the stack she was making.

Her gaze froze him in his tracks.

"What do you think you're doing?" she asked him tersely.

Doyle put the books back where he had found them. "Well, I feel kinda bad that I messed up yer desk again and I was gonna help you to—"

She gave him that withering look. "Don't you think you've helped me enough, Mr. Messy Man?"

Doyle backed away, keeping an eye on her, just in

case laser beams shot from her eyes to strike him. He stumbled into a chair and sat down.

"Would it help if I said I was sorry?"

She picked up the stack of demonology and sorcery texts and dropped them heavily in the corner behind her desk.

Her actions spoke louder than words.

Doyle sat back in the chair, closed his eyes, wished he was invisible, and waited for Angel to return.

CHAPTER TWELVE

They pulled to a stop in front of a dilapidated warehouse.

Angel watched impassively as Meskal switched off the ignition and placed his hands in his lap. He turned to Angel, his blue eyes strangely tired since their meeting in the alley.

"We're here," Meskal said, glancing down at the knife Angel still held precariously to his side. "Would you like me to take you inside?"

Angel gave the man a slight poke with the ancient blade, a gentle reminder that he was still in control. "Just go," he said as he slid across the leather seat to follow Meskal out the driver's-side door.

The sorcerer moved stiffly. Angel could hear popping sounds from the man's vertebrae as he struggled to stand erect. Meskal placed a hand to his lower back and leaned backward. His spine cracked.

"Is there a problem?" Angel asked, though he knew very well that there was. The man appeared to have aged at least ten years on their drive from the club.

"There is a price to be paid for the power I wield," the sorcerer said offhandedly. "The years seek to claim what has long been denied them."

"Then you might want to hurry things along," Angel said as he slammed shut the limousine door. "Wouldn't want the years taking their due before I get what I came for."

Meskal looked toward the darkened warehouse. "We'll find it in there."

Angel gestured with the blade. "After you."

Meskal responded with a slight bow and moved past Angel. Slowly he walked to the gray metal door. Angel remained close behind him, the Fang of Turdakus ready to strike out at any instant. No matter how weak he appeared, Angel did not trust Meskal for a moment.

The sorcerer took a ring of keys from his pocket and searched for one in particular. "I'm curious, vampire. After all the years my little trade has been in existence—why now?"

He found the key and slid it into the lock.

Angel shot a withering glance at him. "Evil like this can only go unnoticed for so long."

The lock clicked and Meskal pushed the door open into the inky darkness of the first floor. Angel noticed that the windows had been painted black.

"Understandable, I guess," Meskal said as he swayed in the doorway at the edge of the darkness. "But when you've lived as long as I have you tend to get a bit overconfident. Nothing can touch you—or so you think."

The smell of dampness wafted out of the blackened room.

"Watch your step," Meskal advised as he stepped into the warehouse and was swallowed by the impenetrable gloom.

Angel followed closely, weapon ready. He plunged into the darkness, his heightened senses suddenly alive, screaming that something wasn't right. But there was no turning back. If this was where Aubrey's soul was to be found, then he would face whatever the sorcerer had in store for him.

He sensed the slightest movement of air near his face and lashed out with the Turdakus blade. It sliced across the flesh of something—something that screamed in surprised agony and moved away.

The savage countenance of the vampire emerged and he bared his fangs in anger, spinning around in the ebony pitch ready for the next attack. They came at him from all sides. He felt their foul hands, tentacles and claws upon him. Angel lashed out with brutal savagery, listening with perverse glee to their cries of pain. But it did not stop them. They came at him, wave after wave. No matter how many he believed he had slain, there were always more.

The ceiling lights snapped on, dispelling the darkness and exposing his assailants. Demons. At least thirty, of various races, all clamoring for a piece of him. Angel stared into their wild, dilated eyes and knew they were all users of the soul drug, Uforia.

Meskal leaned against a far wall, his hand upon the light switch. From the sea of drug-addled demons, Angel roared his name.

The sorcerer smiled weakly. "What I said earlier about overconfidence, Angel? It would appear to apply to you as well."

Angel fought to be free of the demons, to get enough of a footing to cut a swath through their number and make his way to the sorcerer. All he wanted was to rip the arrogant grin from the man's face.

Through the tangle of bodies he saw Meskal slowly walk to a set of stairs that led up to the next level. He was hunched over and appeared to have aged another ten years.

"I knew you would be hunting for me so I set this little trap," the sorcerer informed him.

Angel winced as the demons pried the Fang of Turdakus from his hand. He could see Meskal climbing the stairs, moving as if this simple act pained him greatly. He let loose with a scream more beast than man and with a last burst of strength managed to push some of the demons away—but there were too many, and he was again in their clutches.

A Fyarl demon, its curled horns black and brittle, yelled to Meskal, its eyes wild with need. "What do you want us to do with him?"

The sorcerer stopped and turned, holding on to the railing. His posture was more hunched now. "Kill him slowly—painfully," he commanded. "Succeed and tonight's entertainment is on the house."

The sorcerer's words sent a collective shudder of ecstasy through the demons and they turned their attention back to Angel. They all wanted to be the one that made the vampire scream out in agony. They all wanted to be the one that made him suffer, the one that ended his life.

Angel was not going to give them the satisfaction.

"This isn't over yet, Meskal," he snarled as the demons began to drag his body down.

Meskal hauled his aged frame to the top of the stairs. "I'm afraid it is, Angel."

The drug-starved demons piled on the vampire, their oppressive weight forcing him to the ground. He fought them with all he had left in his exhausted body.

But it wasn't enough.

The darkness of oblivion took him.

Meskal was helped into the laboratory by a homunculus wearing a thick gold chain around its neck. More of the artificial constructs were busily working at a series of lab tables and raised their heads to watch.

"What are you looking at?" the sorcerer shrieked. "Back to work before I destroy the lot of you."

His body was wracked with a series of moist coughs. The battle with the vampire had taken more out of him than he imagined and a tremor of fear passed through him. He could no longer deny the obvious; any expenditure of magic triggered the aging process and could very well kill him if he didn't have a more steady supply of his life-extending drug.

The homunculus brought him to a leather wing chair in the corner of the lab.

"My medicine," he croaked as he eased himself back in the seat. "Bring it at once." He pointed toward his office with a trembling hand.

The homunculus scurried off.

Meskal winced at the pain caused by his body's steady decline into old age. It was excruciating, far more painful than the last attack, and he imagined they would grow progressively worse.

Something to look forward to, he thought, leaning his head back.

"You will not have me yet," he muttered to the specter of death he felt hovering above him.

The coppery taste of blood filled his mouth as his gums began to recede. He leaned over in the chair and spat a wad of pink-tinged phlegm onto the floor.

His eyes grew heavy and he struggled to keep them open. He looked about his lab, at his servants working. It was an inspiration to stay conscious. There were many long, marble-topped tables covered with all manner of strange apparatus and experiments in progress. This was where he shined; this was where his true genius showed through.

On one of the tables in the middle of the room sat four large glass containers where his latest crop of soul collectors grew. A homunculus was carefully replacing the lid on one of the containers after taking the temperature of the solution inside. The infant collectors were beautiful as they floated in the arcane embryonic fluids, their delicate bone structure just beginning to grow a thin covering of protective flesh. It would be at least another six months before they could be put to use. Meskal smiled proudly as he attempted to fight back the call of sleep.

Two other tables nearby were covered with beakers of various sizes, all connected to one another by lengths of rubber tubing; inside the containers, liquids of different color and viscosity bubbled away over Bunsen burners. Homunculi attentively hovered by the tables, waiting for results before moving on to their next tasks.

This was a good batch, he thought, comparing the lab workers with the recent disappointment of his three personal assistants. *Hopefully the next harvest of homunculi will be as good.*

Meskal turned his attention to a series of four wall racks, each holding six twenty-five-gallon aquariums. Each aquarium held two fleshy, translucent sacs. And inside each sac gestated a new homunculus.

The sorcerer struggled with the sudden weight of his head and focused his failing eyes on yet another stone-topped table. This one stretched across the front of the room at a right angle to the others. On it sat his pride and joy; a strange device that shared a kinship with the sorcerer's soul collectors, a machine that appeared to be just as much flesh, blood and bone as gears, cogs and springs. It squatted in the middle of the table, looking very much like some kind of monstrous, independently functioning internal organ. It purred, gurgled and shook as it diligently performed the function for which it had been created.

Meskal watched through cataract-covered eyes as a servant loaded a translucent cylinder containing multiple soul vessels into a pulsing orifice in the back of the living machine. The souls were slowly drawn from the containment shells into the device, where they were processed and distilled into his precious life-sustaining drug. The highly addictive demon narcotic, Uforia, was a by-product of that process.

The sorcerer chuckled, the weight of his head starting to pitch him forward. He remembered

Shugg's condescending words when he had first begun to develop the drug for sale among the lesser species of demon.

You waste your time, sorcerer. No demon in its right mind would pollute its body in such a way for a fleeting moment of ecstasy.

Meskal had proven the Kurgarru wrong. Uforia sales had been slow at first but had grown exponentially over the years. This year Uforia had made up more than half of their net income, more even than the night clubs and the soul trade.

In some ways, demons differed very little from humans. Many looked for a way to escape the humdrum monotony of their everyday existence. And he was more than happy to provide them the means for that escape.

"Where is my medicine?" Meskal cried. He coughed and gasped for air. His lungs had begun to fill.

The homunculus returned with the hypodermic and the four remaining ampules of the drug.

"You . . . you will . . . inject me," Meskal gasped, gulping air through lungs heavy with fluid. "Quickly." Blood had begun to ooze from his mouth down his chin to stain his pristine white shirt.

He watched carefully as the homunculus knelt beside the chair and filled the needle from one of the ampules. It took its master's limp, bony arm and pulled up the sleeves of his jacket and shirt. Dark blue veins fluttered beneath thin, pallid flesh. The homunculus applied a tourniquet, stuck the needle into a vein in the crook of the arm, and pushed the plunger in.

Meskal's mouth opened in a silent scream of agony as the drug entered his bloodstream and began to work its magic on his decaying system.

The faceless servant withdrew the needle and stepped back. Meskal thrashed about in the leather seat. His breath came in short gasps. Though the process was physically and mentally exhausting, in a matter of moments the injection had done its job and the sorcerer was again young and vibrant.

He looked down at his suit coat and shirt with disgust. "Look at me," he muttered.

He stood and quickly removed his soiled clothing. He rolled them into a ball and tossed it at the homunculus. "Burn them and bring me another shirt."

Meskal walked across the lab to where his precious machine worked. A viscous pale green gunk oozed onto a ceramic plate through a winding tube that extended from one side of the living machine. Almost immediately it began to congeal into a thick paste that had the consistency of oatmeal; Uforia in its unprocessed state.

Meskal bent down and carefully examined a line of copper tubing that ran from the front of the device. This was what he really cared about. This was what he needed to stay alive—the age-reversing drug.

He watched it collect. A tiny amount of iridescent green fluid had pooled at the bottom of a rune-covered beaker. It had taken over a year and more than twenty souls to prepare this minuscule amount. He stared at the green liquid beginning to bead on the end of the copper tube. He had to find a quicker way to produce the drug.

Since Shugg had first shown him how to distill the life-sustaining drug from human souls, Meskal had believed he would have all the time in the world. Now he was beginning to fear that luxury might no longer be available.

The homunculus brought Meskal a fresh shirt. The sorcerer handed his servant the hypodermic needle and the three remaining drug ampules.

"Put these back where you found them."

He took the shirt and put it on. *With Angel out of the picture things should return to normal,* he thought as he strolled across the lab and into his living quarters, buttoning his shirt as he went.

Yet something told him his problems were far from over. He tucked his shirt into his pants and went to the bar to make a drink. Angel had friends. Meskal recalled the dark-haired beauty he had met earlier in the evening and the associate his homunculi servants had spoken of while trying to explain the debacle at Bentone's apartment.

He frowned as he finished his drink and poured another. He could not risk jeopardizing the business. But the decision he was about to make pained him.

He had pledged long ago, as he and Shugg were driven from the Roman catacombs by Pope Innocent III's soldiers, that he would never run again. He remembered the anger and helplessness as he was forced to leave his things behind, his tools, his books . . . his writings. They had been no match for the Pope's soldiers, whipped into a killing frenzy as they searched the underground burial chambers for the monsters that had been plucking the citizens of Rome off the streets. They'd had no choice; to survive, they had to run.

Meskal cleared his throat loudly and the homunculus with the gold chain appeared in the doorway. This situation was very much the same. He must take flight. But this time he would control the retreat.

"Pack up the lab. We're moving to a safer location."

"Yes, Master," the homunculus said.

Meskal turned his back on the artificial man, dismissing it without a word. Drink in hand, he went to a large wooden cabinet behind his desk. He reached into his pocket for his key ring and unlocked the cabinet door.

Inside were rows of long drawers. He slid one open.

Lying atop red, crushed velvet were multiple vessels, each containing a soul. Meskal smiled warmly as he gazed down upon them. The vessels were far too precious. He would take responsibility for their transport.

From a closet he grabbed a heavy-duty duffel bag, a promotional gift from one of the many pharmaceutical companies he did business with. He had just reached into the open drawer for the first of the containment vessels when the sound of destruction exploded from the other room.

The lab, he thought in panic.

Meskal raced from his living quarters, his panic turned to rage. *If those homunculi have damaged anything remotely precious, I shall destroy them all.*

The lab was engulfed in thick clouds of billowing smoke. A table that had held many of his chemicals had been tipped over, the jars and beakers smashed on the floor. A fallen Bunsen burner had ignited the chemicals to create the gray smoke that limited visibility. His thoughts raced. *Where are they? How could they be so careless?*

Meskal tore a fire extinguisher from the wall and blasted the spreading flames with suffocating foam. The fire out, he tossed the extinguisher to the floor and stumbled toward his most special machine.

"What have you done?" Meskal shrieked. His heart nearly exploded as he tripped over his new soul collectors lying amongst the debris of their shattered containers.

The smoke began to dissipate and he could see movement ahead of him. "I see you hiding there. Where are the others?"

The figure was silhouetted in the smoke beside the table that held the machine to which he owed his immortality. He calmed somewhat as he heard the sounds of the device still performing its infernal function.

"Answer me, you worthless piece of offal!" Meskal growled as he reached out to shake the silent homunculus.

His feet became tangled in something on the floor and he nearly fell. He looked down to see a trench coat at his feet.

Suddenly he had a very bad feeling. He peered through the smoke as the figure before him slowly become visible. Meskal felt his breath catch. It was no homunculus that faced him.

Angel's clothes were torn and bloody. The head of a homunculus hung from one hand and he held his knife in the other. The vampire's yellow eyes glowed eerily in the smoke-filled air, and he smiled.

"Sticks and stones," Angel said, razor-sharp incisors bared as he swiped the arm holding the head across the table and sent the prized device crashing to the floor.

"No!" Meskal screamed. He moved toward the vampire and then realized the foolishness of his action. Angel swung the homunculus head and smashed him under the chin.

The sorcerer was hurled backward through the air, bounced off a far wall and landed with a bone-shaking thud. He lifted his head and struggled to remain conscious.

"I told you it wasn't over," the vampire said.

Angel dragged Anton Meskal across his ruined laboratory into the connecting office space and living quarters. He propped the unconscious sorcerer against the wall and looked about the office. *If I were an evil sorcerer who sold souls for a living, where would I hide my stash?* he thought, before noticing the cabinet behind the desk.

He went to the still open drawers and gazed down at the multiple vessels. He carefully examined each as he searched for the one containing Aubrey's soul.

Angel didn't find it in the first drawer or the eight drawers beneath. He had seen the crystal that held the girl's life force and could never forget it. The girl's soul was not here among the others.

He heard the sorcerer moan behind him and turned to glare at the man propped against the wall. Meskal's eyes fluttered open and then bulged as they fell upon Angel's fearsome visage.

"Aubrey Bentone's soul," Angel said, exasperation creeping into his voice. "Where is it?"

The magic user wiped dried blood from his swollen lip. There was a look of disbelief on his face. "You continue to impress me, Angel. How ever did you manage to escape from all those drug-crazed demons?"

Angel remembered the darkness that slowly enveloped him as the demons beat him into unconsciousness. But he did not go to a place of sweet oblivion. Instead he had again found himself in the cemetery where his family had been laid to rest.

Aubrey had been there, still dressed in her pink hospital gown, her eyes covered with thick gauze. She sat, weeping, upon the grave of his sister. As he went to her, she had looked up at him and in a voice filled with emotion she had begged him not to give up.

Please, Angel, she had said. *Please don't give up on me.* She had touched the headstone, running her fingers along the inscriptions. *On either of us.*

The child had turned her face to the grave. The earth had begun to churn. Angel had watched with a mixture of wonder and horror as a tiny hand broke the surface like some pale, exotic flower.

The hand beckoned to him.

And, in his head, in this state that was more than dreaming, he had heard her voice, his sister's voice, like the wind whispering through the trees. It had said, *Please.*

Angel blinked away the eerie recollection.

"I made a deal with them," he said, answering the sorcerer's question. "I promised not to kill every last one of them if they let me get to you."

Angel's answer wasn't too far from the truth. He'd

come awake lying on the floor of the warehouse with the drug-addled demons arguing about how to finish him off. He'd solved their problem by putting them out of their misery. Some did escape, though, the need to remain alive still more powerful than the need to get high.

Meskal used the wall to help himself stand. Angel took note of how much younger the man appeared since he last saw him.

"I could offer you the same deal, but something tells me you wouldn't be up for it. The soul. Now."

The sorcerer gave him an intimidating stare. "You realize that everything you hold dear will be forfeit after what you have done here?"

Angel lost his cool. Meskal had the arrogance to think that he could still threaten him. His face morphed to savagery and he brought his clenched fists down onto the glass desktop, shattering it. The sorcerer's phone and a decorative wooden box fell to the floor in a shower of glass.

Meskal made a move toward him. No. He made a move toward the wooden box.

Angel reached the box first and felt Meskal's eyes upon him as he opened the lid. He removed the hypodermic needle and three ampules of the longevity drug. He held them out to the sorcerer. Meskal's face twisted in frustration and rage.

"Give that to me at once," he demanded in a quavering voice.

"Is this how you do it?" Angel asked. "Is this how you cheat time?"

The sorcerer looked as though he might do something foolish.

"Remember the last time you tried to stop me? Cast a pretty nifty spell. Took quite a bit out of you, as I recall."

Meskal fell back against the wall with a heavy sigh. "As they say here in the States, the ball is in your yard."

Angel pointed to the cabinet. "Where is Aubrey Bentone's soul?" Meskal shook his head from side to side; a sly smile began to creep across his face. "Where oh where could that soul be?"

The sorcerer pushed off from the wall; the arrogance had returned to his eyes. "Is that the ball I see rolling back into my yard?"

Unfazed, Angel tossed the hypodermic and ampules down onto the glass-covered floor and crushed them beneath the heel of his boot.

"So much for rolling balls."

Meskal screamed as he watched the green fluid squirt out onto the broken glass from beneath Angel's shoe. He fell to his knees, head bowed, as if drained of his reason to live.

"The girl's soul . . . it's with Shugg. Please . . . don't torment me any longer. I must have time, now. Time . . . Get out. You've done enough."

Angel bent down to scoop the duffel bag up off

the floor where it had been dropped. He turned to the cabinet and began to pluck the vials from the trays and place them inside the bag.

"What are you doing?" he heard the sorcerer ask. "I told you where the soul was. . . ."

"I'm taking these with me—as collateral. Arrange for me to get the girl's soul and you can have it all back."

Angel sensed the sorcerer behind him and glanced around. Meskal looked desperate, as if he might be willing to take a risk.

Angel finished and zipped the bag closed. "Cast your spell, Anton. You might kill me—but the real question is, what if you expend that energy and you don't kill me? You have no idea of the pleasure I'd get watching you rot."

From his coat pocket Angel pulled out a business card and flicked it at Meskal. "Here's my number. Have your boss give me a call and we'll set something up to make the exchange."

Meskal picked up the card. His hand trembled as he looked at it. "He's not my boss, and he's not going to be at all happy when I tell him what you've taken."

"I'm counting on it," Angel replied.

He hefted the bag to one shoulder. It was heavier than he expected. He could hear the vials tinkle like wind chimes and Meskal gasped.

"A word to the wise, vampire? Handle the vessels

with care. The amount of power housed in the containment shells—it could prove quite devastating if released at once."

"Thanks for the tip," Angel said. He turned away from the sorcerer, walked down the stairs to the first floor. Careful not to step on any dead demons, or what was leaking from their bodies, he went out the door and into the night.

Angel could feel it in his bones, a tingling that told him it was almost over.

Soon, he thought. *Soon.*

June Bentone's hand shook uncontrollably as she reached out to the metal door that would take her inside the warehouse.

It swung open with a push from her fingertips.

She was cursing herself. She hadn't had a decent night's sleep since Aubrey had become sick and as she sat in her car waiting for something to happen, she had drifted off to sleep. It was over an hour before she had awakened with a start. She could see the limousine still parked in front of the warehouse but wondered if she had missed anything. She decided she had no choice but to check out the building.

June stuck her gun into the room ahead of her body. It was a Smith & Wesson .38 Chief and she recalled the day she had bought it as if it were only yesterday. A man had come to the house looking for David. But it was one of the few times he was actually putting in a full day of work and he wasn't home. The man had seen Aubrey playing on a blanket on the floor of the living room. *"It would be really tragic if something bad happened to such a cute little baby over something as trivial as money."* She could still hear his voice as clear as a bell.

She had slammed the door, packed up Aubrey and her things and driven to a sporting goods store where she filled out the appropriate paperwork and made her purchase. The thought of a gun in her home had sickened her, but it had been a necessary evil if she was going to keep her baby safe.

A lotta good it did, she thought.

June stepped through the doorway. Her eyes could barely comprehend what she saw. Bodies. Ten . . . fifteen . . . at least twenty lying broken and bloody all around the room.

Bile shot up into her throat and she fought to keep it down. She wanted to run away from the carnage, but felt compelled to walk nearer on wobbly legs. At closer examination she saw that the bodies weren't human. They were monstrous, some with shiny scales, others with mouths filled with black, jagged teeth, and some even had horns.

June felt a powerful current of madness tug at the mooring of her sanity. She thought of Aubrey to keep herself from breaking down and running out into the night. She studied the frozen faces of the monsters lying dead before her. If she wanted her daughter back safely in her arms she was going to have to get used to sights such as this.

Who could have done this? she wondered.

The image of a savage Angel lashing out at the faceless attackers in the alley behind Night School flashed through her mind. She saw his bulging forehead, his piercing yellow eyes and horribly elongated teeth.

Who could have done this? She had a very good idea.

Her thoughts were interrupted by a voice from the second floor. She stepped into the shadows and listened. It was the man from the club; she was sure of it. He must have been talking on the phone because she heard no other voices.

He was screaming and carrying on but she couldn't quite understand what he was so upset about. Did this have anything to do with Angel? And, if that was the case, where was he? If something happened to Angel, who would help her daughter? Who would help Aubrey?

June felt the weight of the .38 in her hand. If something had indeed happened to Angel, it was up to her now.

The man was still yelling as she carefully moved to the foot of the stairs. She thought of her little girl, unconscious in a hospital bed across town, took two deep breaths and started to climb.

Meskal paced around his demolished lab, frantically speaking with Shugg on the phone. "It's all gone. The vampire has destroyed the lab."

Glass crunched beneath his nine-hundred-dollar wing-tip shoes.

The sorcerer took a deep, trembling breath. "And he took all the vessels as well."

Meskal pulled the phone away from his ear as he listened to the bellow of rage that came from the other end. He could hear water splashing. The demon must have been talking from the pool.

"I don't care if he does have a soul," the Kurgarru shrieked, "we will destroy him and any evidence that he walked this world. I myself will plunge the shaft of wood into his thieving heart, take his ashes and—"

Meskal interrupted. "He said we could have the vessels back in exchange for the child's soul."

There was a long pause before the demon spoke again.

"This is not good, not good at all. This kind of extortion . . . it's unthinkable!"

Meskal walked over to the remains of the machine that produced the substance that he needed to stay young—to stay alive; now nothing more than a ruptured casing, glistening internal workings spilled out onto the debris-littered floor.

He had never wanted to kill anyone more than he did Angel.

"At this point we have no choice but to comply. We must have those vials back." Meskal paced, his eyes closed to the ruin that was now his laboratory. "As much as it pains me to admit, the vampire has managed to gain the upper hand."

The sorcerer heard the sound of glass crunching underfoot behind him. He quickly turned, phone still pressed to his ear. A woman he did not recognize, probably in her late thirties, wearing jeans and a tacky silk blouse, pointed a pistol at him, eyes filled with hate.

Shugg continued to rant from the phone. "For now, but when the opportunity is right, we shall strike with the force of—"

"Would you excuse me for a moment," Meskal said into the receiver.

The demon was quiet.

"Can I help you with something?" he asked the woman. He tried to smile warmly, the last thing he needed was a bullet wound.

The woman gripped the gun tighter and squinted down the sight at him. Her voice trembled as she spoke. "What did you do to my little girl?"

Meskal had no idea what the woman was talking

about. "I'm confused, my dear woman. What little girl are we talking about?"

The shot sounded like cannon fire and the bullet buried itself in the plaster wall to the right of his head. He stared into the still-smoking barrel of the pistol and then into the face of the woman. She narrowed her eyes and snarled.

"*My* little girl."

He saw her finger twitch on the trigger again as she stepped closer.

"Where's Angel? What have you done with him?"

And then it all became clear to the sorcerer, like the dark clouds parting to let the sun shine through. He knew exactly who the woman was.

He smiled at her again. This time there was no attempt at warmth. "You're the one who hired Angel, aren't you? You're the one who brought this on us."

Tears had begun to slide down her pain-wracked face.

"Where is it, you filthy bastard?"

Meskal placed the phone casually back to his ear.

"Shugg? Let me call you back. I believe things may have just turned in our favor." He disconnected the call and returned his full attention to the woman with the gun.

She inched closer to him, gun pointed at his face. Her eyes were wild.

"What have you done with my daughter's soul?"

273

Meskal closed up his cellular phone and slid it into his shirt pocket. His movements were slow, completely nonthreatening.

"Calm yourself—Ms. Bentone, is it? Your child's soul is safe."

He sprang at her like a hungry predator.

"And it belongs to me."

CHAPTER THIRTEEN

"Vickie Vale?" Angel stared at Cordelia as he gently placed the duffel bag on top of her desk. "You told Meskal your name was Vickie Vale?"

Cordelia shrugged. "What can I tell you? I got flustered. It was either that or Darva Conger." She quickly changed the subject. "So did you vanquish his sorcerer's butt or what? Let me tell you, if there was ever a guy that deserved vanquishing. Very testy when it came to his father. I don't think they got along."

"His father?"

Cordelia rolled her eyes. "Remember? Clive Meskal? Big-time Hollywood mover and shaker, suspected of being involved with some devil-worshiping cult way back when?"

Angel shook his head. "Not his father, but Anton himself under another name. Looks like our sorcerous friend has been in business for quite some time, with the help of the souls he was stealing."

"Why, that sneaky magic guy . . ." She scowled.

Doyle, who was quietly leaning back against the wall behind Cordelia's desk, gestured to the bag. "So, what have ye got, an answer to a mother's prayers perhaps?"

Angel unzipped the bag. "There have to be over a hundred souls in this bag. But not the one we're looking for."

Doyle and Cordelia both leaned forward to glimpse the contents.

"Wow. They're beautiful. They should come in one of those little blue boxes from Tiffany's," Cordelia said, almost breathless.

"And I thought the one was impressive," Doyle added, equally in awe.

Angel reached into the bag and extracted a vial. "Every one of the souls trapped inside these vials has its own unique look, as individual as the people they were stolen from."

The vessel in the vampire's hand turned from a brilliant yellow to a mute green and then became the color of liquid metal. "We know what happened to Aubrey, but what about this one and all the others? What are their stories?" He looked back into the duffel bag, at the life forces of hundreds. "Why didn't we know about this sooner?"

Doyle stared at the vial in Angel's hand. "It's a

strange world, Angel. Maybe not all of 'em were taken by force."

Angel found the suggestion very disturbing. "You're suggesting that some might have been given up willingly?"

Doyle glanced uncomfortably away. "Who knows what Meskal was offerin' the poor sods. Maybe, like Bentone, they didn't believe in souls anyway and saw it as an easy out."

Cordelia took the vial from Angel's hand and held it up to her face. "An entire soul is supposed to fit in here? I think I'd need more room."

With a shake of her head, she handed it back to Angel. Both he and Doyle stared at her.

"What?" Cordelia said defensively. "I just think my soul's pretty chock full of love and all kinds of other warm and gracious feelings and stuff. It's gotta be pretty big, don't you think?"

The phone rang, relieving Angel and Doyle from the impossible task of coming up with an answer.

"Angel Investigations," Cordelia said as she picked up.

The vampire watched the expression on her face turn from shock to revulsion. She handed him the phone, her palm over the receiver.

"I think it's the Kookookoojoob demon, or someone with a really nasty chest cold," she whispered.

"This is Angel," he said into the mouthpiece.

"My name is Mr. Shugg. I believe you are in possession of some items that belong to me."

Angel gripped the phone tighter. The voice on the other end made his flesh crawl. It reminded him of the days of the Black Death when people would often die from choking on their own blood.

"What a coincidence," the vampire said in a low, dangerous voice. "You have something I want as well."

Shugg's breath was labored, moist sounding. "Perhaps it is time we did some business, yes?"

Angel glanced down into the duffel bag filled with stolen souls. He shut his eyes so as not to be mesmerized by their intense beauty. "As I told your partner, give me the girl's soul and I'll return your property."

The demon laughed. To Angel it sounded like a pipe full of raw sewage backing up.

"You ask me to trust you, vampire?" Shugg laughed again. It was a horrible sound.

"It looks like you trust me as much as I trust you," Angel said.

Angel pulled the phone away from his ear as Shugg growled.

"The exchange will occur at my home tonight. Please forgive me if this is inconvenient, but I have become a bit of a recluse over the years and do not leave my dwelling."

"You're inviting me into your home?" Angel asked.

"What was it Mr. Stoker wrote in his book?" Shugg wheezed and gurgled. *"Welcome to my house! Enter freely and of your own will."*

"I don't read much," Angel lied. The demon was entirely too amused, and Angel was not about to encourage him.

"Tonight then."

"Tonight," Angel responded, as he jotted down the address on a notepad on Cordelia's desk.

Angel handed the phone back to Cordelia.

She held the receiver as though it were a dead rat. "So, was it that demon?" she asked, curling up her nose. "Demons are so gross. They're nasty in person but there's something so pervy-obscene-call about hearing a voice like that on the phone. Know what I mean?"

With a frown, Doyle cleared his throat. "So, looks like it's set to go down tonight, then?"

Angel nodded. "Looks that way."

Doyle rubbed his chin nervously. "Not to be questionin' yer tactics or anything, but yer not actually plannin' on turning those souls over to the demon, are ye?"

Angel zipped the bag closed. "You've always known me to be a relatively honorable man, haven't you, Doyle?"

The halfling was flustered. "I never meant to question yer honor, Angel, it's just that—"

Angel continued. "So what makes you think I'm

the type to double-cross an ancient demon who feeds on the souls of living things . . . including small children?"

The vampire smirked as he removed the bag from the desk.

"Just wanted to be certain I was working fer a guy with standards," Doyle said dryly.

Angel headed for the elevator. "Doyle and I are going downstairs to review Harry's notes," he said to Cordelia. "Would you mind getting in touch with June Bentone and—"

"That reminds me," Cordy interrupted. "I can't seem to find her. She hasn't been at the hospital today and according to the nurse she didn't show last night either."

Angel scowled. "Do me a favor, go over to her house and check it out. She got in the way of some dangerous stuff once and I don't want it to happen again."

Later that night, Angel and Doyle turned up the winding drive at the address Shugg had given him, all of his senses acutely aware of any change in his surroundings. Angel put the car in park before the wrought-iron gates and let it idle.

"Are ye sure you don't want me to check ahead for traps?" Doyle asked.

Angel stared through the windshield. "Why check? We already know it's a trap." He glanced at

Doyle, who clutched the duffel bag in his hands. "And I'm sure they know we know."

"All right, then," Doyle replied, "If they're so cunning, then why are we still waiting out here? Wouldn't this be the perfect opportunity to get the upper hand? They probably don't even know we're here yet."

Angel reached out and rubbed away a smudge on the inside of the windshield. "Oh, they know."

Doyle gestured toward the gates. "Then why—"

The homunculi seemed to appear out of nowhere, emerging from the tall bushes and shadows that surrounded the driveway to stand beside Angel's car.

"Sneaky sods, ain't they?" Doyle muttered.

Angel put the car in drive as the gates slowly opened before him. The homunculi escorted them up to the front of the sprawling home that had gone to seed. He and Doyle got out of the car and stared up at the eccentric Hollywood mansion.

"Nice," Doyle said. "Think I saw it written up in *Better Tombs and Graveyards.*"

"It is kind of cozy," Angel agreed, "in a Frankenstein sort of way."

The front door of thick dark wood opened to reveal a homunculus dressed as a butler. He bowed and extended his white-gloved hand for them to enter. "This way, gentlemen. You are expected."

"So, what's the plan?" Doyle whispered as they walked up the front steps.

"I'm making it up as I go along," Angel responded matter-of-factly.

Doyle did a double take. "Nice a you to tell me, Indiana Jones. If I'd a known your clever scheme I would've called in sick."

They followed the butler down a lushly carpeted hallway to a sprawling living room. "Please go in," the homunculus said. "Mr. Meskal is waiting."

Angel stepped into the room, Doyle close behind. Meskal stood behind an expansive bar, its dark, polished surface covered with alcohol bottles of every size and shape. He dropped two ice cubes into a glass and glanced up, as if only then noticing that he was no longer alone.

"Angel," he said in a voice laced with malice, "how nice to see you again."

"I wish I could say the same," Angel replied.

The vampire glanced around the room appreciatively. It had all the opulence displayed by the Hollywood elite in the 1930s: hardwood floors, an enormous crystal chandelier, a beautiful wall tapestry depicting an English fox hunt.

Meskal poured his Scotch from a cut crystal decanter.

"Can I get you or your friend anything? Beer? Wine? A soft drink, perhaps?"

"If ya don't mind, I'd fancy a—"

Angel glared at Doyle.

"No," Doyle corrected. "Thanks. We're good."

The sorcerer moved around the bar, drink in hand. "Come in, gentlemen, don't be shy. Take a seat."

Meskal walked to a high-backed leather chair and sat down. He gestured again about the room. "Please."

They strode a bit farther into the room but did not sit.

"I must apologize, Angel, for some reason I failed to connect you with your rather notorious past." The sorcerer smiled at him, waiting for a reaction. "Angelus. The Scourge of Europe. How terribly exciting."

He crossed his legs, letting his foot dangle.

"In some ways I owe you a bit of thanks. Your antics in Europe at the time kept the authorities from noticing what Shugg and I were up to.

"Cheers," Meskal said as he toasted Angel, holding his glass high.

Angel stared at him coldly. "Are we almost through with happy hour? I'd like to finish this up and be on my way."

Meskal leaned over and set his drink down on a nearby table. "Of course, of course," he said as he stood. He grinned at Angel. "You know, if you are interested, I could remove the bothersome soul that put such a crimp in your illustrious career." The sorcerer paused. "And it could prove quite profitable for you. Name your price."

The thought of the monster Angelus again free upon the earth sent an icy chill up the vampire's spine. As far as he was concerned, Angelus was locked away for good and he would do everything in his power to see that he never broke free.

"I'm losing my patience, Meskal. Maybe we should do this another time when you're not feeling so chatty."

"I'm sorry, Angel. I was merely attempting to be polite. By all means, let us proceed with the exchange." Meskal clapped his hands together. He turned his attention to an entryway at the opposite end of the room. "Oh yes, and before I forget, there have been some recent developments that may change the dynamics of this transaction."

A homunculus with heavy brows drawn over his eyes in black marker strode into the room with June Bentone in tow. Angel cursed silently, then tensed as he watched the artificial man throw the woman to the floor in front of the sorcerer. Meskal hauled June up by the arm. He had produced a pistol from his suit jacket pocket and now fitted its muzzle against her side.

"After our last encounter, Ms. Bentone dropped by looking for you, and her daughter's soul. Since I suspected I would be seeing you again shortly, I asked her if she would care to join me."

He jabbed the gun barrel into her rib cage, and June winced.

"A gun, Meskal?" Angel questioned. "Thought you were more dangerous than that."

"Not really feeling myself these days, thanks to you," Meskal snarled. He looked at the weapon. "Horrible things, really. Never cared for them myself. But they can be quite efficient in their own crude way."

Angel made eye contact with June.

"I'm sorry, Angel," she said. "I had to do something to help. I'm so sorry."

"It's all right," Angel reassured her, his voice calm. "Everything is going to turn out fine."

Meskal smiled. "Fine for me, yes. But for you? I seriously doubt it."

More homunculi streamed into the living room, bearing down on Angel and Doyle from behind.

"So, what do ye think?" Doyle asked as homunculi placed heavy-gloved hands upon their shoulders.

"Pretty much what I expected," Angel said, as the artificial servants encircled them. "Except for the June part. Didn't see that coming."

"How's that plan working?"

Cordelia hustled up the steps to the office, returning from her assignment. She crossed her fingers and hoped that Angel and Doyle had not yet left.

June Bentone had not been at home; the house was eerily dark and closed up tight. What looked to be two days' worth of mail was still in the mailbox.

The office was locked. Anxiety nestled in the pit of her stomach. They were already gone.

She had checked again with the charge nurse on the children's ward, where Aubrey had been moved from Intensive Care. June still hadn't been in. That was when Cordelia really became concerned.

Where is June, she wondered, *and why do I feel like it's something Angel and Doyle need to know?*

Now Cordelia fumbled through her purse for her keys. She found them at the bottom amongst stray breath mints, lip gloss and a travel-size tube of moisturizer.

"You work with them. Angel and Doyle?"

Startled by the voice behind her, she let out a high-pitched yelp and dropped her keys to the floor. She whirled around, daggers in her eyes, ready to unleash an indignant diatribe on the unfortunate person.

But it wasn't a person at all.

A demon stepped out of the shadows, sweatshirt hood over its head, hands stuffed into its pockets. Its eyes glowed an eerie yellow.

Cordelia thought fast. "I'd stay back if I were you. All I have to do is bang on this door and Angel will come running and kick your butt good."

The demon laughed; liquefied flesh trickled off its chin to spatter on the hardwood floor.

"He ain't in there," the demon said. "I already knocked a bunch a times. I was waitin' for him or Doyle to come back."

She couldn't pull her eyes away from the milky puddles that had formed around the demon's sneakered feet.

"And I'm not here to start any trouble, so you can calm yourself right down. The name's Margus and I got some information they might be interested in."

Cordelia squatted and felt around the floor for her keys. She kept her eyes on Margus and the puddles he made.

"Information? No. We don't need any information. That's what we're all about here at Angel Investigations. Sorry. No need of information today. Thanks for stopping by."

She found her keys and quickly opened the door.

Margus shook his head in dismay, spattering melted flesh an even greater distance. He moved toward the stairs to leave. "Suit yourself. Just thought you might be interested in the pretty lady hostage that Meskal took late last night. Tell Doyle I was by and I'll catch him later."

Cordelia had pushed the door open about an inch when she yelled to the drippy demon. "Wait. What did this pretty lady hostage look like?"

Margus came back up the stairs. "See? I knew you guys would be interested. S'funny. I can't seem to remember what she looked like. . . ."

He held out a drippy hand.

"It's all kinda blurry."

Cordelia realized what the demon was after as he wiggled his fingers at her. She started to go though her purse.

"I'm going to need a receipt for this," she said as she rummaged a bit and came out with a folded twenty.

She came away from the door cautiously, careful not to get anything on herself, and put the bill in the demon's hand.

Margus closed his hand around the money and it disappeared into his sweatshirt. The hand emerged empty and he again held it out to Cordy. "I think I'm startin' to get something. A picture, but it's still a little fuzzy."

"More?" Cordelia asked, her annoyance starting to show.

"Sorry. I got expenses."

Cordelia scowled as she again dug into her purse. "Expenses," she muttered, searching. "The dermatologist's bill alone must be astronomical."

She found a ten and five singles and gave them to him. "That's it," she said, as she pulled her hand away, "and I want you to know that you just took my grocery money for a week. Happy?"

Margus put the money into his pocket. "Happy enough to remember what the lady looked like."

Cordelia folded her arms across her chest and

leaned against the doorframe. "Bang for my buck please, thank you?" Then she shuddered. "Ooh, I can't believe I just said that. You know what I meant."

Margus smiled at her.

"The woman was pretty for a human," he said, "if you know what I'm saying. About thirty-nine or so, curly black hair. I saw her go into Meskal's warehouse after Angel kicked butt on some demons Meskal hired to off him. Then I seen Meskal drag her out to his limo and they were gone."

The demon returned his hands to his sweatshirt pockets.

"And that's what I know."

This isn't good at all, Cordelia thought. *Meskal's got June. He'll try to use her as leverage with Angel.*

Margus started to leave again. "Pleasure doing business with you . . . I didn't catch yer name."

Cordelia eyed the demon. "Good. That's another thing I got for my thirty-five bucks."

The demon laughed and started down the stairs. "Thanks for the business, girlie. Maybe we can do it again sometime."

"Sure," Cordelia muttered as she pushed the office door open, "just let me know in advance so I can get my decontamination suit out of the cleaners."

She had no time for demon nonsense. Deeply concerned, she slammed the door behind her and strode into the middle of the office. There was only one thing she could do. She went to her desk and searched for the pad of paper where Angel had written the address.

Pretty exclusive neck of the woods for a demon, she thought.

A clock had begun ticking in the back of her mind, and Cordelia rushed down the stairs to Angel's apartment. She didn't know when they had left, and if by some slim chance she could get to them before the exchange, it just might save somebody's life. And, if that was what she was going to do, she was going to need some protection.

Cordelia approached a large, oak armoire up against a far wall of Angel's quarters. She pulled open the double doors to reveal a storage cabinet for the weaponry Angel used on his various cases. She eyed the deadly items.

So many ways to maim and kill, she thought, perusing the instruments of death, *so little time.*

CHAPTER FOURTEEN

Shugg felt the vampire's unique soul call out to him as it came into his home. He could feel a soul thrumming with ambrosial power . . . and Angel's called out to him like the world's largest dinner bell.

The demon had been watching a tape of the day-time television show *Dollars and Sense*. The demon loved the game show. Watching as the human contestants groveled and belittled themselves in front of millions for a chance to win patio furniture or an all-expense-paid trip to the Magic Kingdom was his favorite pastime.

This particular episode was one of his favorites and he stayed with the tape as long he could. But the vampire's soul called to him, and Shugg began to salivate uncontrollably. Reluctantly, he turned off the VCR.

❖   ❖   ❖

"All this bother for the soul of one child."

Angel watched Meskal impassively. The sorcerer shook his head and clucked with disapproval, still keeping the gun pointed at June Bentone's torso.

"Can you honestly say it's worth all this trouble?"

Angel struggled a bit against the homunculi that held him, testing their strength. Doyle was also restrained. The vampire glanced at June. Her eyes were filled with the sadness of loss, but there was something else. The burning embers of hope had not yet been extinguished.

Angel stared at Meskal, let his eyes bore into the icy cold blue of the sorcerer's. His resolve was firm. There was no trace of doubt in the simple word he spoke. "Yes."

Meskal sneered and motioned to one of the homunculi that loomed behind Doyle. "Take the bag."

The homunculus tried to grab the duffel, but Doyle pulled it away from the creature's seeking hands. Another clubbed Doyle on the back of the head and the demon halfling fell to his knees.

"Doyle!" Angel exclaimed. He lashed out at the homunculi who were restraining him. He tossed one off him and drove his fist into the face of another. Angel felt the satisfying crunch of the homunculus' face beneath his blow.

"Hold him!" Meskal shrieked, pulling June closer. "And search him for weapons."

It took five of the faceless servants to finally drive Angel to his knees. Their hands reached beneath his duster and patted him down. One found the Fang of Turdakus and held it up excitedly for his master to see.

"That looks familiar," the sorcerer observed with a smirk.

"Take her," he said as he handed June over to the homunculus that had brought her out, "and if she gives you any trouble you have my permission to break her neck."

The creature pulled the terrified woman to him, one of its large, gloved hands wrapped around her throat.

Meskal strolled over to Angel and squatted down in front of him, clearly amused by the vampire's plight. "It's a shame what happened to you. I'm sure Angelus and I could have been good friends," he said with a condescending smile.

Angel's face morphed to one of bestial savagery and with fangs bared, he lunged at the sorcerer. Startled, Meskal nearly fell backward.

"Gotcha," Angel said with a predatory grin.

The sorcerer's face reddened, as much in embarrassment as anger.

"Remind the vampire who is in control here," he spat.

The homunculi attacked, kicking and punching until Angel was practically senseless. He slowly lifted his head. A trickle of blood ran from his split lower lip.

"I'll remember that," he growled, fixing Meskal in his demonic gaze.

"You are in no position to make threats and I doubt you ever will be again," the sorcerer said. "It's over for you."

Angel felt the floor begin to vibrate and his eyes widened as he took in the sight of the monster that emerged from a hallway at the back of the living room. In the two hundred-plus years that he'd walked the earth, Angel believed he had seen them all—demons of all shapes and sizes.

But Angel had never seen anything to equal the sight of Shugg.

Well over ten feet tall and dressed in a flowing robe of black silk, the demon shuffled across the living room. It used two large, ornately carved wooden canes to help move its enormous girth.

Its skin was like an oil slick, black and shiny with unexpected color when light crossed the moist flesh. Strange dangling growths hung from the front of its obscenely fat body.

"Well, that's it then," Doyle said.

Angel looked over at his friend, who had not taken his eyes from the nightmarish visage shambling into the room.

"Hands down that's the most disgustin' sight I could possibly imagine," Doyle added, almost nonchalantly.

Shugg stopped and rested on his canes. He studied the two captives. A thin, nictitating membrane slid across the creature's bulbous eyes as he blinked, taking them all into his monstrous gaze. The demon smiled. A muscular, sluglike tongue protruded from its lipless mouth for a brief moment and then disappeared back into the cavernous maw.

"Anton," it said in a voice sounding as if spoken through thick, choking fluids. "Why didn't you tell me our guests had arrived?"

The demon stood before the visitors to his home. "Anton, introduce me to our company."

The sorcerer seemed annoyed by the request, but then again, when didn't Meskal seem annoyed?

"This is Angel," Meskal told his demon partner as he pointed to the vampire restrained by five homunculi. "Formerly known as Angelus, the Scourge of Europe," the sorcerer added with a smirk. "Though he doesn't appear too fearsome now, does he?"

"Angelus," the Kurgarru happily hissed, as he recalled the vampire's reign of terror. News of Angelus had provided him with many hours of entertainment before the advent of television.

"I admired your work," he added with a slight bow of his gumdrop-shaped head. "I am Shugg, last of the Kurgarru."

"Couldn't think of a better name meself," Doyle said.

The demon turned its malevolent gaze on the man beside Angel. "And this one?" Shugg pointed one of his tree limb–size canes at Doyle.

The demon leaned its head forward and sniffed the air around him. "A half-breed?" Shugg scrunched up his face in revulsion and moved back. "How vile," he sneered.

The demon again let his gaze fall upon Angel. The power of the captive vampire's soul called to him. In all his years he had never felt anything quite like it. The soul was filled with enormous strength and vitality—yet it also radiated a delicious sadness.

Shugg's enormous belly gurgled and popped. He began to drool and looked back to Meskal. "Enough of this frivolity," the demon said. "Let us get to the business at hand."

Meskal responded with a slight nod toward Angel. "The taking of the vampire's soul," the sorcerer said as he reached into his jacket pocket and withdrew a soul collector. "You can't imagine the interest I've had in this specialty item. I had no idea how popular you were, Angel. It seems as though everyone wants a piece of you."

"It's nice to know that all my hard work is paying off," Angel said.

Shugg giggled with anticipation. "Do you know what we have here? Think of it, Anton, the only one of their filthy kind to have a soul. I haven't been this excited since I took the souls of my mate and child. I find it all so very . . . stimulating."

Meskal looked at his partner. "I find the bidding war over his soul far more stimulating."

Shugg shook his misshapen head. "You misunderstand, Anton. There will be no bidding on the soul of Angelus." Thick rivulets of saliva dripped from Shugg's mouth. "You will take this prize and give it to me."

The collector vibrated with life in Meskal's hand.

"Give it to you?" he asked incredulously. "You're not serious."

The demon slid closer, leaning on his canes and bending his head down to the sorcerer's level. "I couldn't be more serious. I want that soul."

Meskal's eyes flashed with anger. "Do you know how much that soul is worth?" He watched as the demon glanced at Angel and then back to him.

"I don't care about the market."

The demon motioned with a cane toward the homunculus holding the duffel bag filled with souls. "We have more than enough souls to satisfy our customers' needs and support ourselves comfortably. My body craves *this* soul and I will have it."

Meskal noticed the vampire smiling, obviously taking great pleasure in the discord.

"If you guys need some time to settle this, we'd be more than happy to come back later," Angel suggested.

At that moment, Meskal didn't care about his partner's desires or the obscene amount of money he could earn by selling Angel's life force to the highest bidder. He just wanted to see the vampire die, to experience the immense satisfaction of driving a stake into his heart. He wanted to watch Angel's flesh wither and crumble away to dust.

Meskal became aware of Shugg moving closer. No matter how much cologne the creature bathed his obscene, glistening flesh in, it could not mask the stench of decay.

"You need me, Anton, do not forget that. Without me, your precious device will not be rebuilt and you will not have the injections your body so desperately needs to remain fresh and young. Without me it is only a matter of time before you die."

Meskal stared into the demon's face, into its bulging, yellow eyes. He could see himself reflected in their watery surface. The days of his needing the Kurgarru demon had passed long ago.

"Do not deny me," Shugg continued in a whispery hiss. "We have experienced far too much to create a rift now. Show me that the partnership is still strong."

Meskal checked to see if the soul receptacle was secured firmly beneath the collector. The words of Julien Cresh echoed through his mind. *Shugg. What exactly does he do for you again? . . . What exactly does he contribute? . . . It's totally obvious that you're the brains of this operation. . . . Y'know what I'd do if I was you?"*

Meskal looked at his partner. The demon grinned obscenely.

"I'd find a way to get rid of Shugg and take over the whole ball a wax."

The sorcerer turned toward Angel and took aim with the collector.

"For the whole ball of wax," he said as he squeezed the trigger.

Angel tried to escape the clutches of his homunculi captors but they only tightened their hold and moved him into the path of the collector. The bolt of crackling blue fire spat from its mouthlike barrel and traveled the distance to him in the blink of an eye. The energy's tip pierced his chest and hurled him violently back.

Angel tossed his head back in agony, screaming as the magical force burrowed its way inside of him.

The pain was excruciating. All he could think of was that a helpless child had endured this misery.

The torment triggered Angel's transformation. His forehead thickened and his teeth grew pointed and sharp. He snapped at the air like an animal driven to madness.

Above the roar of his agony, he heard the sound of his friend calling to him.

"Fight it, Angel!" he heard Doyle say. "Fight it with everything ye got!"

The collector's power found what it had been seeking and began to draw it from him. The pain grew even worse and his body was wracked with bone-breaking convulsions. The homunculi struggled to hold him firmly in place.

Angel could feel his soul begin to pull away from its spiritual mooring within his being. No matter how hard he struggled to hold on, he could feel it gradually slipping.

And he could feel the evil he fought so hard to restrain scramble hungrily forward to fill the void.

"Nature abhors a vacuum," he heard himself say in a voice that filled him with dread. Wickedness dripped from every word as the monster within began to assert control.

Angel screamed in rage as he realized that it was almost too late.

And Angelus laughed when he saw he would soon be free.

CHAPTER FIFTEEN

June struggled in the grasp of her faceless captor, panicked by Angel's roar of pain and the demon's horrible laugh; something awful was happening to the man she had entrusted to save her daughter. Somehow she had to get to Meskal. She had to stop him.

The homunculus pulled her closer. "Stop squirming or I'll—"

Like an answered prayer, an arrow whispered past her face to embed itself deep into the creature's forehead.

June felt its hold loosen as it fell away from her. Her eyes searched the room for the source of her salvation and she saw Cordelia standing in the doorway, reloading an ancient crossbow.

Now, she thought, her mind moving at lightning speed. June launched herself at Meskal, who was

301

too engrossed in the agony he was causing Angel to notice her attack.

"No!" she heard the obese demon shriek as it noticed she was free. It shifted its bulk to intervene.

It wasn't fast enough. June slammed into the magic user and knocked the device from his hand to the living room floor. She gazed down on the perverse instrument with disgust. It looked like the rotting remains of an animal washed up on a beach.

This is what they used on my daughter, she thought, taking in its every revolting detail.

"You'll pay for that," Meskal hissed as he dove to reclaim the collector.

June blocked him with her body and raised her foot up over the cruel device. "This is for Aubrey, you miserable sons of bitches," she said as she stamped her foot down.

Angel's soul rushed back into his body, the threat of Angelus's return narrowly averted. He felt the monster struggling to remain free, but he forced it down deep. That was where Angelus belonged, where he would stay forever.

He was still in the grasp of the homunculi, and he feigned weakness, slowly shrugging off the harrowing effects of the soul collector. One of his homunculi captors began to scream and claw at its back. It stumbled away from him and that was when Angel saw Cordelia in the doorway, crossbow in hand.

He watched with a faint smile as she loaded another bolt. She *had* been paying attention when he showed her how to use the weapon a few months back.

Cordelia's appearance had thrown the room into chaos and set in motion a chain reaction. June was free, the soul collector was destroyed, Angel was once again in control of himself, and the homunculi were in a frenzied state of utter confusion. One of the faceless creatures held the Fang of Turdakus in its hands. Angel was not about to let the diversion Cordelia had created go to waste.

With a sudden burst of strength he reared up, throwing off his captors, and dove for the blade.

Doyle brought his elbow down on the head of a homunculus with a long ponytail. Things hadn't been looking too good for the home team, until Cordelia came to the rescue. He didn't think he'd ever seen anyone look quite so lovely and stylish while wielding a crossbow.

His reverie was interrupted as a homunculus jumped on his back. Doyle quickly bent forward, flipped the creature over his shoulder, and slammed it to the floor.

When Angel had said he didn't really have a plan as they strolled into the lion's den, Doyle's first instinct had been to turn tail and head for the nearest pub. This whole marching into the valley of death business really wasn't his style, but it had become all too common since the Powers That Be had hooked him up with Angel.

As Doyle drove the heel of his foot into Ponytail's face, he thought about what Harry had said earlier, about how fighting the good fight alongside Angel might help change his opinion of his demonic nature. Maybe there was some truth in that.

Doyle spun around to sucker punch another of the faceless attackers. A crossbow bolt breezed by his left cheek and he turned in time to see it *thunk* into the wall directly behind his head. He looked back at Cordelia lowering the bow. She scrunched up her pretty face, shrugged her shoulders and mouthed the word, *whoops*.

"Don't ferget whose side yer on now, darlin'," he yelled before returning his full attention to the homunculi attackers, and any stray bolts.

Angel drove the Fang of Turdakus into the chest of a homunculus that had red, white and blue stars painted on its face. The creature began to decay as Angel withdrew the blade, spun around and severed the head of another attacking from behind. Its ring-covered hands went to the spurting stump of its neck as it fell to its knees, its body liquefying.

Angel turned to find a new wave of homunculi converging on him from the side, and wondered how many of them Meskal had created. He waded into them, lashing out with hand and foot and blade.

The creatures met the attack with fury, but were no match for his vampiric savagery as he hacked and slashed them into steaming piles of waste. Angel knew the homunculi numbers had to be dwindling, but still they came. Two more of the faceless creatures perished beneath his blade. Then he turned his attention toward the back of the room where June still struggled with Meskal. Shugg shouted in anger at this turn of events, its gelatinous mass quivering with rage.

Angel glanced quickly about to be sure Doyle and Cordelia were holding their own, then started toward the trio in the back. The remaining homunculi threw themselves at him, doing everything in their power to prevent the vampire from reaching their creator.

Nevertheless, he forged a path toward Meskal by cutting down homunculi like wheat at the harvest.

"You're beginning to try my patience, Ms. Bentone," Meskal said. Viciously he backhanded June across the face with her pistol and watched as she crumpled in a heap to the floor.

He straightened his suit and tie and turned his attention to the scuffle behind him. His breath caught as his gaze fell on Angel cutting a bloody path directly toward him. Things were spinning out of control. He needed time to collect his thoughts, but sadly, he no longer had that luxury.

"Follow me," he ordered the homunculus carrying the bag of souls.

He had taken only a few steps toward the exit when he felt Shugg's heavy hand on his shoulder. "We have to do something. The vampire will ruin everything."

"It's over, Shugg," Meskal said, his voice void of emotion.

"Don't be ridiculous, Anton," Shugg blustered, clutching his hand into a fist and shaking it at the ceiling. "One vampire against Shugg . . . against us? Angel will scream for mercy as I—"

Meskal wanted to laugh but there was precious little time for humor.

"Look at you," he said, drawing attention to the demon's corpulent frame. "Look at what has become of the last Kurgarru. What will you do? Nauseate him with your eating habits, or maybe bore him with your foolish television game shows?"

Meskal scoffed. "Where once you filled me with awe and fear, now you make me sick." He turned his back on the demon.

The blow to the back of his neck came suddenly and ferociously, driving him to all fours. Meskal rolled onto his back to see the snarling Shugg raise one of his canes above his head, preparing to strike at him again. After all this time, *here* was the savage Kurgarru he so fondly remembered.

"You will learn that the last of the Kurgarru is still one to fear," the demon roared.

A magical spell of defense was upon Meskal's lips

when he stopped. To utter the arcane words would trigger the process that would steal away his vitality and rot his flesh. He might as well allow Shugg to bash in his brains.

Then he realized that he still clutched June Bentone's pistol. He raised the gun and fired into the demon's face. The first shot put out one of its eyes. A milky white fluid exploded from the gelatinous orb and streamed down its face.

Shugg dropped his canes and stumbled backward, clawing at his face and screaming in the guttural tongue of the Kurgarru. Although he was not as fluent as he had once been in the demon's language, Meskal was fairly certain it was shrieking something about betrayers and the fate that awaits them in the afterlife.

Meskal fired until the weapon was spent and the hammer fell on empty chambers. He tossed it aside and watched with relief as Shugg stepped on one of his canes and slipped, falling backward to the floor with a horrendous crash that shook the house to its foundations.

But his relief quickly turned to trepidation as the Durge, agitated by their master's pain, exploded from the demon's chest in a voracious fury.

Cordelia couldn't have imagined anything more gross than having to play *Let's Make a Deal* with Margus the drippy demon. But that was before the enormous, revolting Shugg was shot in the face. Her stomach convulsed as what she had thought were just disgusting growths hanging on its fleshy body came to life and flew into the air.

She was glad she hadn't eaten since lunch.

"So we've got mutant bats now?" she asked, gripping Doyle's arm with one hand as a hint of panic crept into her voice.

Some of the screaming creatures flew helter-skelter toward them. "I think it might be worse," Doyle said.

"Worse than mutant bats?" she glanced at him, horrified. "What could be worse than mutant bats?"

One of the things glided to the ground near her foot, looked up at her and hissed.

"Scratch that last question from the record," she said, staring down into the tiny beast's cold, shiny-black eyes.

The animal skittered closer and Doyle lunged forward. He stomped his foot down onto its body with a wet crunch. "Maybe if we show 'em who's boss they'll leave us alone," he said hopefully.

Cordelia waved the crossbow around her head and knocked some of the squealing monstrosities from the air. Beside her, Doyle stamped them into the floor.

"Yeah, and maybe if we make smoochie noises we can get them to eat popcorn out of our hands. Keep stompin'!"

One of the creatures swooped down and became entangled in her hair. Cordelia let out a shriek and dropped the crossbow. She reached up to grab at the monster and it nipped at her fingers. "Doyle!" she called out.

"Hang on, girl." Doyle tore one of the clinging beasts from his pants leg and threw it away.

With his help, Cordelia extracted the flapping horror from her hair. She threw it to the floor and they both took turns stomping on its writhing form.

The batlike demons were everywhere, the air of the living room a storm of flittering, screeching monsters. The creatures became bolder and began to attack in larger groups.

"Get offa me, you little pervert," Cordelia screamed at a tiny predator climbing up the front of her shirt, moving toward the soft flesh of her throat. She grabbed the creature in both hands and squeezed. Despite the horror of it, the crack of the bones in her hands was gratifying—she could kill them—but there were so many now, and she doubted she could do any real damage without the help of a flamethrower or some low-yield nuclear device.

"This is mad!" Doyle swatted at the air above his head and took her by the arm. His face was bleeding where he had been bitten and scratched. "They got us cut off—we'll never reach the door. We have to find some kind of protection or these things'll strip us to the bone in no time."

She squinted through the storm of flying bodies, her eyes falling upon the tapestry of an English fox hunt hanging on a wall nearby.

"The wall thingie," she cried leaning closer to Doyle's ear so she could be heard over the high-pitched shrieks of the flying demons. "If we can get to it we can cover ourselves."

They began to move as one across the room, swatting and plucking the beasts away as they fought to reach what might be their only chance for survival.

Angel had almost reached the sorcerer when the life-forms hanging from the Kurgarru's chest erupted in a black cloud of leathery wings and screeching ferocity. He covered his head against the maelstrom of flying creatures. Through the living storm he saw Meskal grab the bag of vials from one of his homunculi. Nearby, June struggled to stand.

"Meskal!"

Angel's voice boomed across the room as he pushed on.

The sorcerer turned. An expression of unadulterated loathing spread across his face as he shoved the homunculus toward the vampire.

Angel still held the Fang of Turdakus and he charged. But this homunculus proved smarter than the others. It sidestepped the blade and brought its arm down, trapping Angel's arm against its side and loosening his grip on the knife. The homunculus smashed Angel across the face and brought a knee up into his midsection. Stunned, Angel fell to the floor as the artificial construct advanced to finish what it had started. Past the faceless creation of sorcery, he could see Meskal, a smile upon his malevolent face, waiting to see if the vampire would finally meet his end.

On the floor, June slapped at the batlike creatures tearing at her clothes and flesh. Angel heard her scream and knew that time was short.

The homunculus reached down just as Angel surged up from the floor and plunged clawed fingers through the flesh of its chest. The homunculus struggled as the vampire reached beneath its ribcage and grasped its cold, synthetic heart. Angel crushed the organ in his hand and tossed the shuddering body aside.

The Durge swooped down on the body, sensing a fresh kill and easy prey.

Meskal was trying to get away, his progress hindered by the flying beasts. But as Angel fought his own way through the flurry of animals, his concern was not for the sorcerer but for June. She had fallen to her knees, nearly covered by the vicious attackers.

"We have to get you to cover," he shouted above the din as he began to drag her across the room.

The tiny, winged demons landed on both of them

now, sinking needle-sharp teeth into their flesh. June screamed again as Angel tore the snapping beasts off her and crushed them in his hands. But the things were relentless; no matter how many he killed there seemed to be twenty more to take their place. Nearly blind in the storm of leathery bodies, Angel wasn't sure where to go.

Doyle called out to Angel and June as he and Cordelia peeked from beneath the wall hanging, making their way through the maelstrom.

"Always wondered what these things were for," Doyle announced as they came closer. "The little buggers can't get at us under here."

Doyle reached out and pulled them beneath the tapestry, he and Cordelia tearing at the winged annoyances that still managed to cling to them. The flying demons landed atop the tapestry like savage rain, raking their claws across and biting into the material.

"So what now?" Doyle asked looking into his boss's steely gaze. "Shugg is dead and Meskal can't be too far behind 'im."

He saw a look come into Angel's eyes that he'd seen many times before. The vampire turned away. Doyle reached out and grabbed his arm, stopping him.

"What the hell are ye doin', man? These things'll eat ye alive."

Angel answered his question with a look. "You three stay under here. There's still a soul to find and only one person left alive who can tell me where it is."

He tugged his arm away and Doyle watched as Angel charged out into the living room.

Who was he to argue with the boss?

Angel hadn't gone far when he discovered Meskal. The sorcerer was covered in the black-skinned demons and struggled feebly to be free.

"Did I catch you at a bad time?" Angel asked. He grabbed the sorcerer by the back of the neck and threw him to the floor, then knelt and began to help the man tear the creatures from his body.

"Filthy beasts," Meskal hissed. "Like piranha with wings."

Angel pulled the last of the thrashing Durge from Meskal's leg and crushed it in front of the man's scratched and bitten face.

"The girl's soul," he demanded.

Meskal's eyes were filled with hate as he reached into his jacket pocket.

"I'm signing my death warrant by giving you this," he began.

Angel held out one hand while swatting away Durge with the other. "Now, or I'll feed you to these things piece by piece."

The sorcerer fumbled inside the pocket. "But it'll be worth it."

Meskal suddenly bellowed a string of words in an ancient, sorcerer's tongue and withdrew his hand, burning with arcane power. A blast of white fire, like the sun, exploded from the hand, throwing Angel back.

"I'll give you nothing," he heard the sorcerer snarl.

Angel's coat was ablaze. He tore it from his body and threw it to the floor, suffocating the hungry flames. He was burned but felt the healing process already starting. He stood, preparing to charge.

Meskal stood also, burning the Durge out of the air with his flaming hand. Already, the man looked considerably older.

"Why, Angelus?" the sorcerer demanded. "Is this about paying for the past? Save a girl's soul and go to heaven?"

Angel moved closer. "It's a start."

Meskal chuckled, flames leaping from his finger to sputter and die upon the hardwood floor. "That's the difference between you and me, vampire, I'm repentant of nothing."

The sorcerer raised his arms, murmuring yet another destructive incantation, but the spell died upon his lips when Shugg rose up behind him like some leviathan from the depths.

"Not repentant, Anton?" it bellowed in a voice brimming with rage and madness.

Meskal turned, hand still weakly ablaze, and aimed it at the demon's leering, bullet-riddled face.

"You should be," Shugg spat. He swatted Meskal aside like some petulant child grown tired of his toys.

The sorcerer sailed through the air, collided with the bar in the room's far corner, and flopped like a rag doll to the floor. His supernatural fire extinguished, Meskal tried to rise. He coughed, blood flying from his mouth to dapple the front of his white shirt.

He reached a hand out to Angel as he leaned his broken body against the bar. "Help me . . ." the sorcerer begged. "Help me . . . and I'll tell you where the girl's soul is." Again he coughed blood.

Angel began to move toward him but saw the Durge begin to swarm above the injured sorcerer. Some had glided to the floor and were scrambling eagerly toward him.

"That's it, my babies," he heard Shugg wheeze. "Try not to choke on his treacherous black heart."

Meskal screamed and struggled weakly as the demons dropped down to land upon his broken body, biting through the material of his Armani suit to get at the soft, fleshy prize beneath. One crawled onto the sorcerer's face, holding on tightly with razor-sharp claws, plunging its pointy muzzle into the soft meat of his left eye.

Angel looked away as the muffled screams became more frantic and pitiful. Soon there was no noise at all except for the sound of feeding.

A horrible way to die, he thought, *but it couldn't have happened to a nicer guy.*

"Angelus," the demon hissed, laboring to lift its bulk from the floor. The Durge, sated, screeched happily as they flitted about its head.

The vampire growled low and angry. "Why do you people keep calling me that?"

Angel watched as the demon lumbered closer, and saw how it craned its awful head so its one good eye could see the duffel bag Meskal had dropped in his struggles.

Cautiously Angel began to move toward the bag as well.

"Maybe you'll have more sense than your partner did," he said to Shugg, glancing briefly at the bloody remains of Anton Meskal propped against the bar. "Give me the little girl's soul and you can have the bag."

The demon self-consciously swatted at the Durge that circled its head. "Give you the vessel in exchange for what you stole from me?"

Angel nodded as they started to circle the duffel bag. "You got it."

Shugg blinked his single eye and nervously stroked the bodies of the demons that had returned to suckle at his chest.

"Do you think this is some game show, Angelus, and I, a pathetic contestant starving for beautiful prizes?"

Angel stopped as an idea began to form in his mind. He remembered what Harry had said about how the demon's voracious appetite would be its undoing and what Meskal had said about the volatile power within the vials.

The Kurgarru was dangerously close, its good eye tilted toward the prize, saliva dribbling from its mouth.

"I'll take the bag now," Shugg growled, beginning to lunge.

Angel was faster. He snatched up the duffel bag as the Kurgarru's clawed hand fell upon empty air.

What happened next seemed to occur in slow motion. Angel slammed the bag on the floor, and the delicate vials shattered at the demon's feet. There was a heartbeat of a pause, and then the soul energy exploded with unearthly power that lifted Angel off his feet. He was tossed backward through the air and landed on his stomach, stunned.

Through eyes blurred with pain, he watched as the collected soul energy at ground zero writhed and pulsated with life, spreading up to engulf the demon Shugg.

"What have you done?" the demon shrieked as its body was devoured by the mordant energies that had sustained it for centuries.

"This cannot be! I am the last of the soul-eaters . . . the last of the Kurgarru!" he bellowed pathetically.

The Durge met with a similar fate, many flying directly into the soul energy, like moths drawn to the ever-destructive flame.

Shugg's screams grew weaker as the rainbow-colored energy continued to dissolve the oily black flesh to expose blood-flecked bone.

"I am Shugg!" the demon cried out to the disinterested heavens. "I am—"

Its voice was suddenly silenced as the voracious soul energies ate away the last of the monster's flesh, leaving behind the frozen skeletal remains, which then collapsed, clattering noisily to the floor.

June crawled from beneath the tapestry and made her way toward Angel. Her face was scratched and bitten, a result of the Durge attack.

"Angel?" she asked. "Are you . . . is everything all right?"

He gazed up at the ceiling, unable to take his eyes from the wonderful sight. "I don't know," he said as he watched the swirling soul energies separate and reestablish their individualities.

Cordelia and Doyle had joined them and were watching as the souls flew about the room.

"Look at them go," Cordelia said. "They must have been pretty cramped inside those tiny little crystals."

"They're . . . they're beautiful," June whispered in awe. She brought a trembling hand to her mouth. "Is . . . is Aubrey's soul up there?"

Angel didn't answer. He studied each of the souls that playfully dipped and wove through the air, searching for one in particular.

With heavy heart he answered. "No. I don't think she is."

June gasped. She reached out and grabbed his arm. "But where—?"

He continued to study the souls' activity and noticed that many seemed to be concentrated above Shugg's skeletal remains.

"I intend to find out," he said, walking toward the demon's bones.

The hardwood floor at ground zero had been seared a powdery white, years of wax buildup scoured away by the explosive release of the powerful soul energies. Shugg's skeleton lay at the point of detonation. The strangely shaped demon skull gazed up at him from the floor, mouth agape in a silent scream of rage.

The souls darted down to the skeleton, moving freely in and out of the empty eye sockets and mouth, squeezing their delicate iridescence between the rib cage of the chest cavity and then back up again to circle about the ceiling.

Something faintly glowed from a side pocket of the tattered remnants of Shugg's black silk robe. Angel squatted down and from the pocket withdrew a crystal, which, at that moment, was the most beautiful thing he had ever seen.

Aubrey's soul.

He smiled at the vessel lying in the palm of his hand. He stroked the etched glass with his fingertip, wiping away some lint and dust that clung there. The color of the soul within turned from a brilliant yellow to a sky blue and then to a vibrant orange that reminded him of a beautiful sunset. It was perfectly lovely and made everything he had endured since taking the case seem inconsequential.

The liberated souls flew above his head as if urging him to set the last of their imprisoned kind free.

Angel closed his fingers around the vial and gently applied pressure. He felt the glass give and his hands were thrown apart by the searing power of the soul's release. They were burned but hurt only briefly as the child's life essence washed over him.

Aubrey's soul was within him now and he was driven to his knees, overwhelmed by the intensity of the child's innocence and purity. It spoke to Angel in a heavenly voice, thanking him. The souls were free; they could finally return home.

Then Aubrey's soul left his body to join the others that danced about the ceiling. He looked up from where he knelt and saw that they had begun to depart, to pass through the wall of the mansion, to begin the journey either back to the bodies from which they had been torn or to the other side.

June, Cordelia and Doyle hurried to his side.

"Angel?" Doyle touched his shoulder.

He had closed his eyes again, still experiencing the residual presence of the essence within him. His own soul pulsed with life and he knew the answer to the question of its beauty.

Yes, it too is a most wondrous thing.

Angel shivered with joy at the thought of his sister's smile and how much they had loved one another, joy that he hadn't allowed himself to feel in centuries.

"Hello? Earth to Angel, are you all right? Hello?" Cordelia asked.

He finally opened his eyes and his hands. They were bright pink and blistered but had already begun to heal. He showed June the broken and empty vial and smiled.

The woman's eyes widened with understanding and filled with tears.

"Oh, my God," June said, her body trembling with emotional release and relief. "Thank you. Thank you so very much."

"She's fine now," Angel said, letting the pieces of glass fall from his hands to the floor. "Everything is fine."

EPILOGUE

Angel watched Aubrey sitting behind Cordelia's desk. Doyle and Cordelia squatted on either side of the busy child, supervising the arts and crafts project she was working on.

"She's been talking about visiting you all week," June said as she watched her child scribble on a piece of white construction paper. "She said she wanted to make you a special present."

Angel felt the warmth from the mother's thankful gaze upon him and began to feel a bit uncomfortable. "How's she doing?" he asked, crossing his arms and avoiding eye contact.

Doyle handed Aubrey a yellow crayon from the super-deluxe box with built-in sharpener that Cordelia had bought for her.

"We've had some bad nights and she insists on

sleeping with the light on, but other than that, nothing."

Aubrey had finished her coloring and was now cutting into it with great vigor. Angel was amused by the tip of her tiny pink tongue protruding from the corner of her mouth as she concentrated on her project.

"Have I thanked you for what you did for us?" June asked him.

Angel looked away from the happy child and held out his hand. He ticked off on his fingers. "Phone calls, cards in the mail, a lovely basket of fruit, balloons; yes, you've said thank you in many ways and I appreciate it."

"I just want you to know that what you did . . ."

He looked at the woman and smiled. "You're welcome."

Angel noticed that Aubrey had begun to cut smaller pieces from the paper, raining yellow colored confetti onto the desktop.

"You should try an' be a bit neater, hon," Doyle said to the child as he attempted to sweep the pieces of paper into his hand. "Auntie Cordy doesn't take kindly to her desk being messy."

"It's all right," he heard Cordelia say to Doyle. "Let the cute little thing cut to her heart's content. I'll just clean up when she's finished."

Doyle appeared visibly shaken by the woman's nonchalant attitude about the condition of her desk.

"But all the times I've been workin' at yer desk and left it a tad disheveled, you—"

Cordelia helped the child manipulate the scissors to get the desired shape from the construction paper. "Well, that's *you*. She's much cuter."

Angel smiled as Doyle shook his head in defeat and began to put the crayons back into the box.

Aubrey set the scissors down and looked at what she had done.

"Finished," she proclaimed proudly, a look of accomplishment on her beautiful, cherubic face.

For the first time in as long as he could remember, Angel felt content. He was satisfied with the knowledge that he had saved Aubrey's soul as well as the souls of others taken by the sorcerer Meskal and the demon Shugg.

The child's mother approached the desk. "What did you make, honey?"

"It's a present for Angel."

"Wow, that's really something. I think you should go and give it to him right now," June said to her daughter.

The child slid from the office chair and came around the desk, her special gift in her hand. She was wearing a pair of blue overalls with an embroidered rose on the front, and colorful sneakers with a thick white sole.

The child stood before him, hiding the present behind her back.

"You're gonna hafta kneel down so's I can give it to you," she said, looking up at him seriously.

Angel squatted. "Is this okay?" he asked.

She nodded her head and brought out what appeared to be a crudely cut ring of yellow paper. Aubrey grabbed him by the front of his shirt and pulled him closer. She put the yellow ring on top of his head. "This is your halo," she said to him, making sure that it was perfectly straight. "Now you're a *real* angel."

The child's smile warmed him like a sunrise as he knelt in the middle of the office with the construction paper halo atop his head. He again thought of his sister Katherine.

Angel knew there would probably never come a time that he would be able to forgive himself completely for what he had done to his sister. But, at that moment, he found within himself the ability to believe that perhaps someday, she would forgive him.

Aubrey threw her hands about his neck and hugged him tightly. Tentatively he put his arms around her waist and returned her affection.

What he had done? It wasn't necessarily the equivalent of averting the apocalypse, but it was another victory for the Powers That Be.

More importantly, it was another step on the long and winding road toward his own redemption.

One soul at a time, he thought, holding Aubrey in his arms. *One soul at a time.*

About the Author

Thomas E. Sniegoski is best known as a comic-book writer who has worked for every major company in the comics industry, including DC, Marvel, Image, and Dark Horse. Some of his more recent works include *Batman: The Real World* for DC, and *Star Trek: Embrace the Wolf* for Wildstorm. Sniegoski is also the only outside writer ever invited to work within the universe that award-winning artist/writer Jeff Smith created for his series *Bone*. Sniegoski was the writer of *Stupid-Stupid Rat-Tails: The Adventures of Big Johnson Bone*, which was published by Cartoon Books in 1999. With Christopher Golden, he is currently working on the *Angel* comic for Dark Horse Comics and several other *Buffy* special projects. Sniegoski has recently expanded into other areas that showcase his interests and talents. He was one of the writers on Pocket Books' *Buffy the Vampire Slayer: The Monster Book* and is currently completing the thriller *Force Majeure* for Pocket Pulse with fellow *Monster Book* collaborator Christopher Golden. Sniegoski is also working on several other book projects for children and young adults. He lives in Stoughton, Massachusetts, with his wife, LeeAnne, and their four-year-old Labrador retriever, Mulder.